His Fantasies, Her Dreams

Other Ellora's Cave Anthologies Available from Pocket Books

Master of Secret Desires
by S. L. Carpenter, Elizabeth Jewell
& Tawny Taylor

Bedtime, Playtime
by Jaid Black, Ruth D. Kerce & Sherri L. King

Hurts So Good
by Gail Faulkner, Lisa Renee Jones & Sahara Kelly

Lover from Another World
by Rachel Carrington, Elizabeth Jewell
& Shiloh Walker

Fever-Hot Dreams
by Jaci Burton, Sherri L. King
& Samantha Winston

Taming Him
by Kimberly Dean, Summer Devon
& Michelle M. Pillow

All She Wants
by Jaid Black, Dominique Adair & Shiloh Walker

His Fantasies, Her Dreams

SHERRI L. KING
S. L. CARPENTER
TRISTA ANN MICHAELS

POCKET BOOKS
New York   London   Toronto   Sydney

POCKET BOOKS, a division of Simon & Schuster, Inc.
1230 Avenue of the Americas, New York, NY 10020

Published by arrangement with Ellora's Cave Publishing, Inc.

ISBN-13: 978-1-4165-3616-1
ISBN-10:   1-4165-3616-7

This Pocket Books trade paperback edition July 2007

10 9 8 7 6 5 4 3 2 1

POCKET and colophon are registered trademarks of Simon & Schuster, Inc.

Manufactured in the United States of America

For information regarding special discounts for bulk purchases, please contact Simon & Schuster Special Sales at 1-800-456-6798 or business@simonandschuster.com.

Contents

The Jewel

SHERRI L. KING

1

Samantha Gaynes tripped over her own feet and went crashing down in a boneless heap onto her couch. Her head swam dizzily and she let out an unladylike burp, grimacing when the after burn of too much Southern Comfort stung her throat. What a way to spend her Valentine's Day. What a way to spend her birthday! Drunk, unemployed, lonely and horny as all get out. It was shameful and pathetic—she knew that—but that was one good thing about being alone. There was no one around to see you when you finally hit rock bottom.

She had hit the bottom so hard that she'd fallen straight through it and found an entirely new level of low.

How could she have been so stupid—to think that the worst wouldn't happen and she'd lose her job? Everyone knew that their company was giving thoughts to downsizing, but she'd foolishly held out hope until the very last. Of course she should have known better than to ignore the warning signs. She should have been putting money aside for such an emergency, should have been scouting for another job just in case. But she hadn't. She was flat broke and without prospects. The job market was pure hell because of the recession—especially for anyone in her field—so all she had to look forward to now was perhaps a job at a fast food restaurant to help her earn some living money until something better could be found.

Sam groaned as her head spun out of control again and berated herself for her pessimistic thoughts. It wasn't like her to look at the dark side of things. Her pathetic attitude must be from the effects of too much drinking. Feeling sorry for herself would get her nowhere—she knew that—and as soon as she sobered up she'd put all of these lugubrious thoughts behind her and start looking for a job. Surely there would be something for her out there in the great wide world; she just had to keep her chin up and her hopes buoyed with happy thoughts.

But first . . . she needed to pass out.

Her eyes became heavy and her sight grew dim. Her head swam round and round, making her feel as though she were riding a loop the loop roller coaster ride at an amusement park. At times the feeling was almost euphoric and utterly delicious—at others it made her stomach churn and go queasy. She held a shaking hand to her head, closed her eyes and laughed drunkenly. What a way to end a perfectly horrid Valentine's Day.

With one last little burp she lost consciousness.

* * *

Hot breath spilled over her swollen nipple just before a tongue rasped over it with torturous slowness. Samantha couldn't help but arch up against that mouth, silently urging it to take her nipple deeper, to ease the empty ache that had been inside of her for what seemed an eternity. It had been so long since she had felt the touch of a man. Too long. She had almost forgotten that ripe, heavy throb of attraction and desire that could instantly drug her body and mind more thoroughly than any hard liquor.

Countless long, powerful fingers stroked her from neck to toes, as if a hundred different hands were running over her. It was impossible for her to focus on any one area of her body as it was bombarded with so many different sensations all at once. The mouth at her nipple roved upward and pressed a slow, firm kiss against her already panting mouth, testing her response until she moaned into it with rising need. Fingers ran through her hair, sifting the strands over and over again, making her scalp tingle oh so pleasantly. The mouth on hers moved up to press against her hair and she sighed and stretched, the better to savor each and every delicious sensation that was being visited upon her body with such patient carnal knowledge.

Hands forced her thighs apart with immovable strength and she gasped. Immediately countless fingertips moved to spread her vaginal lips and stroked her wet, swollen flesh until her hips were bucking, hungrily seeking more of the sweet caresses. Gentle tugs at her pubic hair had her trembling, and the pulling and pinching of her swollen clit made her cry out shamelessly in her passion. Her nipples were hard as diamonds and straining toward the heavens as yet more hands caressed her there, tugging them mercilessly until they were as plump and rouged as juicy berries.

Sam wanted to open her eyes, to see the phantom lovers that were pleasuring her so thoroughly, but was afraid that in doing so her dream would disappear before it could reach the conclusion that she so longed for. Her mind was still fogged from the consumption of too much alcohol and surely that was why her dream seemed so real, for never had her sober imagination produced such a heady sexual vision or dream. Better to keep her eyes closed for now and savor the fantasy while it lasted, than to tempt fate and wake up too soon.

It was so erotic, the way her body was being fondled and explored by the many hands that roved over her. No part of her body was left untouched. Even the tender flesh between her toes was caressed in turn. When the feel of a hot, wet tongue laved her open and quivering sex, she keened and undulated her hips against it, aching for more. The tongue lingered for a moment, then pulled away, and she groaned her disappointment aloud.

A deep voice chuckled and her body was spun over so that she lay on her stomach. The unexpected move caused her eyes to open in shock, but she may as well have been blind for all she could see. It was black as pitch around her, darker than a foggy, moonless night. Her senses reeled anew until she closed her eyes once more, and rested her forehead on the pillows beneath her.

Hands roved over the flesh of her back and squeezed the globes of her bottom until she was sighing and moaning once again. She dipped her back, raising her hips and presenting herself more fully for the convenience of her sexual tormentor. Again came that deep chuckle and the hands at her rear spread her cheeks wide so that the tongue could lave the puckered moue of her anus.

Rearing up on her elbows, she screeched—whether from indignation or surprised pleasure she couldn't have said because she felt both emotions with equal strength—and tried instinctively to move away. The hands that anchored her bottom would have none of that, however, and a gentle slap was administered to reprimand her for the attempted withdrawal. The tongue moved away, but the hands that held her did not falter from their handle on her cheeks. Instead they lifted her higher and yet more hands moved in to caress her exposed labia and anus.

Only her head and arms rested on the couch now, so that her breasts swayed beneath her as she was moved this way or that to better accommodate her phantom lovers' wills. Her entire body, front to back, head to toe, was caressed over and over again until she was weeping for culmination. Her body felt swollen, heavy and moist. It was all she could do to keep from screaming with each pass of those fingers and lips over her body, so sensitive had she become to the tiniest of touches. Never before had she been so completely aware of her own flesh, so receptive to each and every nuance of erotic sensation that was visited upon her.

This was lust. This was passion. This was pure, animalistic need . . . and god help her she wanted more of it.

Then, just when she thought that surely she would be driven mad with her own need, her every orifice was penetrated by long, strong fingers. Her mouth, her vagina and—yes—even her ass was gently stretched by these fingers so that she came with a violent shudder that racked through her body over and over, in rhythm with each tremor of release that washed over and into her. It was enough to make her mind swim even more drunkenly, until she faded out of the dream and entered into a deeper sleep to escape the throes of her exquisite climax.

Just before her senses faded she heard a thoroughly smug and satisfied voice whisper into her ear. "You are worthy of Him, worthy beyond price. You have done well . . . indeed you *will* do quite well . . ."

2

Samantha swam in and out of consciousness for what seemed endless hours. Her mind was a haze of disjointed and confusing images as she struggled to find wakefulness. Flashes of light and color stabbed at her brain until over and over again she was forced to swim down into the depths of sleep in order to escape the annoyance. But at last she was able to pull free from her drunken slumber long enough to open her eyes fully and assess the damage her hangover would inflict on her this morning. If morning it was and not afternoon as she feared it might be. Judging from the strength of the sunlight that filtered through the covering over her head it was probably, regrettably, the latter.

With a gasp she awoke fully and tried to claw at the sheet that covered her head. Her claustrophobia, most of the time not much of a nuisance for her, now reared its ugly head and had her in a near panic when she realized that the sheet was wrapped around her nude body, hindering her movements. She was moaning with anxiety before she was finally able to wrest the sheet from her body and fling it away. She buried her face in her hands and struggled to regain some composure over herself before moving on to face the day.

It wasn't until she lowered her hands and flung back her tangled hair that she noticed her surroundings. Having fallen asleep on the sofa in her living room she naturally expected to see her television, coffee table, and hanging collection of animation cels cheerily greeting her as she looked around. But with a jolt she realized that this was not the case. Instead of the homey lived-in space of her small apartment sheltering her, she found herself . . . somewhere else entirely. Suspecting her booze binge from the night before was still playing tricks with her mind, she rubbed her bleary eyes, shook her head and took another look around.

Instead of lying on her comfy couch she was reclined in the middle of a monstrously huge round bed heaped high with creamy vanilla satin comforters and deep carnelian velvet pillows. The bed was sunken into the stark white marble floor that surrounded it, so it felt and looked as though she was swimming in a lake of pillows and mattress. It was too much for her senses to bear. She moaned and flopped back onto the mound of pillows at her back and closed her eyes again. She waited for several minutes, taking deep calming breaths, before she rose once again and dared to take another peek about her.

The vanilla hue of the bedding that cocooned her seemed incredibly rich and inviting to her wide, searching eyes.

Oh god, she was losing it. She groaned and snapped her eyes shut once more. Who was she kidding? She had *already* lost it. Too much stress and worry over the past weeks coupled with an overindulgence of whiskey the night before had finally snapped her brain. Yep, there was no denying it—she needn't worry about looking for a job now—she was destined for the loony bin. Oh well, she sighed, and in a mercurial switch of mood that she was famous for among her friends and family, decided she might as well face this new challenge—her own insanity—with a smile on her face instead of a scowl.

It wasn't easy but somehow she managed to fight her way out of the lake of pillows and comforters to reach the edge of the bed. Because the bed was below the level of the floor she had to pull herself out of it—a clumsy task at best as the bedding was quite slippery—and rise to her unsteady feet beside it before she could risk taking a look around. The room she was in now was as different as night from day in comparison to her living room. It was indeed more suitable for a pasha than a graphic artist, with its lush designs of texture and color that made her senses reel, along with the thick perfume of spicy-sweet incense that permeated the air around her. It was by far the strangest and most luxuriously beautiful room she'd ever been in.

The ceiling was incredibly high, perhaps twenty feet or more, and that was a conservative guess on her part. And like the floor and walls it seemed to be made of a type of marble or similar stone, as if the entire room had been carved out of a giant solid block. And from that ceiling hung silk and satin scarves of every imaginable color and hue. Some were short with elegant embroidery lining the edges, and others were long—reaching nearly to the floor—and devoid of all decoration but no less attractive because of it than the others. They all swayed gently with the soft breeze that was playing through the high, narrow windows that appeared here and there in the wall farthest from her, creating a lazy symphony of movement that was extremely hypnotic.

It was to the windows that Sam now wandered. They were several feet high but perhaps only two feet wide at most, rounded at the tops and adorned with beautiful carvings of baroque-styled figures in various states of undress and sexual hedonism. There was no glass to shield the room against the elements—an oddity that brought a puzzled frown to her face. But it was what stretched beyond them that had her gasping in shock and her face draining of all color.

"Holy crap, that was some strong whiskey," she breathed in shock as her eyes took in the scene before her. Past the open windows lay an alien landscape that was surprisingly no less beautiful or exotic because of its strangeness. Hundreds of feet below the window, glittering copper and black sands and rocks stretched in rolling hills as far as her eyes could see, soaking up the warm rays of a golden-white sun that hung low in the sky and seemed fully three times the size it should have been.

After an age of looking in wonder at this scene, she backed unsteadily away from the windows, closed her eyes and shook her head to clear it again. It was no more successful an endeavor now than it had been earlier and when she opened her eyes again the scene before her was still unchanged. "Omigod, omigod, omigod," she repeated over and over to herself as her senses reeled and confusion took hold of her.

Where in the hell was she? Was this a hallucination? A dream?

Sam stumbled over an incredibly thick rug and landed with a jarring thump on her bare bottom. The floor covering was so deeply cushioned it saved her from a more bruising landing and her hands sank down to the wrists into its padding as she steadied herself. All about her the floor was littered with similar rugs in various shades and textures, along with plump divans, ottomans and enormous pillows—giving credence to her first estimation of the room's purpose as a pasha's haven.

Wasting no time now worrying how she'd gotten here—if here was even a place outside of her fevered imagination—she rose and took flight toward the only thing in the room that resembled a door. It was a golden diamond shape in the wall, barely a foot taller than she was, with a baseball-sized handle that looked alarmingly enough like a genuine multifaceted emerald. Sam was no expert on gemstones but the handle was definitely made of some kind of translucent green stone. It *was* a door—and she flew through it as it opened. Then stumbled to an immediate and abrupt halt, stunned in her tracks.

Dozens of women, all nude but for strange golden cages about their mouths, stood before her. Delicate chains and colored stones adorned their bodies, glinting in the light as they turned to look at her as she stood there staring dumbfounded. Well, she assumed they were all women . . . more than a few of them were creatures outside of her scope of imagination until now, so it was difficult to tell for sure. She knew she looked like an idiot, standing there with her jaw hanging to the floor as she looked around at them with wide eyes, but she couldn't school her features into anything more intelligent or polite than that. This new situation was more than she could bear to cope with rationally just now.

The women moved closer and gathered about her, some being so bold as to stroke her hair or skin. She tried not to back away as a purple-fleshed, six-breasted woman came forth and cupped Sam's breasts in her webbed six-fingered hands. She barely managed to hold her ground. The woman giggled and made odd twirling notes with her tongue—obviously communicating with the others—and they joined in her laughter.

The purple woman tweaked her nipples with her fingers and laughed again. True to the redhead's reputation Sam's temper rose with her indignation over this treatment and the group's obvious humor at her expense. The women spoke amongst themselves in strange languages and continued to grope her even when she tried to back away.

"I don't know what you're saying, but I doubt I'd find it funny," she gritted out with a scowl.

The women seemed to understand her words well enough because they twittered amongst themselves and made soothing motions towards her with what appeared to be friendly smiles. Sam couldn't help but notice that one of the women had two mouths, one had sharp teeth—another, none at all—and one even had what looked like a vagina in place of a mouth. It was hard to tell because the delicate, golden, cage-like masks they each wore around the lower part of their faces obscured her view of them a little.

Most of the women had vibrantly colored skin, in shades of purple, yellow, silver, green, and mauve. Some were possessed of scales, others with what looked like moist, amphibian flesh. A few of the women looked as though they were made of velvet or feathers, and still others appeared as if they weren't made of any familiar substance at all . . . perhaps water or gas or a cross between the two. Suffice it to say these women surrounding her now were anything but human.

"Where am I?" Sam had to swallow nervously before continuing when a centaurian-looking woman came forward on four hooves and patted her hair. The mythological creature seemed to be trying to comfort her, though it only made Sam incredibly skittish to be standing so close to the giant half-woman half-horse. "And who are you . . . ladies?" The last word almost didn't make it out of her mouth as she saw a sexless, anamorphic creature smile at her with tentacle-laden lips behind her mask.

All about her the odd-looking women began to speak in what sounded like dozens of different languages. Clicks and twirls, grunts and slithering sighs assailed her ears, but Sam understood none of what they were saying. They seemed to have no trouble understanding her, or each other though, but after a few moments they seemed to realize that their attempts at communication only confused her, and quieted down.

The centaur smiled at her reassuringly and motioned for her to precede the group deeper into the room. Well, "room" wasn't exactly the right word for it, Sam thought as she looked about her. It was more like an enclosed courtyard or stadium. In the middle of the massive enclosure there was an immense, round pool filled to the brim with crystal clear water. A grand fountain erupted like a geyser in the center of it, from a set of golden sculptures. What was so unusual about this—aside from the great scale of it all—was that the fountain's sculptures depicted three headless male forms, back to back, facing outward—all nude—and the water spewed forth from their huge erect cocks which they palmed in their sculpted hands. Sam paused upon seeing this but the giant centaur at her back nudged her forward once again and she was forced to tear her eyes from it or trip over her own feet.

The ceilings of the room were even higher than those of the room she'd just exited, standing hundreds of feet high. The better, perhaps, to accommodate the towering trees that bloomed colorfully beneath it. How these trees existed without direct sunlight, Sam couldn't have guessed, but they were real—not artificial—and they flourished in their sheltered garden. Other vegetation—strange, exotic flowers, shrubs and fruit bearing vines—decorated the courtyard, giving it a welcoming appeal. The scent of incense, flowering blossoms and fruit were heavy in the air, but not overpowering. Indeed it was a delicious aroma, this mixture, and served to calm Sam's nerves a little.

The centaur made elaborate motions with her hands and after a few moments of watching this Sam deduced that the woman was suggesting that she bathe in the pool. Her deductions were confirmed as several of the women then splashed into the sparkling waters, frolicking like children with each other and joining the centaur in motioning her forward to join them. Sam shook her head and gave them a weak smile. She wasn't one for modesty among other women nor was she the least bit ashamed of her body, but she'd never bathed in public before and just now wasn't inclined to start the habit.

What she really wanted was to get out of here and figure out what the hell was going on.

She tried several times to convey this desire to the centaur woman, who seemed to be the unspoken leader of the bunch, but either she didn't understand Sam's awkward sign-language or she refused to comply. Either way, Sam was getting rather frustrated with the whole situation.

Just then, a great doorway appeared—from out of nowhere it seemed—in one of the walls of the room and two men strode through it. Both men were tall, with caramel-colored skin and exotic features. In fact, to Sam's dazed mind they looked like the ancient Egyptians might have, if the images of antique busts and hieroglyphic-adorned walls could be believed. They even dressed like Egyptians, with wide golden cuffs on their wrists and upper arms, elaborate golden collars with intricate inscriptions upon them, and long split skirts that hung low on their hips and ended just above their sandaled feet. One of the men was shaved bald so that the top of his head gleamed in the light of the room—whose source Sam had yet to discover—and the other had thick black hair that reached nearly to his waist.

Now Sam felt a wave of modesty overcome her, so she quickly pulled her long red hair forward to cover her bared breasts and surreptitiously crossed her wrists over her pubic mound to conceal it. As she did this she noticed that the women had moved forward to flank the men and were openly fawning all over them, touching them all over just as they had done to her in greeting. The bald man smiled warmly at them, patted some gently on the head, kissed others in like manner—on the head—and received their adoration with good cheer. The long-haired man, however, remained stoically reserved, merely nodding in response to the women who caressed him affectionately. The two men were completely different from each other, though they were obviously of the same nationality, and Sam could only wonder what they were doing here. Who were these men? And why did the women so obviously revere them?

As these thoughts and observations filtered through her mind, the two men took notice of her and approached. The women moved away as if instructed to, letting the men pass unhindered through their numbers, until they stood directly before her. Sam took a step back. The two men followed, taking one step only as she had, coming to rest a few feet away from her. Sam's eyes shot from one to the other and she wondered what new shock her hallucination had in store for her.

"This is no hallucination, Sa-man-tha. You are in the palace of our King and you are welcomed."

Samantha tried not to choke on her surprise as the long-haired man spoke to her in heavily accented English.

"I don't understand. I went to sleep in my living room—"

"I brought you here, as a birthday present for my Master. You have been chosen for Him. It is a great honor and one you should be proud to boast of." He offered her a deep bow and the other man followed suit with a warm smile.

"W-what? *Birthday present?* I'm not—"

The man cut her off once more and she felt her temper soar at his highhanded manner. "It is time for you to be prepared for Him. We have only so many hours before the light ends and our Master's birthday celebration will begin with the rising of the Satellite Moons. You must be made ready to please Him along with the other two."

Good lord, what was going on here? All this talk of birthday presents, preparations and . . . the other two. The other two *what?*

The man laughed and shook his dark head, reading her thoughts again. "You think you were the only one to be given this honor, out of all the females in all the worlds in all the universe, you think you alone have been deemed worthy for my Master this year?" He laughed some more and the bald man joined in, speaking rapidly in a foreign tongue between hearty guffaws.

"Hey!" she barked out, definitely angry at feeling like she was the butt of some great joke. "I don't exactly follow what you're saying so quit laughing at me because it's not fair. Just take me back home. *Now.*"

The men's laughter ceased abruptly and they turned incredulous looks to her. The bald man, who until now had seemed the cheerier and more approachable of the two, scowled darkly and the women each looked at her with something like disappointment and pity in their eyes.

"This cannot be undone, Sa-man-tha. You have passed all tests, been chosen carefully for your many virtues and strengths and given the honor of a place in the King's collection. Already your friends and family begin to forget you back on your homeworld. No one would know you, were you to return now. You would be adrift. So you see, you cannot go back home. *This* is your home now."

Sam swallowed hard around a sudden lump of fear in her throat. "I don't understand," she managed to whisper.

"You will soon enough. Now come, we have much to do and little enough time to do it in." The man motioned for her to join him as he turned and spoke to the bald man, who had yet to cease scowling at her. In fact, the man was giving her such a harsh look that she felt goaded enough to stick her tongue out at him in defiance. If the look on the man's face was any indication, he was shocked at her action and perturbed even further by it. Sam didn't care—let him be angry with her—for now she would follow the other man to . . . wherever he was leading her . . . and find out just what the hell was going on.

3

Samantha followed the dark-haired man through the magical doorway and down a long corridor that led away from the courtyard. She was highly conscious of her nudity but unable to do anything about it besides try her best to ignore it. It was difficult but she managed. Thankfully there were many distractions for her to focus on along the way.

Along the corridor stood many doors, similar in style to the diamond-shaped door in her bedroom, though there were many different geometric shapes, and each sported a large jeweled handle. She would have, at any other time, been curious to see what was behind these doors but her guide led her on past them and she was obliged to follow him. It seemed a long walk but at last they came to a door. The dark-haired man waved his left hand—his fingertips were encased in gold and a strange emblem appeared to be floating over his palm—before the door and it disappeared as if it had never been there.

"How . . . ?" Sam tried to find the right words to ask how he'd performed such a trick but lost the thought as she saw what was beyond this new doorway.

A room, seemingly carved whole from the fieriest of diamonds, lay before her dazed eyes. Within it, dozens of odd golden devices—the purposes for which she dare not guess—decorated an area surrounding a large steaming pool of water. The pool was lined with what looked like pure gold, so that the golden-hued water reflected dazzlingly against the diamond walls that ensconced it. It was so bright and blinding—this room—that Sam had to squint her eyes to see her guide as he motioned her to follow him into it. But once within it, the light seemed to dim to a bearable wattage, and Samantha was able to see clearly once more.

"This is the preparation bath. Here you will be made ready for our Master's Collection."

At that moment, the bald man entered behind them with two other women in tow. One of the women had skin the color of bubble gum with matching eyes and hair—a monochrome confection of palest pink—while the other was covered almost from head to toe with a pelt of thick, white fur. What little of her skin could be seen—her breasts, belly and pubis—was a beautiful, shiny ebony color that contrasted wonderfully with her snowy pelt. The two women moved to join Sam before the dark-haired man and surprisingly enough looked far more comfortable than she felt she did.

The dark-haired man was reading her mind again. "To give you your due, Sa-man-tha, these two have had more time to grow accustomed to their new role in life. I only hope that you will adapt as well as they have." This last was said with an unmistakable hint of warning in his tone.

"Are all of you mind readers around here?" she asked unsteadily.

"No. You need only accept my intrusion into your mind. It is part of my job, I guess you would say, to know what you are thinking at all times."

"And what is your job, exactly?" she couldn't help asking.

"Forgive me for not following the formalities, Sa-man-tha. You are a unique individual and have thrown me off my pace with your questions." He gave a small chuckle. "I am The Collector, you may refer to me as such, and my job is just that—to collect. I scour the universe in search of new additions—such as yourself—who are worthy of a place here in the King's palace."

"And what is my place? Am I supposed to be a slave or something?"

"Of course not!" He sounded insulted at the very idea. "You are to have a high place at court. You will be a consort to our Master and treated with great deference. Your every wish shall be granted, your every comfort seen to with great care. You will be provided for all the rest of your days. You will never have to work again, never have to suffer or worry."

"Oh be still my heart," she scoffed, not believing his words for a second. "And what's the catch, oh great Collector? I'm sure that there is one."

"The *catch,* if you want to consider it thusly, is that you must always be ready and prepared to accept our King should He have need of you."

Sam felt her eyes bug out of her face as realization dawned. "You mean I'm going to be a prostitute?"

The bald man spoke rapidly then, gesticulating with angry motions towards her but directing his words to The

Collector. It was obvious that he was displeased with Sam's words and attitude.

The Collector ignored the other man and with a dangerous glint in his eyes addressed her once more. "You will not be a prostitute! You will be a Beloved One. You should be honored by this, not angered. I will forgive you your insulting behavior because I know much of your culture—having studied you for nigh onto a year now—and am aware that your kind does not have such honored ones among them. You have no King, no higher court, and therefore do not understand the great honor that has been bestowed upon you.

"Sa-man-tha, you have been chosen out of countless other women, out of countless other worlds across the universe, for this honor. It was your unique beauty that first drew my eye—your vibrant coloring, red hair, green eyes, and white skin—but after I began my study of you it was your unique personality that ultimately decided me. You are loyal to your friends and family. You revel in life's adventures and are not afraid to enjoy them to their fullest. You have a strong character and will, and above all you are capable of compassion and understanding in a world where such things are often scoffed at or misunderstood.

"The new life I have gifted to you is not one of suffering or worry—as you would be doing now after the loss of your livelihood—but of pleasure, happiness and joy. My Master will treasure you as He treasures all of His Beloved Ones and will shower you with all the creature comforts that are His to give. You need only yield to Him, love Him, and all of your days you will be cared for and given your every heart's desire."

"But what if my heart's desire is to return home? Will that wish be granted to me?" she gritted out.

"No, and why should it? Is it not better to reside here in

safety and comfort, than back on your own world where there is dishonesty, poverty and sorrow? It is better that you put this thought of return from your mind now, because it can never be. You are here with us now, and here you shall remain."

Her own world? Holy moly, she was in far deeper than she'd thought. What to do now but let her anger give her courage and ignore the fear that threatened to take over. Better to focus on the most direct issue at hand and worry about the rest later, she thought. "I. Will. Not. Be. A. Whore!"

The bald man interjected again, spitting out his words, clearly enraged by her attitude.

"And just what the hell is he saying anyway? It's hardly fair that everyone can understand me in this place, when I can't understand anyone but you."

"Let me rectify that immediately then, Sa-man-tha," The Collector gritted out impatiently. He then placed his hand over her head, golden-tipped fingertips splayed wide, and the strange branded symbol floated over his palm once more then was gone as quickly as it appeared. Sam noticed that the golden caps on his fingers were each connected by intricate, hair-thin chains that crossed over his fingers and palms numerous times, forming a sort of glove over his hand. This image branded itself into her brain for later study. The Collector withdrew his hand then and quite suddenly Sam could understand what the bald man was saying.

"—not worthy of this honor! She is disrespectful and undeserving of her place in the Collection."

"Be at ease, Cerebus. Give her but half a chance to grow accustomed to her place. Have I once failed the King in all my years of service? Trust me to know that all will be made right in the end," The Collector said, obviously trying to calm the bald man's tirade.

"*Learn my place*? Learn my place—how can you talk like that and tell me I'm not going to be a slave? You're already treating me like I am!" she shouted.

It was then that the furry woman stepped forward and laid a soothing hand on her arm. "Do not be frightened, red hair, for there is nothing to fear. You do not yet understand and so your anger must be forgiven." The woman's pearly black eyes beseeched the men before them to hear the plea in her voice on Sam's behalf. "Please be at ease until you know more of this new world which you have been asked to be a part of."

The woman's words and demeanor automatically helped to cool Sam's temper and she couldn't help but feel grateful to her for it. The woman was right—anger would get her nowhere just now—and all of her questions and doubts would be allayed enough if she could find a little patience and see how the next few hours were to play out. Unfortunately patience was not something she was known for having an abundance of. It would take a lot of self-control to sit back and watch things unfold before she completely blew her top. But she would do it if she had to . . . and it looked as though, right now, she had no choice but to do otherwise.

"I will not be a whore," she reiterated.

"We are not asking you to be," The Collector said gently. "You will soon see that your indignation is misplaced. We do not want to subjugate you, Sa-man-tha."

"My name is Samantha," she slowly pronounced it for them, "or just plain Sam, to save time."

"And this is Cerebus, keeper of the Collection, or Collection master. It will be to him that you will make all your needs known." The bald man gave Sam a hard glare and she was of the impression that he really didn't like the thought of catering to her just now. "And these two females are Ferd," the pink woman nodded and offered a shy smile, "and Haliatyde Se Duri'ann an Malvindosaide."

The furry woman smiled, too. "Since you like small names, you can call me Hali if you like." She pronounced the word Hah-lee, giving it an exotic, foreign sound. Sam repeated it to her and greeted them both with her own smile.

"Now, enough of our talking. We have much to do. Let us begin your preparations." The Collector waved his hands and there appeared before them a table heaped high with food-laden dishes. "Eat now, so that you have the strength to face the hours ahead, for they will be busy indeed."

"First will come the cleansing. These waters are highly medicinal and will calm your nerves and ease any aches you may have so that afterward you will feel refreshed and free of all stresses," The Collector said some time later.

Cerebus led Sam, Ferd, and Hali into the giant sunken pool. When he entered the bath before them his long skirt floated up about his waist, as he hadn't bothered to remove it beforehand, and Sam frowned as she began to suspect that he meant to assist them with their bathing.

"Do not worry, Sam. You have nothing to fear," The Collector murmured at her back. "Cerebus is here only to help you. It is his duty and privilege to do so." Sam had to bite her lip to keep from voicing her thoughts on that assessment of Cerebus' feelings towards her.

The water was pleasantly warm when Sam stepped into it and the steaming vapor that rose up from it possessed a sensual aroma that lulled her senses. When she stood in the deepest part of the golden tub, along with Ferd and Hali, the water reached just below her breasts, lifting the hair that concealed them and baring her to the gaze of anyone who cared to look. Oddly enough, this didn't trouble her now as the comforting waters worked their special magic on her inhibitions and worries. Cerebus moved to Hali, took her gently up against him and dipped her backward over his arm—as if baptizing her in the waters—until she was completely submerged. Then he pulled her slowly back up, gave her a kind smile and moved on to Ferd. He repeated this process with her, once again gifting her with a soft, kindly smile before moving on to Sam.

When Cerebus came to stand before Sam, the warm light of welcome in his eyes vanished completely and he was perhaps less than gentle as he lowered her into the water. As the liquid closed up over her head she felt her entire body relax, though she hadn't even known she was tense, and her blood throbbed with a delicious, tingling warmth as it pumped through her veins. All too soon Cerebus plucked her up from the water's embrace and, without the smile he had bestowed upon the other two women, left her, went to the edge of the tub and climbed out.

He turned and motioned for them to follow him and it was then that Sam noticed the same strange glove adorning his left hand as the one she had seen on The Collector's—golden caps for the fingers, connected by thin golden chains that crossed over his palm. Other than her initial noting of it, however, she gave it no more thought. She was too relaxed now to think on anything so inconsequential as a man's jewelry.

The three women exited the bath and Cerebus gently toweled off Hali, then Ferd and lastly Sam, though he was a bit more brisk with her. If Sam had been any less at ease just then she would have laughed at the bald man's obvious show of displeasure with her. He was treating her like a child, giving her a taste of his parental censure because of her earlier attitude—though now she wasn't sure why she'd been so irritable a few minutes before—and he was clearly expecting her to hang her head in shame in the face of it. But she felt no shame, only warm acceptance of her current position, despite Cerebus' irritation with her.

Cerebus next took a large crystal bottle filled with oil, poured a dollop into his palms and began to rub them down with it. Sam could only watch as each woman purred and stretched beneath his hands as he stroked them, before he came at last to her. His hands were warm when they touched her, even the golden metal of his glove. He massaged her from neck to toe with the oil, which smelled of honeyed almonds, soothing her muscles until she was arching against each pass of his strong, firm palms, eager for more. When at last he was finished, her skin felt softer than she'd ever known it to feel, and she was flushed a healthy pink from all the pleasant friction his hands had made upon her flesh.

"Now comes the time for your new vestments." The Collector's voice broke through her thoughts and Cerebus led them deeper into the diamond walled room, away from the steaming bath, to an area where strange golden gadgets were laid out and waiting. "These are the only coverings you need ever wear, unless the King should decree otherwise. Lie down, all of you."

Sam glanced down, along with Ferd and Hali, and saw three narrow piles of velvet pillows appear at their feet. As one they moved to lie down upon them and Sam couldn't help but snuggle her head into the deep cushioned softness. It was heavenly, this bed, especially when she felt so relaxed and heavy limbed. Perhaps she could even catch a quick nap, she thought, uncaring that she'd only just awakened from sleep.

But no, it was not to be. Cerebus was moving towards Ferd, with tiny golden rings in his hand and Sam was too curious not to watch the scene as it unfolded before her.

Cerebus laid a small golden loop down upon Ferd's erect pink nipple, waved his gloved hand over it slowly, and magically—when he moved his hand away—the ring was pierced neatly, and painlessly it seemed, through her flesh. Ferd smiled up at Cerebus and he responded in turn before moving onward. Hali was next, receiving the same piercing as Ferd—a golden loop through her nipple—though she toyed with hers as Cerebus moved over to Sam. As Cerebus laid the golden circlet onto her nipple, Sam felt enough of her natural self return so that she laid her hand over it before Cerebus could complete his magic.

"I don't want to be pierced," she said in a husky voice she normally wouldn't have recognized as her own.

"What you want and what will happen, at this juncture, don't necessarily have to agree with each other," Cerebus said flatly, with no small amount of irritation burning in his dark eyes. He waved his hand over hers and beneath her palm she felt the puckered flesh of her nipple seem to rise up and swallow a small portion of the hoop. She took her hand away and looked down at her breast. Sure enough, the golden ring was pierced cleanly into her flesh, though it hadn't hurt in the least. Cerebus gave her one more dark look and turned away.

Next Cerebus retrieved three long, delicate golden chains. In turn he attached one end of a chain to their nipple rings, trailed it down over their ribs and stomach, then wrapped the rest of the length around their waists, securing it at the last with a tiny jeweled lock that was no bigger than Sam's pinky nail. The jewels on the locks matched the eye color of the wearer, Ferd's was cotton candy pink, Hali's was a pearly black, and Sam's was an emerald green. If it weren't for the fact that Sam strongly suspected it was some sort of brand she might have found the jewelry quite beautiful, in an exotic and other-worldly sort of way.

The three lounging women were fitted with wide golden arm cuffs. One was affixed to Sam's upper left arm, another on the wrist of her right hand. It was the same for Hali and Ferd. They were given narrow wire necklaces, also made of gold, for these men obviously treasured the stuff, to wear about their necks. Another delicate chain was attached to their necklaces and then to their arm cuffs so that when their arms or necks moved about even the slightest bit, a trail of fine gold flashed in their wake. They were given golden earrings, thin chains that trailed to their shoulders and were weighted at the ends with the tiniest of jewels—again colored to match their eyes. Sam's ears were already pierced but Hali's and Ferd's were not and again came the waving of that gloved hand as Cerebus magically affixed the jewelry to their ears. All of this preparation must have taken a good solid hour, but it was clear that they were far from finished as The Collector spoke once again.

"There is but one official rule that you each must follow here at the Palace and that is this; under no circumstances are you to ever allow the entrance of man or beast into any of your orifices. Beyond eating or drinking you will at all times wear a Veil, to keep your mouth locked away from the insertion of foreign objects. And unless in the presence of the King, or when nature deems it necessary, you will always be fitted with an anal and vaginal plug so that you will at all times remain chaste for Him."

Before Sam could sputter her indignation over this "rule," Cerebus moved forward and blew some sort of brown powder into her face, which smelled of honeyed almonds just as the massage oil had. That quickly, after she'd breathed in the dust of this powder, her objections were gone and a wave of carnal heat rushed through her body like wildfire. The other women were given the same puff of brown powder into their faces and they reacted just as Sam did. They writhed upon their beds, spreading their legs wide and arching their backs as if posing for a lover. Sam moaned and bucked her hips and vaguely noted that Hali and Ferd followed suit.

"We call this *phuq* dust. It comes from the treasured Nipey seed after it has been harvested, aged, and ground into a fine powder. It is a potent aphrodisiac and we use it here only to prepare you for the comfortable insertion of your chastity plugs," The Collector informed them gently.

Sam felt the lips of her sex splayed wide by the hand of Cerebus and arched up against his gentle fingers, craving more of the contact on her aroused tissues. Cerebus seemed to soften towards her then and brushed his fingers over the soft hairs of her pubis in a soothing manner. She felt a warm probing between her legs, looked down and saw the sleek golden dildo grasped between Cerebus' golden brown fingers slip between her legs and into her pussy. Her channel felt stretched for only a moment by this dildo before her muscles relaxed and welcomed its intrusion into her body eagerly. The plug was held in place within her by the use of two long chains that wrapped about her hips and waist and was fastened with yet another jeweled lock at her navel. Cerebus then moved to the other women and repeated this process.

When Cerebus returned to her he knelt between her splayed legs and gently placed the soles of her feet upon his shoulders. He leaned in against her, pushing her rear up off of the pillows so that he was given easier access to insert a short, thin butt plug into her anus. The plug's dry intrusion made her gasp and jerk away so that Cerebus removed it and went to re-trieve the bottle of oil, which he had massaged into her skin earlier. He rubbed some of this oil into the soft puckered flesh of her ass with two blunt fingers and attempted to insert the plug once again. After a few moments of uncomfortable resist-ance her anus seemed to quiver and then the warm golden probe was sliding tenderly into her. Sam felt spitted, impaled, but was so completely aroused by the whole ritual that it was a welcome feeling indeed.

After the insertion of her chastity plugs, Sam lost track of time and before she knew it she was fitted with one of the grids that she had seen upon each of the women earlier that morning. The mask, or Veil as The Collector had named it, was light as a feather but strong as steel as it rested just below her nose over her mouth and jaw. It wasn't fastened in any way that Sam could easily discern, but hovered immovably over her face in such a manner that nothing could enter her mouth without its removal.

Jeweled anklets were fastened about her ankles and she was given thumb rings that matched. Cerebus brushed her hair patiently until it glistened—which couldn't have been easy considering how tangled it was—and she was given a vial of perfumed oil with which to scent herself. The scent was indescribably beautiful—fashioned solely for her by The Collector she was told—based on her special personality and physical attributes. Ferd and Hali were also gifted with their own unique scents.

Cerebus then waved his hand over Ferd and Hali's pubic mounds, magically removing any and all traces of hair from their sexes. The King, it seemed, liked his women bald be-tween their legs. However, at the last, The Collector in-structed Cerebus to leave a small swath of hair upon Sam's mound, and Cerebus did so. A patch of hair in the shape of a diamond graced the top of her pubic bone and with a last wave of his hand tiny rubies were weaved into her fiery red pubic hairs, leaving her sex to glisten and twinkle with every slight nuance of movement. Other than that, her pussy was now completely bald and smooth to the touch, as if the hair had never been there. She felt beautiful, decked out in her new finery, swollen and ripe and utterly feminine.

It was only later, after the effects of the *phuq* dust had long faded, that she would lament the loss of her normal reactive self during these proceedings.

4

Now that you are prepared you will join with the other women of the Collection and be brought forth to meet our King. He is most anxious to see His newest Beloved Ones and if you are lucky He will choose some of you to entertain Him tonight in His private chambers."

Lucky? Sam was not so far under the *phuq* dust's influence that she couldn't still give a sarcastic thought to The Collector's words. *Who would feel lucky to be used by some boorish royal guy who's obviously quite too full of his own importance? Certainly not me!*

But she couldn't quite voice the words, even though she longed to—if only for her own amusement to see the indignant look on Cerebus' face that would surely greet her comments—and she was silent as The Collector led them from the room. The plugs that filled her were surprisingly comfortable and she was able to walk with ease. In fact, she practically forgot that they were even there. The tingling spell of the *phuq* dust still coursed through her veins and surely that helped. Her pussy was gently thrumming, her clit swollen and wet. Her nipples were hard as pebbles and her breasts were heavy and aching. Her mouth, she knew, was pouting behind her mask, full and yearning to be kissed. All in all her body was deliciously aroused, not quite to the fever pitch it had been right after the *phuq* had been administered, but still softly awakened to desire.

After a long walk through yet another winding corridor the group came upon a grand entranceway marked by hundreds of different geometric symbols etched into a set of immense solid gold doors. The Collector waved his hand and the doors swung outward, away from them, and they proceeded beyond. What greeted them was beyond anything Sam had ever seen. Before them, at the end of a room that must have been the size of a football field, was a shining throne made of a rainbow of jewels piled high with gorgeous soft pillows and swatches of silk, satin and velvet. The throne was several feet up off of the floor, on a raised dais littered with thousands upon thousands of flower petals. Soft music sounded in the background, otherworldly and ambient, reminding Sam once again of the Egyptian or perhaps Arabian facets to her surroundings.

At the foot of the dais lounged several women and as she drew closer Sam noted that they were bedecked in finery that was similar to hers, though their "chastity plugs" were noticeably absent. One of the women had three breasts and each of her nipples were pierced and chained. Another woman appeared to have two sex organs between her spread legs—a penis and a vagina—and the penis was pierced by golden bars three different times through the glans in a Prince Albert position. She also sported a guiche-styled piercing—a horizontal golden bar at the base of her small scrotum—with jeweled weights attached at the bar's ends. Each woman was uniquely different in shape, coloring and form, and Sam was struck dumb by the sight of so much exposed alien flesh.

Inevitably Sam's eyes rose up the dais and settled on the reclining figure of a man who sprawled lazily out upon the throne. He was very tall—Sam could easily discern that even though he reclined—lean and long of limb. His fingers were especially graceful, artistic-looking on his broad palms, bedecked with jeweled rings and the same type of golden-tipped glove that The Collector and Cerebus both wore. His hair was the color of dark sorghum syrup. Thick and long it trailed down in a fat braid onto the pillows beneath him and was woven with the occasional tiny jewel or glistening threads.

His face, hidden partially by shadows, was an exotic study of slopes and planes. He was possessed of a high forehead and flaring sculpted brows. His eyes were rimmed with a thick line of sooty black kohl and they turned up like a cat's at the corners. His eyes were a dramatic contrast against his dark caramel skin, light and translucent, they were the color of watered-down sherry. His lashes were long, no doubt at least an inch in length—enough to make any vain woman go positively green with envy—and they gifted him with a borderline androgynous look that oddly enough made him appear that much more exquisitely masculine.

He wore a large jeweled golden collar about his neck and matching cuffs on his toned upper arms. His torso was tightly muscled but not heavily so. His nipples were dark and small on his hairless chest, like tiny chocolate drops, and they kept drawing Sam's eyes, no matter that she valiantly fought the urge to gawk at him. He wore a long glittering ebony skirt, split high on one side so that as he reclined his one bent leg was bared from foot to hip, exposing yet more of his beautiful honeyed skin. The skirt rode dangerously low on his hips giving hint to the fact that he was quite possibly hairless all over his taut, exotic body.

Instantly Sam was attracted to the man and she was exquisitely aware of her own jewelry adorned nude body as she and the other two women were led closer to the throne. The plugs in her body felt heavier now; more noticeable as her erogenous zones began to vibrate with arousal. If just looking at this man caused her juices to flow, Sam grew breathless to imagine how potently his touch might affect her.

Perhaps being a love slave wouldn't be so degrading a chore as she had initially thought . . . for a short while anyway. Or maybe it was the aftereffects of the *phuq* dust making her feel this way, Sam couldn't be sure of her own reactions it seemed.

She hadn't even noticed when the other women of the Collection had come to join them, but suddenly she was surrounded by dozens of women who were all quite clearly preening for the attention of the King. Sam ignored them as best she could; she had eyes only for the man on the throne as he rose up on his elbows and regarded those in the room about him.

Cerebus moved forward and sank to his knees, bowing his head before the King. "Happy Birthday, My Master. Your Collection is ready and waiting to join you in celebration tonight, prepared especially for this joyous occasion."

Slowly, in graceful motions like a giant jungle cat, the King rose up from his position on the cushioned throne. An enigmatic smile played about his delicately sculpted lips as he descended the steps of the dais in his thong-sandaled feet. He came to a stop before a round green-skinned woman who couldn't have stood higher than four feet at most. With a flourish he swept aside the front panel of his skirt, unashamedly exposing his phallus—Sam couldn't get a good glimpse of him as she stood behind too many taller females, though not for lack of her trying—and pulled the woman's plump face towards it. Even though Sam couldn't precisely see what was going on she could clearly hear the unmistakable sounds of the woman's greedy suckling as she went down on her Master's cock. The King must have removed the woman's veil to have free access to her mouth.

The King petted the woman's head as it bobbed over his erection, and though the scene was shocking in the extreme to Sam—she who had never seen such a public display as this beyond the occasional pornographic film, which was viewed only in the privacy of her own home—she couldn't help feeling a growing hunger unfurl within her because of it. After a long moment the King gave one final pat to the woman's head and pulled his cock free of her mouth with an audible popping sound. He gave her a soft smile and moved on past her, easily righting his clothing as he went.

"She is the King's favorite just now," said the centaurian woman who'd been so nice to Sam earlier that morning. She stood now by Sam's side, dwarfing her with the mass of her four-legged horse body.

"I can understand you," Sam said with a smile.

"I know. I hadn't realized this morning, at first, that you weren't yet given the gift of understanding us. My name is Keln, by the way."

"Mine is Sam. You say that woman is the King's favorite? Does he have many or just the one?"

Keln laughed softly and leaned down to speak more quietly in Sam's ear. "That depends. Some nights He picks almost half our number and pleasures each to within an inch of their limitations, and others He only picks five or six and pleasures them but once or twice a piece. But recently He has been choosing an equal ten, and Dennota—the short green woman—is always among those ten. Our Master likes to be suckled and Dennota is His most talented mouth apparently."

"Were you . . . captured . . . like me?" Sam asked, more than a little hesitant to broach the subject.

Keln sighed and shook her head a little sorrowfully. "It is perhaps best if you do not view your being here as the result of a capture. Think more along the lines that you have been chosen, blessed even. Life here at the palace may seem strange to you at first—it did to me too, in the beginning—but it is one of luxury and ease. We are all lucky to be here, cared for by the most powerful ruler on this world, our every wish granted by Cerebus—our keeper."

"What world is this?" A lump of fear almost choked off her words. The thought of being on an alien world was not one she would grow accustomed to any time soon.

"It is named Valeo. It is a planet in the Ysault Dimensional Plane, in the middle of the Sord Star System. Quite far from where you are from, I dare to guess."

Another solar system! Good grief, how could this be happening? How was she ever going to get back home?

"Are you from around here?"

"No. I am far, far removed from my place of birth. But do not pity me," Keln rushed on as Sam sent her just such a look, "I am much happier here than ever I could have been back on my native soil. Here I need never worry or toil. And whenever I am called on to entertain my Master—which I am sorry to say is only rarely now—I am more than happy to do it. Eager in fact, for He is a spectacular lover. I love Him. We all do. You will soon too, if you but let yourself."

Sam highly doubted that. He was a sexy, appealing man—there was no doubt of that—but love him? She'd never loved anyone in her life, besides the love she had for family or friends. She very highly doubted an autocratic harem owner could inspire such a depth of feeling from her.

Just then she caught a glimpse of him through the crowd, standing before the heavily pierced hermaphrodite. The King was stroking the woman's small penis with one hand and diddling her large clitoris with the other. It was obvious that he didn't find such a thing as the fondling of male sex organs taboo . . . or perhaps the fact that the penis was in fact owned by a female made it okay in his book. Whatever the circumstance, the woman was obviously enjoying herself as the King massaged her two sex organs, if the newly engorged length of her cock was any indication of her arousal. A few more strokes and the woman gave a heavy moan, coming onto the hands of the King, gushing pearly liquid from both her cunt and her cock as she shuddered before him in release. Cerebus came forward at once with a towel and cleaned his Master's fingers and the King moved deeper into the crowd of women.

For the first time Sam was afforded a full look at his face. He was indeed a work of contrasts with smooth unblemished skin, sharp high cheekbones, a lushly curved mouth and hard stubborn jaw. His eyes were quite pretty, outlined as they were by kohl and long dark lashes, but they had a decidedly bored look within their sherry depths, which surprised Sam. How could a man of such obviously hedonistic leanings such as Himself be bored while surrounded by so many ready and willing females?

How indeed?

As the King proceeded through the throng about him he paused here and there to fondle or be fondled by his women. But never did he kiss any of them and it seemed a significant thing to Sam. A kiss was the gentlest, most affectionate of all sexual overtures. A lot could be learned about one's partner through a kiss. Love itself could be won or lost with the power of a small kiss. So why did the King not bestow them, at least to the favored in his Collection? Did kisses mean nothing to the people of his race? Were kisses only practiced among humans, perhaps? Surely not, Sam scoffed at the idea. How sad life would be indeed, here on Valeo, if there were no such things as kisses.

The Collector came up behind her then and herded her forward where she joined Ferd and Hali. "These are the newest members of your Collection, Master, your birthday presents."

The King turned away from the woman whose single breast he was presently fondling as the Collector spoke. His eyes roved lazily over them as he approached, but at the last settled unflinchingly on Sam. His eyes took in the fiery warmth of her red hair, the bright emerald of her eyes and the porcelain white of her skin as if he'd never seen the like of it before. With a sinking feeling Sam realized there was a good possibility that he hadn't; she'd yet to see a woman even remotely resembling herself within the Collection. The sinking feeling was because she wasn't quite ready to be noticed by the King. And she certainly didn't want to be noticed because she was considered "odd" or "unique" in her coloring and shape among the other women of his harem.

Dramatically the King walked up to Sam, standing impossibly—proudly—erect as his long legs closed the distance between them, ignoring the other women at her side, and came to stand almost on top of her. Her eyes were only just level with his nipple and it was a little disconcerting to have him standing so very close to her.

Against her will, Sam's eyes rose to meet his as they burned down onto the top of her bent head. She felt dwarfed by him, dangerously so, especially when he began to slowly circle her—almost touching her with the bared skin of his chest as he prowled around—studying her entire form. Never had Sam been so aware of her nudity as she was then, and the chains and jewels that dangled on her form seemed suddenly heavier under his perusal, like brands of ownership instead of decorations. At last the King came back to face her, locking his eyes to hers once more. She couldn't help a spark of defiance from entering her gaze and she was too angry to think of the folly such a sign of spirit might be in her current situation.

All she could think about was how he dared to treat her like an object, as if she had no feelings or say in the matter. Looking her over like a vase or painting he wished to purchase . . . but then he had *collected* her, hadn't he? It was no different than if she *had* been a piece of art that happened to catch his fancy. He saw her as such and would treat her accordingly. Well she would have none of it! The other women of the Collection might be resigned to their station as the King's playthings, but she would be damned before she joined their adoring ranks.

The King sidled up even closer to her, so that their skin was just barely touching. He bowed his head, seemingly entranced by her hair, and softly pressed his lips to it. One of his hands came around and lightly settled on the flare of her bare hip, making the chain that was fastened about it jingle slightly as it was caught between them. Sam tried and failed to suppress a shudder of pleasure at his gentle caresses and had to reassure herself that the loss of her control was most likely due to the lingering effects of the *phuq* dust and not to any real attraction she might be feeling for the King. The King pulled back, sent her a dangerous, enigmatic smile, lifted the hand at her waist and placed it on her unadorned breast.

The heat from his golden-gloved hand scorched her breast nearly to the point of pain, sending shivers of forbidden desire through her entire form. A second more of the erotic torture and he pulled away. Without a second glance in her direction he turned around and threaded once more into the crowd of women, heading back towards his throne. Sam looked down at the breast he had touched and was surprised to see it was now encased in a solid cup fashioned from a bright green emerald. She pulled at the jeweled stone cup, but it would not budge from her skin even the slightest as a result of her efforts. How the odd covering stayed in place Sam couldn't have guessed, but she assumed it functioned no differently from the veil that even now hovered immovably over her lower jaw and mouth.

What did it mean, this jewel over her breast, for surely it meant something? She was given too little time to ponder it. The King's voice broke out over her thoughts—stunning her with its husky beauty—and instantly commanded all of her attentions. "I have made my choice. Let the birthday celebrations begin."

There came then an outpouring of murmurs and cries from the women that rose in volume to a dull roar.

"Fates, Sam, but you've surprised us all." Keln was at her side once more, smiling brilliantly.

"What do you mean?"

"I have been a part of the King's Collection for nearly seven years and never have I known Him to choose less than five partners for an evening. Let alone during a birthday celebration."

Sam felt a sinking sensation in the pit of her stomach. "Keln, suppose—just for a moment—that I am totally in the dark about all of this and explain to me as plainly as possible just what the heck is going on."

Keln laughed, though not unkindly, and patted Sam's hair soothingly. The woman seemed fascinated by her hair. "Well, for one thing, tonight we will celebrate the King's birthday. It is a very special event as you can see by the revelry about us—for many reasons. Every year The Collector finds new females to add to the Collection and gives them to the King as gifts, so we all get to celebrate the new additions to our family.

"Also, tonight is the night that the Satellite Moons will be at their highest peak in the sky. This is important because the natives of this planet believe the two moons will promise a fruitful season among mated couples—and it is also significant because this event only occurs once every three years. I say you have surprised me, Sam, because the King has crowned you His jewel for the night, evidenced by that jeweled cup over your breast—you alone will receive His attentions in the royal bedchamber this night. He has found such favor in you—you, who are new to our family. The King, you see, generally prefers His jewels to be older, more seasoned members of His Collection. I hope you're ready for a magical night indeed."

Sam reeled. "But I don't want to be chosen," she whispered, going white.

Keln's eyes filled with soft compassion. "Do not be afraid, Sam. The King will see to your pleasure in all ways. He is caring and tender. He will not hurt you."

"Doesn't it matter that I am unwilling?"

"Unwilling! But why would you not be willing to give and

receive pleasure? Are you," Keln's voice dropped to an incredulous murmur, "untouched?"

"No," Sam hurried to say, though on second thought she wondered if it might have been better to lie and say that she was. "It's just that I would prefer to be given some choice in the matter of who I have sex with."

"If given a choice would you not find some attraction to our Master?"

Sam wouldn't lie to this woman who was so clearly kind and open. "Well, probably, but it would be different because then I wouldn't be *forced* to choose him. Do you see what I mean?"

"What I see is that you are determined to dig in your heels about this when to do so can only cause you harm in the long run. Do not dwell on the past. Embrace your new future here at the palace. Embrace your new King. Who knows, you've already impressed Him quite a lot, perhaps one day He will choose you as His *chastity keeper*."

"And just what is that?" Sam asked in exasperation. Just when it seemed she was gaining a small understanding of the place, she was thrown some new tidbit to dwell on and mull over.

But Keln wasn't given time to answer her as the King's voice boomed out over the murmuring throng of people once again. "Cerebus, bring my chosen Beloved Ones to me, posthaste. I have great need of them."

Almost immediately Cerebus was at Sam's side, ushering her to the throne beyond the crowd and away from Keln, who waved goodbye to Sam as she went. As they went, the hermaphrodite, the one-breasted woman, and Dennota—all of whom had been fondled in some way by the King, Sam was quick to note—joined them. Too soon they were on the steps of the dais that led up to the lounging King on his throne.

"My beauties. Come. Join me here on my pillows." The King's voice was like a velvet finger trailing down Sam's spine and she shivered. With one last hard look of warning in Sam's direction, Cerebus left them alone with the King.

Sam didn't know how to react. She felt cornered and had to fight the instinctive urge to flee as the King's translucent eyes settled unwaveringly upon her. He must have seen some of the indecision on her face because he gifted her with another of his enigmatic, but not wholly unkind smiles and turned to Dennota instead, motioning her forward.

"I have a longing for your mouth, Beloved One," the King said and swept aside the front of his skirt as he had done earlier for the green-skinned woman. It was then that Sam was afforded her first view of the King's sex. It was a mighty weapon indeed and she felt positively faint just by looking at it.

He was massive in both girth and size, at least twelve or more inches in length and so thick that she couldn't have possibly wrapped her fingers around it comfortably. Sam had never been one to find a man's penis attractive in and of itself, but the King was possessed of the most beautiful cock she had ever seen. It was a delicious caramel color, golden and smooth. His testicles were heavy and—as she had suspected—completely hairless, as was the rest of his form. There was a small golden bar pierced delicately through the base of the head on his shaft, and it glinted in the light a scant second before it was enfolded in the plump lips of Dennota's mouth.

The King looked at Sam once more as the green woman's head began to bob up and down on his phallus. "Do you like what you see, Beloved One?" he asked her silkily.

Sam looked away, refusing to answer him, and he laughed

at her show of spirit. But, too soon, the sounds of Dennota's suckling reached Sam's ears and she couldn't contain her curiosity for long. She glanced back and discovered that the King was waiting for her to do just that.

"Come here," he beckoned and reached out his gloved hand to her.

Against her will it seemed, Sam felt her feet moving her to him and then his hand was resting on her waist.

"Your skin is as soft as the finest down," he murmured raking his eyes from her head to her toes.

Uncomfortable under the intense amber gaze of the King, Sam looked away and studied the room about her. All throughout the throne room, men—who looked much the same as the King, The Collector, and Cerebus so presumably they were all natives of Valeo—and women mingled sharing much talk and laughter. They seemed deferent—respectful— to the King and curiously unfazed by the fact that he was being orally pleasured by a woman between his legs, stroked and fondled by still two more at his side. Footmen brought out golden platters piled high with aromatic food and drink, to the delight of all in attendance. Exotic music was played at a pleasing volume and the revelers enjoyed much dancing. Sam had never seen such a carefree and easy bunch of people. They were all quite obviously happy to be there in the presence of the King and each other.

The King drew her attention once more. "You needn't be hesitant or afraid with me, Beloved One. I will treat you with great care, you have my word on that."

"I'm not afraid of you," Sam bit out, ignoring the shiver in her body as the King's fingers stroked lazy circles on the skin of her waist.

"Good," he said and pulled her forward. When she was

close enough, the King bent his head and buried his face against the swell of her belly. Sam gasped and jerked back reflexively.

"Ah, you smell as good as you feel, though I had little doubt that it was so." The King's eyes glittered wickedly up at her as he allowed her a small retreat.

All of a sudden the King's eyes shuttered—Sam noticed then that the black lines rimming them were tattoos and not kohl powder as she'd thought—and he let out a soft groan. He turned his attentions then to Dennota, pulling her mouth deeper over his cock with a hand in her hair. A few seconds later he groaned again and bucked up against the green woman's mouth, spending his release within the plump seam of her greedy lips. Eagerly the woman lapped up every last creamy drop of the King's come, stroking the large, erect shaft with her hands, milking him for all he was worth. The King's hand had tightened on Sam's waist during his release but now it eased once again and stroked away the little discomfort he had caused while he relaxed as Dennota finished with him.

When Dennota's mouth left him, the King's cock was glistening wet and heavily weighing down between his knees as he began to fall flaccid. The hermaphrodite moved then between his legs, rubbing his cock with her own much smaller one. The King looked up at Sam once more and moved his hand to cup her breast in his palm. He gently flicked the golden ring in her nipple and that quickly he grew erect once more, obviously pleased and fascinated by the glittering jewelry that speared her flesh. The great length of him stabbed skyward as the hermaphrodite climbed over him and impaled herself upon his marble cock. The King pulled Sam closer and pressed his mouth to the underside of her breast as the woman rode him.

Sam was in a quandary. Her body was alive with arousal—both from the scene that played out before her and the erotic ministrations of the King's hand and mouth at her breast. But her mind was a storm of indignation at being treated with such familiarity by a man she had only just met. If *met* was even the right word for the situation—she didn't even know his name! She was afraid to openly rebuke the King's advances, his people might not forgive such a thing lightly, but she would be damned if she would return any of his affections. There was only so much she was willing to surrender at this juncture.

His back was pillowed by the one-breasted woman at his back, her arms wrapped around his chest, hands stroking his chest and belly from behind him. He raised one hand and fondled the woman's large nipple as he was fondling Sam's, clearly not one to ignore his women as they serviced him. Dennota seemed to be in her own little world as she writhed on the floor at the King's side. It was clear that she had found her own release when seeing to the King's needs and was content to be ignored for the moment.

The King seemed to notice her failure to participate in the festivities and pulled back from her breast to look deep into her eyes. "Won't you touch me, Beloved One? I need your touch so badly." His words pulled at Sam's heartstrings in a most unusual and unexpected way. It was as though he was tortured with the knowledge that she didn't want to touch him. As if he emotionally craved her surrender. But Sam pushed away the feelings, considering them an unforgivable weakness, and reminded herself that this man was too used to getting his own way. He was quite obviously spoiled by all of his women and expecting the same treatment from her.

"Is it not enough to have these three women touching you? Why not focus your attentions on them and leave me be?" Her voice was low and her words were intended for his ears alone. The last thing she wanted was to involve anyone else in this conversation.

The King's head recoiled as if he'd received a physical blow. His eyes when they met hers were full of angry pride and tinged with hurt, though Sam was dubious as to the sincerity of the latter emotion within their amber depths. He opened his mouth to say something but was swept away in the throes of another orgasm before he could lay voice to those words. The woman that rode him bounced up and down on his cock, crying out as her own release shook her until both her cock and cunt were creamy with ejaculate. The King's face went slack with passion and he groaned brokenly as he shuddered and spent himself within the slick folds of his partner's sex.

After a long moment the King unceremoniously plucked the hermaphrodite off of his body and set her down beside him on the dais. He turned and gave another hard glare to Sam and jerked the one-breasted woman to him with less than gentle care. He spun the woman about, bent her over and without so much as a by your leave stabbed the long, thick mass of his cock into the woman's ass. Luckily the woman appeared to have a very willing and eager ass, because the aggressive penetration of her nether region by the King was met with nothing less than a wailing moan of pleasure from her parted lips. The King pounded furiously into the woman, causing her single breast to bounce up and down vigorously with every motion. And all the while he kept his eyes locked to Sam's, clearly goading her, taunting her, as he fucked the woman before him with calculated ferocity.

All too soon the woman cried out and experienced her release. The clenching of her anal muscles milked the King of yet another explosive climax as well, causing Sam no end of embarrassment as the King's eyes remained steady on hers as he came. It was far too personal suddenly, her being witness to these acts of carnality. Where before she had merely been uncomfortable she was now excruciatingly aware of her own part that was yet to play out in this game and it was obvious that the King was deliberately heightening her awareness of that fact. The promise in his eyes spoke volumes without his even opening his mouth to speak the words.

When the woman was limp and spent in the King's arms he gently lowered her to the floor at his feet then moved to catch Sam's arm none too gently in his gloved hand.

"I have seen to their pleasure as is my duty, it would have been unforgivable of me to leave them unfulfilled. But for the rest of the night, Beloved One, you will get your wish. You and I will be a duet. Just we two. Alone. Now come!" He needn't have bothered to bark out the command, not when he so easily dragged her unwilling body behind him as he stalked down the dais and across the great throne room.

"Cerebus!" the King called out in a hard, authoritative voice. "Prepare a service for two in my chambers at once."

Sam had to tamp down once more on the primitive and instinctive urge to flee as it became clear where the King was taking her. Oh if only she hadn't opened her big mouth, but then she never had been one for diplomacy. It seemed that she was about to reap the consequences of her actions. In a big way.

5

The King's chamber was a direct mirror in design as that of the room in which she'd awakened just that morning. However, the color scheme was perhaps a bit more volatile, with a heavier usage of crimson and black and gold. The exotic barren landscape beyond the high windows of his room reflected the rays of the setting sun as though a torch had been lit to the dark coppery sands.

"You are uniquely beautiful. But then that is why you were chosen I have no doubt," The King said into her ear, causing her to jump in surprise. She'd been standing there, riveted by the opulence of her surroundings for longer than she would have thought possible under the circumstances, and his voice had startled her.

"I am not beautiful," she said firmly.

"Yes you are," he responded in kind. "I have never seen such coloring." His voice grew hoarse and he reached out to capture a lock of her hair between his fingers. "You are truly one of a kind."

"My coloring is garish, I'll have you know. And it's not all that rare on my world."

"You are trying to goad me. Why?" He seemed truly puzzled over it.

"I'm not sure," she admitted and wondered over the truth of it. "I can't seem to help it. I guess I just get a little surly after being kidnapped and carted off to an alien world. Call me crazy but that's just my initial reaction to all of this."

"You have a very independent nature. That much I can clearly see and it pleases me that it is so despite your anger. Now come, let us forget our tempers—I have already forgiven you yours—and enjoy our evening repast. Cerebus has already come and gone it seems." He turned from her then and led her by the hand to a short table flanked by plush cushions on the floor, which was piled high with aromatic foods.

"Recline a bit and allow me to help make you more comfortable." Before Sam could reply he had pushed her back against the pillows on the floor and removed her veil with a wave of his hand. Then, gently but insistently, he spread her legs wide with his hand, intending to remove the chastity plugs.

"You are breathtaking," he said and kissed the seam of her sex between her spread thighs. Sam squeaked in surprise and jerked away. "Do not fear me," he implored her in a coaxing voice, gazing up at her from his perch between her legs. He dipped his head again and drew her swollen clit into his mouth, stroking the soft tissues of her inner thighs in a soothing manner. His lips and tongue were searing hot against her aroused flesh and she couldn't help the moan of pure bliss that escaped her lips. That her body could go from uncomfortable embarrassment to full arousal in so short a span of time was shocking to her in the extreme.

There was a sudden, intense feeling of relief as his adept fingers removed the golden dildo from her drenched pussy, but it was short-lived as his fingers took its place, stretching her even more fully than before. The King kissed her clit—hard—and pulled back to watch his hands move between her legs. He thrust his fingers into her three more times then withdrew them. He brought his shining wet fingers to his mouth, keeping his eyes locked to hers, and licked away every last trace of her arousal from them with his tongue. Sam moaned again but it ended in a choking sound as he neatly removed the butt plug.

"Now you can relax and enjoy your meal to its fullest," he murmured, sending her a truly devilish look with his sherry gold eyes, quite obviously well aware that he'd left her in a state of razor-edged arousal with his erotic attentions.

"You're a beast," she grumbled inelegantly, reached forward to snare what looked like a slice of pineapple from her dinner tray and popped it into her mouth, eyes bulging their surprise at its robust and sour flavor. It wasn't pineapple but it was tasty nonetheless.

The King's eyes widened in surprise and he let out a laugh. "I like your sharp tongue, I think. Perhaps you will find that you like mine as well?" He leaned forward and licked a trail of stray fruit juice from the stubborn point of her chin before Sam could even think to move away.

"Why are you teasing me? I thought you were mad at me?" Sam couldn't help asking.

The King smiled and toyed with a lock of her hair. "I admit I was a little taken aback by your harsh words to me in the throne room, but I am not one to hold a grudge. I can see that you are still adjusting to the thought of being here, being part of my Collection. I cannot say that I blame you for that. But in time I am sure that you will bless the day you were chosen for me by The Collector."

"That'll be the day," she mumbled and rolled her eyes. What arrogance . . . but then he was probably used to females treating him like the sun rose and set in his pants.

The King put two fingers beneath her chin and forced her to meet his eyes dead-on. "Give yourself a chance. Give me a chance. I am trying my best to woo you, the least you can do is let go of your negativity for the time we spend together tonight. Enjoy yourself. If there is one thing I believe in implicitly, it is the healing power of pleasure . . . and I promise you I will give *that* to you in spades."

"What if I don't want pleasure from you?"

"Not want pleasure? Now I know you are just joking with me." He sent her a killer smile full of charm and the dark lure of sex. "All beings desire pleasure, a surcease of need or want, and there is no shame in that. Come, let me show you." He leaned forward and buried his lips in the hair that draped across her shoulders.

"But I haven't eaten yet," she protested, stalling for time.

"What need have you of such trivial sustenance when I am in your arms?"

"Such conceit!" She started to push him away but stopped when she saw the wicked look in his eyes.

"I just wanted to get a rise out of you, Beloved One. There is no need to get physically aggressive."

"I am not getting aggressive," she growled.

The King merely laughed at her contradictory behavior and nuzzled her neck with his lips. "Your hair is the color of the brightest flame. I fear it will burn me if I am not careful. And your scent," he breathed deeply at her throat, sending pleasant tremors racing through her body, "it is enough to drive me wild with lust."

"Perhaps I should bathe it off then," she said sullenly, trying her best not to respond to the seductive tone of his voice and the close cage of his arms as they braced on either side of her on the pillows.

"A bath . . . yes. Let me bathe the other women from my body so that you are more comfortable in my arms." He pressed a soft kiss to her shoulder and pushed away from her, rising to his feet. "Eat your fill, my jewel, so that your strength is at its peak when I rejoin you on the pillows."

Sam expected him to leave the room for his bath and was therefore surprised when, in the marble floor behind her, there appeared a deep round pool filled with water. The King stepped into it, skirt, jewelry and all, and dunked his head under the water. When he reemerged his hair was long and loose, trailing like a cape into the water all about him. He dunked once more then exited the bath, trailing water onto the floor in his wake—water that miraculously disappeared after little more than a few seconds, as if it had never been spilled.

The King shamelessly pulled the dripping skirt from his body, exposing firm round buttocks, which made Sam's mouth water just to look at, and shook the water from his body. Moments later he was dry, his hair falling in glistening ringlets down to his knees. He didn't bother to redress, but came back to her side gloriously nude but for the golden adornments on his body.

"You were too busy watching me bathe to eat your meal," he teased her with a satisfied smile.

"You didn't bathe, you just took a quick dunk in the water!"

"And how else would you bathe?" he asked with a curious look.

"With soap and a cloth or sponge," she said with no little amount of exasperation.

The King chuckled and he responded as if he were informing a child of the obvious. "But these waters are enchanted so I have no need of harsh cleaning agents or exfoliants. You were given such a bath but a few hours ago in the preparation chamber. I assure you that I am as clean as it is possible to get."

Sam swept her eyes down his length and felt her body suffuse with the warmth of arousal.

"You like the way I look. I can see it in your eyes."

Sam huffed, blowing her long bangs out of her eyes. "You are attractive, I'll give you that. But just because you're good-looking doesn't mean I'm going to hop into bed with you like that." She snapped her fingers for an example. "I'm not that easy."

"You want me," he urged.

"Maybe. A little. So what? I'm sure you're used to that kind of response from women. It doesn't mean anything."

An arrogant and wholly dangerous look entered his eyes. "It means that I can use all of my wiles without guilt. Because there is already some desire in you for me, I can do this for example," he raised his hand and blew and generous amount of *phuq* dust into her face, "in order to entice you into my arms without it feeling like an unfair coercion."

Sam's body immediately went up in flames. Her head grew light and her mind dreamy. Why she was fighting her attraction to the King but seconds before she couldn't begin to fathom, but it was better late than never to rectify her mistakes in dealing with him. She launched herself into his arms, throwing them both backwards into the depths of the cushions that littered the floor. The King's voice chuckled darkly into her ear, the delicious sound causing her body to shudder with the force of her lust for him, and settled her more easily against him. Sam's lips sought out his but he deftly turned his head before they could reach their destination. She moaned out her disappointment and settled her lips at his jaw instead.

Oh such bliss was this! Her mouth was swollen and tingling, so that by pressing her mouth against his smooth caramel skin they felt an immense wave of relief, enticing her to bury them deeper against his flesh. Her body felt heavy and thick with arousal. Her King sensed this and swept his hands lovingly down her back and buttocks, making her nearly swoon with rapture. In turn she raced her own eager hands down his firm, muscled stomach and thighs before zeroing in on the object of her greatest desire—his long, thick cock.

"Nah, ah, ah," he admonished, gently taking her hands from his arousal. "We will play this out my way this first time, Beloved One. Come. Let me show you what it is like to be loved by your King." He rose, lifting her with him—which was a lucky thing since she had no strength to stand on her own—and carried her to a large cushioned bench in a curtained corner. The bench was upholstered in something resembling leather or vinyl and was just as smooth against her skin when he laid her down upon it. He positioned her legs just so on either side of the bench so that she straddled it, leaving her wet sex open and vulnerable to his gaze.

The King turned and retrieved a large silver pitcher from its resting place beside the bench. He held it over her body for a moment then deliberately poured its contents over her body with a flourish. Silvery, glistening oil splashed its warmth onto her body, covering her from neck to feet in a thick river of the stuff. Sam gasped and instinctively raised her arms to shield herself but only succeeded in getting her hands and arms drenched as well. When the vessel of heated oil was empty the King tossed it carelessly aside and straddled the bench so that his spread knees butted against hers.

He reached out his hands and massaged the oil into her thighs, sweeping his palms in broad soothing motions, deliberately easing his ministrations on her inner thighs so that they were more of a caress than a massage. Before long Sam was spreading her legs wider by pushing her knees against his, seeking to bring her sex that much closer to his magical hands. The King only chuckled at her motions and purposefully avoided the place that most needed his attention.

Sam moaned when his hands moved up and kneaded into the flare of her hips. That such a seemingly innocent press of his hands could bring her so close to the pinnacle of pleasure would have stunned her had she been capable of any rational thought. His hands then proceeded up to her belly, ribs and breasts. Her nipples were swollen and hard from her arousal and the slip slide of his hands over them was both a torture and a gift. The oil was positively burning against her flesh now as he rubbed her down with it, but it was such a pleasant fire that it only served to heighten the pleasure of his touch.

Suddenly the King lifted her and turned her over onto her stomach on the bench, again positioning her legs so that she straddled its girth. He pushed aside her hair and ran his oily hands down the dip of her spine. Her toes curled and she sighed, more than willing to let him continue his massage. After long, wondrous moments of his kneading the planes and slopes of her back, the King turned his attentions to her buttocks, plumping and squeezing them as if they were ripe fruits. He spread her cheeks and administered a heavy dollop of the oil into the crease and rubbed it silkily into her most delicate skin.

Soon Sam was panting and moaning with the pleasure of his attentions. Her rear rose up off of the bench, until she was presenting herself like a lioness for her mate. The King chuckled but this time it was a strained sound and then he bent forward and laid his lips to the dripping wet heat of her pussy. The thick moisture of the oil had mingled with her own arousal and created an exquisite, silky friction between the flesh of her sex and the flesh of his lips and tongue as he moved his face deeper against her.

Too soon—oh the torture of it!—his rooting mouth moved away and he turned her back over to face him. His lips came down onto one of her swollen nipples and his large sex prodded at the portal of her cunt. A moment of tight fullness and he was through, causing Sam to gasp with the shock of his heavy girth that quickly stretched her full to bursting. He was so long that it seemed an eternity that he came into her, filling her with each delicious, hard and meaty inch of him until at last his balls rested against the oiled wetness of her behind.

The King groaned long and loud against her nipple, before biting down gently upon that tender flesh until she too was groaning with the torturous pleasure of it.

"You feel like fire and silk around my cock, Beloved One," he gasped against her breast. "Squeeze me with your muscles, tight."

Sam did as he commanded and moaned with the resulting pleasure of her motion. Immediately she repeated it, closing the inner muscles of her vagina around his impaling thickness until she was aching with delight.

"Yes. Just like that," he moaned, clearly enjoying the

movements of her body as much as she was. "Milk me with your sweet, juicy pussy."

Too soon, without his even having moved once inside of her, the clasping and unclasping of her inner muscles around him brought them both to an explosive climax. Sam cried out and raked her nails down his back. The King squeezed her breasts tightly in his hands and groaned against her chest as he filled her full of his ejaculate.

Sam was already spent and tired, but the King had no such weakness. He pulled himself free of her, glistening and still fully engorged. Without a word he crawled up her body, placed his mighty cock between her breasts, plumped the globes up with his hands and pumped himself in and out of the valley he created between them. The oil eased his way as he moved and the feel of his cock there between her swollen breasts, butting against her chin on each up thrust he made, had her wet and ready for more of him in mere moments. Sam couldn't resist palming the clenching muscles of his buttocks in her hands as he moved against her and was pleased when the King moaned his pleasure at the caress.

His thumbs stroked over her nipples with each movement he made, causing them to tingle and swell even further than before. The effects of the *phuq* dust flooded her with hot molten lust, but had nothing to do with the soft aching jerk of her heart that occurred every time his exotic eyes met hers. He was truly a master, playing her body, heart and mind with the skill gained from his life as a sex god and she was powerless to resist his potent allure.

With a mighty shout the King's hot seed spurted against her chest, breasts, and chin as he found yet another release. Breathing hard he moved down and rubbed the thick essence of himself into her skin, even smearing some onto her lips and she eagerly licked it away with her tongue. He bent down, heedless of the sperm that covered her flesh, and took one swollen breast deep into his mouth, sucking it clean.

The King threw her legs up over his shoulders and impaled her once more with his mighty cock. He pumped into the farthest depths of her, reaching her very womb and scraping against that most perfect place within her with the bar that pierced the head of his shaft. It was too soon for her and Sam fought instinctively against the approaching release that threatened to rack her body with a mixture of both pleasure and pain. But the King would have none of that. His skillful hands reached down and rubbed into the soft wet flesh of her sex, pulling on the full, bald lips, the swollen clit and ruby-threaded hair with his fingertips. Sam screamed and felt her inner muscles clamp down like a vise onto the invading flesh of the King as she reached an explosive climax. The King, unbelievably, joined her in the culmination, once again filling her to the brim with the wet heat of his come.

Sam lost all track of time as the King continued to love her throughout the long, sultry night. They did not get any rest or sleep until well after the dawn.

6

The light of early morning stabbed at Sam's bloodshot eyes and she moaned in protest as the satin covers were jerked unceremoniously from her body.

"Wake up, my Jewel. A new day is upon us."

"Mmplf," she mumbled in response to the overly cheerful voice and snuggled back down into the pillows.

"Get up sleepyhead." A hand smacked loudly against the exposed flesh of her bottom. "The day is wasting away while you sleep."

"Let it, I'm too tired to care," she grumbled.

The King laughed and lightly jerked her to her feet, tenderly brushing her tangled red hair out of her eyes with his fingertips. Sam winced as the sudden, unexpected movement caused her much used and tender flesh to protest vehemently. A silvery trace of semen ran down her leg but she was far too tired to bother wiping it away. The King had filled her; let him see the results, she thought sullenly, trying her best to forget how incredibly pleasant the night had been. How sweet and beautiful it had been, despite her initial misgivings.

The *phuq* dust had worn off sometime during the evening, but her ardor for the King had not cooled. It had only flamed brighter and hotter in the deep hours of the night.

"You are truly beautiful, my Jewel, and you have greatly lifted my spirits with your generous body and heart. I have a gift for you."

Sam's tired eyes immediately widened and grew more alert. The King chuckled once more. "I knew that would get your attention," he boasted arrogantly.

The King went down on his knees before her. His white silk skirt was split on both sides today and exposed a generous amount of caramel skin as he lowered himself and nudged apart the love-swollen lips of her sex. He pressed a light kiss to the rise of her clit and with a flourish of his hand presented her with his gift. It was a delicate hoop with a small emerald suspended by a chain dangling down from it. The King's eyes gleamed their satisfaction as she gasped in appreciation of the jewel's beauty and he nodded his satisfaction at her reaction. He placed the hoop against the flesh of her clit, waved his hand over it, and when he pulled away the jewel was pierced painlessly through her flesh. When Sam moved, the dangling emerald hung down past the bald mound of her vagina and tickled against her inner thigh, glinting in the light with every movement she made.

"Do you like it?" he asked in a husky whisper.

"Yes," she couldn't help admitting, though she never would have willingly gotten such a piercing back at home. She'd never thought herself the type to enjoy such adornments.

"The jewel has a name. Sar'chesh. It is a shard from a much larger stone—Sar'cheih-a—which rests in my royal scepter and therefore makes this offering quite priceless. I hope you treasure it. As I treasure you, Beloved One."

What else could she say? The gift humbled her, if not the gesture, which she was sure he made to each and every one of his nameless "Jewels." "I will treasure it," she vowed, because it was true.

"Now come. You must return to your quarters and break your fast." The King rose once more.

"I need to bathe," she protested, feeling the sticky essence of him coating her practically from head to toe. He had loved her long and thoroughly during the night, of that there could be no doubt. He was truly an insatiable beast.

"Won't you keep my scent on your skin for a little while longer?" he asked silkily.

"But I look a mess! Everyone will see—"

"Shh. Wear my seed proudly before the others in the Collection. They will see it as a sign of your power over me, as evidence of your prowess as a woman and they will respect you highly. As you deserve."

Sam was silent as the King led her from his chambers, walking her back to the women's chambers with a hand placed lightly at the small of her back. The emerald cast that enclosed her breast still remained, feeling heavier now that the night was over. During the hours spent in the King's arms she had forgotten for a little while the situation in which she found herself. But now, with the harsh light of the morning, she remembered and was troubled.

Had her friends and family back home truly forgotten about her, as The Collector had said? True, it had only been a little over a day since she'd left, but it felt to her like ages had already passed her by. Long ages. Perhaps so much time had passed that she really was just a memory to those she'd known before. Or perhaps The Collector's magic was so powerful it could change history. She was afraid to ask and find out the truth either way.

Down through endless winding corridors they went and Sam again noticed various doors sporting large jeweled handles as they passed. She wanted to ask the King where they led to but suspected that he wouldn't tell her so she decided not to waste her breath on the question. Perhaps she would find out from the other women later. Then, too soon it seemed to her, they came to their destination. The King waved his gloved hand over an unadorned wall and there appeared in the middle a doorway through which they proceeded without pause.

The women of the Collection were already gathered and waiting to greet them. The women acted surprised to see their King escorting her and Sam had a moment to be grateful that she didn't have to face this group of strangers alone, for it seemed plain that the King didn't normally accompany his Jewels back to their chambers after a night spent in his.

The King turned to her and before she had any inkling of his intentions he positioned the Veil over her face with a flourish of his hand.

"To keep your mouth chaste for me, Beloved One," he said softly. He went down on his knees before her, pulling her with him after one long searing look into her eyes. He laid her out before him, putting on a grand show for their audience. He trailed his fingers over the seam of her vagina, which was still creamy and wet from his many orgasms spent between her legs during their night together. He spread her nether lips wide apart, bent down, and licked the exposed flesh of her cunt with the flat of his tongue. Sam moaned. She couldn't help it.

Her body was so sensitive to the slightest touch that it would have been impossible for her to find no pleasure in his erotic caress.

"And to keep your body chaste for me as well." A moment later and her chastity plugs were inserted carefully and pleasurably into her nether orifices. The King tongued her clit one last time then rose, bringing her to her shaking feet with him.

The King leaned down from his considerable height over her and bestowed a soft, chaste kiss to her forehead. The back of his unadorned hand stroked lazily over the swollen peak of her breast before he pulled back and gifted her with a sultry smile. "Until tonight, my Jewel, think only of me and the untold pleasures I have yet to show you." With those last heady words of promise he turned on his heel and left the courtyard with Sam staring dumbfounded after him.

Of a sudden she was in the midst of an army of giggling females, each begging to hear some specific detail of the night she had spent as the King's Jewel. A few women were even so bold as to approach her and lick a trace or two of the King's sperm from her skin, their veils having been removed by Cerebus in anticipation of a meal no doubt, until Sam growled her displeasure over such forward behavior and they refrained from further advances.

"Let her be. Give her some space, girls, she is still new here." Keln's voice broke over the din as she moved at once to Sam's side. "Come, Sam. Let us move now to the bath where we can all relax. Perhaps after your muscles have eased you will see fit to share the details of your evening with the rest of us." She winked reassuringly at Sam, who was immensely grateful to the woman for her intervention.

As one the group of women moved to the large fountain pool and entered the sparkling waters. Sam gave a sigh as the water lapped around her thighs and mons. The steaming warmth healed and soothed the chapped flesh of her tender sex almost immediately. She dunked her weary head beneath the water and was amazed to feel the last of her aches and worries flee from her as if they had never been. What she wouldn't have given for a bath like this on an early Monday morning back at home.

For the next few hours Sam and the women frolicked in the healing waters of their bath. Sam was so relaxed by the end of it that she found herself content to let the others feel her hair or flesh, as they seemed wont to do. Her hair, its color and texture, fascinated the women and in a way it was most flattering though under any other circumstances it would have made Sam a little uncomfortable. When a hand or mouth strayed too close to her breasts or sex she pulled away—not out of shyness or disgust—but because she was still far too tender after the King's loving to tolerate such explorations no matter how gentle they might be.

Too soon Cerebus entered the courtyard and bade them exit their bath. With a wave of his hand there appeared long tables laden down with foods of which the women were invited to eat their fill. He removed Sam's veil so that she could eat with the others. Sam was famished and ate until her stomach was quite full, eager to try a little morsel from each exotic dish. When they were finished with their meal Cerebus offered them each a bowl of lightly scented water and a small towel to clean their fingers and mouths.

Cerebus, it seemed, was quick to forgive his earlier displeasure with Sam, offering her kind smiles as he passed just as he did with the other women in their turn. It was clear that Cerebus was a gentle soul deep down; a man loyal and committed to his King and the women under his care. Whenever one of the women voiced a need or want he was quick to see that their wishes were carried out. Not once did he deny a request and not once did he balk or complain. In fact it was clear to Sam that no one in this new world was given much to complaining or negative feeling. These people as a whole were given more to gentle pleasures and the pursuit of happiness than to lugubriousness.

Before Sam really understood what was going on, the women had all moved away from the table to gather in a large circle around Cerebus by the fountain pool, lying back on pillows and cushions they had gathered along the way. Sam joined them, sitting between Keln and Ferd as they had thoughtfully reserved a spot for her amongst them. Keln's large equine body folded down on itself so that she rested on her side with her long horse legs curled in front. It was then that Sam noticed the very human sex organ that rested between the centaur's legs, a puffy red vagina, bald and filled with a chastity plug just as hers was. It was a strange sight, but then Sam was surprisingly growing more and more accustomed to such things.

Cerebus exited the circle and fetched two large silver tureens and several small matching bowls from an alcove in the wall. The bowls he deposited, one apiece, with the women and filled them with oil from one of the tureens. From the other he took a pinch of *phuq* dust and dashed it into the bowls. Sam wondered what new ritual was about to be played out. After long moments in which Cerebus fetched more and more bowls to provide each woman with her own, she grew increasingly more curious. When Cerebus was through and every woman had a bowl full of glistening oil, the women dipped their fingers into the bowl, spread their legs and began to masturbate, uncaring of their audience. Their golden plugs and piercings glinted between their oily fingers as they stroked themselves shamelessly and with eager abandon. Sam was shocked to her toes but—sooner than she would have guessed—accepting, because the women seemed oblivious of Cerebus and one another as they played with themselves like eager sirens.

Cerebus noticed at once that Sam was hesitant to join the group and moved to her with a concerned look in his soft dark eyes. "Is something wrong, Sam?"

"No," she said, voice husky and embarrassed despite her efforts to remain aloof.

"Yet you do not join the others."

"I'm . . . I'm a little sore," she admitted and was glad that it was true and she didn't have to admit to her prudish embarrassment of the proceedings surrounding them.

"Forgive me, I should have realized." He gently pushed her back against her cushions and attempted to spread her legs. Sam instinctively protested, clamping her knees firmly together.

"I will not hurt you, Sam. I just need to make sure that your flesh is soothed and healed. It would not do to have you tender and bruised when my Master comes to fetch you tonight." He smiled at her with the last words, obviously pleased that his King had found favor with her.

So Sam dropped back and allowed Cerebus to spread her legs wide apart, the better to inspect her with his dark, knowing eyes. Cerebus gathered oil in his fingertips and warmed them with his breath before laying them against the swollen flesh of her sex. The oil instantly soothed her tissues, but also awoke a need within her that had her breathing harder and she willingly spread her legs further for Cerebus' attentions. Gently, Cerebus removed the plug that filled her pussy and poured a dollop of oil into her channel with the bowl. He rubbed the oil into the saddle of her sex, the full outer lips and the soft skin within, but was careful not to penetrate her channel in any way with his fingers.

Sam sighed and began to relax beneath Cerebus' gentle ministrations. Her body thrummed with a soft arousal but after the initial starburst of sensation it dimmed and left her feeling dreamy instead of lustful. Cerebus poured another generous dollop of oil between her legs and reinserted the golden plug. All of Sam's discomfort had eased away and she was left dozing against the pillow as Cerebus moved on and supervised the care of the others in the Collection. Before long the moans of the women increased in frequency as one by one they found release under their own hands, rolling their hips into the air as if accepting the thrust of a lover.

Sam needed her sleep and Cerebus and the other women left her to it, seeming to understand without having to be told that she had gained no rest during her night with the King. It was several hours later before Sam awoke and time already for another meal. The women primped and giggled amongst themselves, preparing themselves for the King should he choose them for the night—or so Keln informed her. It was a given that Sam would be amongst the women chosen, but no one held it against her or showed jealousy that she was so favored. In fact the women seemed happy for her, perhaps a little in awe of her—she was a newcomer and that in itself was a rarity—and definitely friendly to her. Before much time had passed, Sam was already feeling more and more at ease, as if she had a true place among them, as if she belonged.

The day passed by for Sam in a blur of relaxing naps and lazy swims in the fountain pool. The sun sank low on the horizon of the coppery black sands of Valeo and the Collection was once more gathered in the throne room to stand before the King. Sam wondered what kind of night lay ahead of her . . . and how many women she would have to join at the King's side. Though she was the King's Jewel for the night and allowed the time alone with him in his bedchamber, she knew she would not be the only woman to pleasure him at his throne. Already she was learning much about this new world around her.

The King, surprisingly, chose only two other women that night besides Sam. Keln seemed especially proud of Sam, telling her plainly that it was her ability to please the King that made him choose so few partners from the Collection. Sam had no such illusions about herself; probably the King was just too tired after his long night with her to have the stamina for too many women tonight.

The revelry of the people in the throne room was not conducive for brooding and Sam joined the King and his chosen few at the throne with fewer and fewer sarcastic misgivings in her mind. It was that easy to let herself go with the flow and simply enjoy herself as the others seemed eager and willing to do. The King greeted her with a smile and a soft press of his face into the swell of her stomach.

He surprised her and every other listening ear with his first words. "My Jewel. You are lovelier now than you were yesterday. Come. I know you are territorial so I will not touch any woman but you tonight so that you will find favor with me. I have chosen these two because they find completion with the consumption of seed and do not need further stimulation." Sam immediately noticed Dennota amongst the two women. So that was why the King hadn't needed to have sex with the woman the night before to help her find her release. "They will take the edge off of my need with their mouths," he continued. "Afterward you and I shall retire for the night." He seemed pleased with himself over the gesture and was boyishly handsome as he smiled at her.

Sam couldn't help it, she smiled back and stepped closer to him as the first woman stepped up the dais and wrapped her lips around the swollen flesh of the King's cock. Sam felt her body react to the sight and let out a soft sigh when the King's fingers moved to stroke her exposed breast. His mouth soon followed, his lips pulling and his tongue licking at the swollen flesh of her nipple. His hands gripped the flare of her hips, plumping and kneading the flesh gently. Soon he found his first release and he moaned against her nipple, vibrating it pleasantly. The creamy white milk of his come filled the woman's mouth to overflowing but she cleaned up every last drop, crying out too when she found release.

Dennota moved to follow the first woman, taking the King's cock deep within her greedy throat. The King's fingers moved down to cup the hairless flesh of Sam's sex, delving between the seam to find the silky wetness beyond.

"You're ready for me already," he sighed appreciatively against her breast before taking it deep into his mouth, suckling it with noisy abandon.

Sam was soon bucking against the King's mouth and hand, seeking more and more of the delicious torment he visited upon her. The King groaned and pulled away, throwing her a searing look from beneath his long dark lashes.

"I find myself ever eager to retire to my bedchamber," he said huskily.

The King reached down and gripped the base of his cock in his hand. Dennota's head bobbed upon him as she fucked him with her mouth and he aided her ministrations with a pumping motion of his hand. Sam watched in fascination as the King stroked himself to completion within the woman's mouth. He pulled back to afford Sam a better look as he spurted another thick wash of semen into the green woman's mouth. Dennota moaned and swallowed it down eagerly, bucking her hips, finding her own release as she did so.

The King groaned loudly, squeezing the last pearly drops of his release into the woman's mouth with his fist. Dennota licked his cock clean and moved away from him with a gentle, friendly smile in Sam's direction. Immediately the King captured Sam's hand and raced with her to his chambers, commanding Cerebus to prepare them a meal as he had the night before. Sam's body was tingling with giddy excitement.

And much as the night before, she gained no sleep until well past the dawn.

7

Two weeks passed and a sort of routine became the norm for Samantha. As unusual as that routine might have been in her former life, Sam found herself enjoying it nonetheless. Each evening the King had Cerebus fetch Sam from the Collection. Each night Sam and the King spent endless hours making love and sharing lovers' secrets with one another, for the King was ever interested in the life she had led before coming to him. And each morning the King escorted her back to the women's courtyard, kissed her lightly on the forehead, and bid her goodbye for the day. It would have been lovely if Sam weren't reminded each passing moment that their tryst would not last forever. She would not be his favorite for long, though the emerald cup stayed firm over her breast.

She didn't even know his name.

And since the King never called her by anything other

than his usual endearments she assumed he didn't know hers either.

What a travesty that she should be losing her heart to the one man who would never want it. The one man who would never really have any use for it. He was kind and caring to her, seeing to her every need in bed and out of it, but from all accounts that was how he treated all of his women. It was why they all revered him so much.

Just now Sam and the other women were gathered in their circle masturbating—a pastime that Sam had of late begun to participate in. As the days wore on it seemed to her that she missed her King more and more with each passing hour and she needed the relief of self-pleasure to sustain her until their evenings together. Her body positively ached by the time her royal lover sent Cerebus to fetch her, weeping for the King's touch so that even the slightest shift of her chastity plugs tortured her with a mix of pain and pleasure. She needed release more and more, no matter if it was from her own ministrations.

Sam moaned and bucked her hips as she rubbed the *phuq* oil into the swollen button of her clit with her fingers. The slippery skin of her vagina tingled with each pass of her fingers and she spread her nether lips farther apart, gasping when the sensation nearly undid her completely. Cool air teased her splayed sex, contrasting with the warmth of the *phuq* oil. She imagined in her mind that the fingers touching her belonged to her King. That her clit was being manipulated not by her own fingertips but by his skillful lips and tongue instead. She cried out and rolled her hips, enjoying the feel of her chastity plugs shifting deep inside of her body. She was so wet, so swollen . . . oh if only He could be here with her now.

And then, as if her wish had indeed come true, she opened

her eyes and there he was, staring at her from a distance across the courtyard. His golden eyes fairly blazed with heat as he watched her stroke herself to completion. Sam's sex pulsed and throbbed, as if his gaze had the power to physically caress her, and her fingers rubbed frantic circles into her clit as she approached the fury of her orgasm. She closed her eyes on a sigh and that quickly the King was at her side.

He came down upon her like a beast covering its mate, growling and throwing aside his skirt. He removed the chastity plugs that filled her and the Veil that covered her face with deft and hurried motions. Grabbing his cock at its thick base he positioned himself at her portal and came into her with one long thrust. Sam was so wet and ready that she easily accepted his girth, her body easing his way with a spurt of heated moisture that made him groan and buck deeper into the depths of her. Eagerly and without shame Sam wrapped her legs about his waist, locking him to her as he began to rock within her.

The King breathed hot warmth into her mouth but Sam knew that was as close as he would come to kissing her. She accepted it, knowing it was his way, and savored the sweet breath he gave her with every ounce of love and passion within her. His chest was adorned with a gold-plated rib corselet and it scraped against the tender flesh of her breasts with each movement he made. His hair was dressed in long thin braids and threaded through with tiny sparkling diamonds all of which tickled against her face, arms and sides. All over her body there was the sensation of his touch as every portion of his form caressed her in its way.

Deeper and deeper he moved, harder and harder, shaking her frame against the soft pillows that cushioned her. He was as close to losing control as Sam had ever seen him, obviously greatly affected by the sight of her masturbating. His forehead came down upon hers, the perspiration dotting his brow mingling with hers as he looked down into her eyes.

"Your pussy belongs to me. Only to me. Say it," he commanded.

"My pussy belongs to you. Only to you," she repeated, meaning every word with every fiber of her being.

"Who is your Master, my Jewel?"

"You are."

"Say it!"

"Master. You are my Master," she panted, clutching at him with desperate hands.

"I am the Master of your luscious pussy. No one will ever fuck this juicy piece but me. Only me," he groaned brokenly.

"Yes. Yes!"

The King increased the tempo and force of his thrusts, jarring Sam's teeth and making her wail with the pleasure that swamped her senses. The muscles deep within her sex pulsed and gripped the King's impaling weapon and she was flying.

Sam screamed and shuddered in his arms. The King threw back his head and roared triumphantly to the heavens as he too found his release. He filled her with his hot cream, continuing to thrust in and out of her as he spent himself. Sam bit into his shoulder as her climax reached untold heights and he roared again, bucking into her mindlessly. Slowly their passion abated and his thrusts eased and slowed until he was softly, gently moving his hips between her weak legs. He kissed the curve of her jaw and rested his head on her shoulder, silent but for the pounding of his heart and the rasp of his breath.

After long moments the King pulled away with one last kiss to her shoulder. He smiled down at her softly and withdrew his cock from her spent body with gentle care.

"Rest now, my Jewel. Regain your strength. I'll be back for you tonight," he promised.

He righted his clothing and turned to speak to Cerebus. Sam was in a daze after the whirlwind of passion she'd just been a party to. Her eyes lazily followed the form of her lover as he moved with the Collection master to a small gray woman on the far side of the circle. It was with no small amount of shock that she witnessed the King, the man who had only moments before been thrusting into her eager body, take the woman's hand and lead her from the Courtyard.

Had the time come so soon then, that he needed other women to see to his needs? Sam's heart constricted painfully and her eyes filled with tears. The King hadn't even looked at her as he'd left through the doorway, his hand firmly grasping the gray woman's as he led her through. Though she had suspected that this day would come, she hadn't envisioned it playing out only moments after she'd been in the King's arms. On that thought she felt her pain swell, but along with it there came a spark of anger.

He hadn't even cared to spare her feelings! Here she was full of his come, creamy with it still, and he'd dared to claim another in plain sight of her. He knew by now how she felt about sharing him. She could only bear to share him with his sucklers—mouths as he called them—in the throne room before they retired to his chambers together. He had seemed more than accepting of her feelings on that matter, had even gone so far as to promise not to fuck another woman so long as she was his willing Jewel.

How dare he lie to her so blatantly? She seethed and dashed away her tears, ignoring the pitying look coming from Keln, her dearest friend in the Collection. Instead of dwelling on her pain at the King's defection she nurtured the rage that was slowly gathering and building in her heart.

A plan began to form in her troubled mind.

So the King would play her false under her very nose, without a care for her feelings? Well let him see her revenge for this inflicted injury. Let him witness her fury and retribution for her loss of pride. He had stolen her heart, forget that she had almost been ready to give it to him of her own free will. He deserved swift and brutal punishment. She would see that he received his due . . .

And then she would leave for home. Somehow. Someway. She must leave this place, this velvet heaven that had for a few shining, blissful weeks been her truest home.

8

Before the night had come to Valeo, Sam had thoroughly worked out a plan of escape from the Courtyard. She waited until Cerebus came to assist them in their afternoon bath, as was his habit. While he moved to the fountain pool, Sam brought forth the tureen of *phuq* dust she had collected from its home in the wall earlier in the day. She wasted no time getting a handful of the stuff as she'd seen him do. Instead she threw the entire contents of the jug at Cerebus' head, holding her breath as a great plume of the stuff rose about them, and waited for the madness she expected to ensue.

It did and quickly. The women, unwisely breathing in the fumes of the dust launched themselves at Cerebus, who opened his arms and went down in a pile of horny women beneath the water of the bath. Sam, still holding her breath though she was beginning to see spots, rushed forward and wrested the golden glove from Cerebus' hand while he was occupied with the women and unable to stop her. She shoved the glove onto her hand while making a dash for the wall that hid the magical door, which led beyond to the corridors that would take her to the King's bedchamber.

Finally she had untangled the chains that crisscrossed her palms and the glove was secure on her hand. She paused before the wall, waved her hand and though she had expected no less she was amazed to see the magical doorway appear before her. She wasted no time, but raced through the doorway into the corridor behind. There was no telling how long the effects of the *phuq* dust would last, or how long Cerebus would be occupied with the women of the harem.

As she ran she took note, as she always did, of the doors that lined the corridor. Soon enough she would have her answers about those mysterious doors, she promised herself. She did so long to open one of the doors to see for herself where they led or what lay beyond them, but she hadn't the time for such frivolous pursuits just now. For now she was on a mission and the rest would have to wait. Quickly she weaved through the hallways that were by this time very familiar to her and within moments she had closed the distance, standing before the side door that led into the King's chambers. Without preamble she burst into the room, fully expecting to see the King locked in an embrace with the gray woman.

He was alone, lounging back against his heavily canopied bed with an arm flung gracefully over his eyes. Sam's panting explosion into the room had him rising up with a wide-eyed look of surprise.

"What is wrong, my Jewel?" he asked with no small amount of concern and alarm. "What is amiss?"

Sam was afforded her first real look of danger and anger on the King's face as he rose from his bed and rushed to her side. The strength and nobility of his face impressed the fact of his royalty on her and almost had her thinking twice about her chosen course of action. Who knew what this King was capable of when moved to extremes?

"Where is she?" Sam demanded, throwing all caution to the wind and plunging headlong into the situation as she'd planned.

"Where is who?" the King asked, perplexed.

"The gray woman." Sam racked her memory for a name. "Nantiqua."

The King looked at her for a long moment, searching her face. Sam wanted to squirm beneath his sherry gaze but stood firm by the force of her will alone. All of a sudden the King threw back his head and roared with a mighty burst of laughter. Sam wouldn't have been more shocked if he'd hit her upon the head with an anvil. How dare he laugh at her while her heart was breaking in the face of his faithlessness!

"Where is she?" Sam screamed, enraged at his reaction.

The King was beyond answering her, busy as he was clutching at his sides, doubling over in laughter until tears poured from the corners of his eyes. Sam rushed at him, pounding her fists into his chest in a rage of anger and hurt. The King stumbled back, not from the force of her blows, but with the force of his own mirth. He fell back against his pillows once again, taking Sam in his arms as he fell so that she joined him. He buried his face in her hair and laughed and laughed until Sam was openly crying with heartache and sadness and unchecked rage.

The King noticed the wetness of her cheeks and pulled

back, his laughter immediately subsiding into chuckles. He brushed away the tears that spilled from her eyes and kissed her lightly on the nose, unable to keep from smiling.

"You were jealous of Nantiqua, weren't you, love?"

Sam broke down and began to sob, hating herself for her weakness and loss of pride. "You didn't even care that I saw you leave with her right after you had your way with me." She buried her tearstained face against the bare ridge of his chest and pounded it with her fist for good measure.

"I had to leave with her. Her groom was waiting for me to fetch her."

Sam hiccupped. "What?"

"Her groom. One of my men at arms has desired a match with her for several moons now. I put the offer before Nantiqua and she accepted. They will be married in the throne room tonight and a great feast will be given in their honor."

"You mean you didn't take her back here with you?"

"Of course not, my Jewel. Did I not promise you that I would lie with no other but you so long as you would have me? Does my word bond mean nothing to you?"

"But you have so many women at your beck and call. How do I know that you haven't grown bored with me yet?"

"I could never grow bored with you." He chuckled and nuzzled her nose with his. "Especially when you throw such glorious tantrums like this. I will never know what to expect where you are concerned. I love that about you."

Sam took his face in her hands. "I don't know what I would do if you pushed me away," she said, knowing she was giving him a weapon should he ever choose to wield it. But he wasn't like that, her King. He would never willingly hurt her. More like accidentally, which was why she'd been so quick to jump to conclusions.

"You'll never have to know," he promised and did the most surprising thing he could have done.

He kissed her.

Oh it was no ordinary kiss, this. It was the kiss to end all kisses. If Sam had held the illusion that she had ever known love before, it was dispelled altogether as his lips closed softly over hers. No man on Earth could have ever hoped to kiss this way. So perfect. So much the physical manifestation of love that Sam's eyes filled once more with tears . . . tears of joy. The sweet, gentle press of his lips against hers caused her senses to dance and sing with euphoric delight. The flavor of his kiss was the taste of a future resting just within her grasp. A life of beauty and love and happiness, of children and grandchildren between them, and long nights spent in each other's embrace.

His mouth was soft and hot and moist against hers, a living, breathing silk at play over hers. Sam sighed, a broken sob, and his tongue slipped inside like a warm ghost past her lips. It was so gentle, this storm of love that swept her up, and her only anchor was his cradling arms cupped around her shaking body. The current pulled her deeper, the world around her growing paper-thin—like a dream—and all that she knew was the taste and feel of Him. Her love. Her King.

Sam clutched him to her tighter with a desperate aching need. Not for the physical pleasure of his bed, but for the spiritual haven of his love. How she wanted him to love her. As she loved him—more than time or place or life. More than anything ever dreamed of. He was her everything. Her always and forever.

A dizzying spiral of sensation and his lips had left hers, trembling and moist with the memory.

"My Jewel."

"Please . . ." She faltered, overcome with emotion.

"Please . . . what?" he urged softly, breathing the words into her mouth.

"My name is Sam," she said with a soft sobbing breath.

"My Sam. My Sa-man-tha. I have always known your name, but I waited for your permission to use it."

"Why?"

"It is just my way. Your name is precious above all things and I wanted you to gift it to me of your own free will."

"Please use it. I don't want to be just a Jewel to you anymore."

"You were never 'just a Jewel.' You have always and always will be *my* Jewel."

Sam leaned into him and pressed her mouth to his once more, feeling all of the same wondrous, magical things she'd felt in their first shared kiss. Such bliss, such delicious completion, this. He completed her, this man, in all ways.

Long moments later the King pulled away from her once more, breathing raggedly with the force of his own emotions. "You came storming in here like a goddess. I didn't know if something horrible had befallen you or the Collection or Cerebus—"

"Cerebus!" she exclaimed. "Oh no, he's going to hate me."

"Cerebus is incapable of hate." The King laughed at the very notion. "But why do you think he would?"

"I stole his glove and left him in a predicament back in the courtyard," she said with a look of chagrin.

"You stole his glove?"

Sam raised her hand and brandished it before his surprised eyes. "It's how I escaped the women's quarters. How did you think I got here?"

"Why would you need that to leave the women's quarters?" he asked, perplexed.

"You know. To make the door appear with the glove's magic."

Suddenly the King erupted into laughter. "You thought you needed the glove to open the door? Oh, my Jewel, you are a treasure beyond price in your innocence."

"What are you talking about?"

"The door is not magic. You do not need this glove to open it. In fact this glove has no magic—it is merely an insignia of Cerebus' station as Collection Master. The door is open to any who wish to use it. You are not a prisoner, Sam. You are free to come and go in the palace as you wish."

"But no one ever leaves the courtyard without being escorted by someone."

"That is likely because the women are content to stay where they are. The better to be served by Cerebus and have their needs taken care of with all haste."

"Oh man," she moaned, blushing with embarrassment. "I thought that because Cerebus and The Collector and you always wave your gloved hand around before magic happens that it was the glove that gave you power."

"My people are born with power. We wave the glove out of vanity mostly, showing off our insignia." He laughed and kissed her on the nose.

"We have to go save Cerebus."

"Save him from what?"

"The women." She quickly told him what she had done in order to "escape" her prison and make her way to his chambers.

All through her explanation the King's sherry golden eyes widened more and more with a mixed expression of shock, awe and perhaps a little bit of fear.

"Remind me never to make you angry, my Jewel," he said

with a small, nervous laugh. "Come, let us save Cerebus then. I only hope there is a little of him left after the women have had their way with him."

As they hurried down the corridors, back to the courtyard, Sam gave in to the urge at last and asked the King about the doors that lined their path.

"They are the personal chambers of the women from past Collections who have chosen to stay here at the palace."

"What do you mean by past Collections? How many have you had?" Her voice rose on the last.

"Not me, Sam. My father's Collection and his father's before him and so on and so forth."

"So when you . . . die," she choked on the word, "the women in your Collection are allowed to live on at the palace?"

"Not exactly. When a King chooses his chastity keeper—his Queen—he releases those women in his keeping and vows monogamy with his mate for all the rest of their days together. Some women choose marriage with men at court, others a life of simple ease here in the palace, others still choose to return to their native lands, restored to the memory of their loved ones by The Collector as is necessary. A King cannot play with his Collection forever, he must breed heirs to continue the line."

"What about love?" she couldn't help asking.

"Love is very important too," he agreed with a smile, gathering her close beneath his arm as they walked on. "The most important."

At last they came before the courtyard and hurried within. The sight that greeted them was total chaos, with Cerebus trying his best to disentangle himself from a mountain of women who each wanted one thing and one thing only—him. The *phuq* dust had obviously taken care of Cerebus' inhibitions—

none of the women had their veils on and many had been divested of their chastity plugs.

"Master, help me!" Cerebus cried out.

But the King was too far gone in his mirth to offer any assistance. Sam stepped forward and pulled Cerebus free, with no small amount of difficulty, and was immediately blasted with a hard glare from the much abused man. Poor Cerebus was completely nude, swollen with arousal and covered in hickeys. The women behind him turned and reached again for him but Sam pulled him away and they turned back to each other, an undulating swarm of arms and legs and swaying bodies.

The King wiped tears from his eyes and joined them. "Never have I laughed so much in so short a span of time. Thank you for that, Sam. Are you all right, Cerebus?"

"Master, forgive me. I have lain with your women and for that I deserve the ultimate punishment, but I beg of you, do not believe the worst of me. I did not mean to—"

"It is all right, Cerebus. There is nothing to forgive."

"But my King, I have failed you most grievously."

"You have failed no one, Cerebus. Sam told me everything and there is nothing to forgive, as this was all her doing. Think of it no more. In fact, I think you deserve some accolades for weathering the storm . . . that was a lot of *phuq* dust Sam used." He laughed again. "Oh. There is one more thing before I forget—before the gathering and feasting tonight I will need to see you in my chambers. We have much to discuss." The King turned from Cerebus and moved to Sam once more. "My Jewel. Until tonight . . . think of me." He kissed her forehead and was gone, chuckling as he went.

Sam looked nervously at Cerebus and then immediately wished she hadn't. The look on his face promised retribution—swift and punishing. The man was truly angry with her and Sam couldn't blame him. The poor man felt he had failed his King in the worst way possible, by soiling the members of his Collection. Sam thought back to her first day on Valeo and remembered that the one rule of the Collection was that no woman was to allow penetration of her body to anyone other than her King. That most sacred of rules had been broken and Sam was to blame for it.

"Come with me." Cerebus' voice was as hard as steel and cold as ice.

Sam turned to run, but the man caught at her arm brutally and dragged her along behind him as he headed across the courtyard.

Sam fought him every step of the way.

9

Sam yelled out in the long endless dark, pounding her fists against the walls of her prison until they blistered and bled. But no one came for her. No one heard her cries. If Cerebus had planned it he couldn't have punished her in a more brutal way. Her claustrophobia was upon her like a monster, causing the unseen walls to squeeze in against her until she was mindless with fear.

How long she had been there Sam couldn't say, though it felt like an eternity had passed since Cerebus had taken her here, beyond the walls of the palace and into the glittering desert sands beyond. With a wave of his hand, Cerebus had erected a large black box—this isolation chamber—and closed her within it, snuffing out all light as he went. It was perfect, this punishment. No matter how loud Sam shouted or cried or begged, no one heard her. She was completely alone.

Sam beat her fists against the walls once more, choking and sobbing as the last of her strength began to wane. Her hands were coated in warm sticky blood, torn and bruised and aching, but still she pounded them against the imprisoning walls, praying for someone—anyone—to hear her. Endless time passed and the walls closed further in on her. Curling up into a ball in the corner of the cell, Sam lost all touch with reality.

And began to scream.

"Sam! Sa-man-tha, my love, wake up."

Sam's eyes opened and blearily took in the worried face of her lover as he bent over her, wiping away the tearstains on her face with unsteady hands. Her eyes felt like swollen grapes in her head, aching and bruised from too much weeping.

"Oh, Sam, my Jewel, are you all right?" The King's words were a tangled rush as he ran his hands up and down her body as if trying to reassure himself that she was going to be okay. "You scared me so."

Sam's breath came out in a choking sob and the King immediately gathered her into his arms. His hands stroked down over her hair in long soothing motions as he began to rock her back and forth.

"Sa-man-tha, please forgive me. I did not know you would react in such a way to the punishment box." Cerebus was at her back, his voice frantic and full of worry.

"You needn't have punished her, Cerebus! When have you ever used the punishment box on a member of the Collection? Why now and with my Jewel of all people? Did I not tell you that all was forgiven for Sam's impetuous deeds? I should have you banished for this monstrous act," the King growled, never loosening his hold on Sam as he addressed the Collection master.

"I would docilely accept such a punishment, Master. It would be no less than I deserve."

Cerebus' sincerity and sorrow broke through to Sam and she pulled away from the King, wiping the tears from her face with the back of her hand. "No, Cerebus. You couldn't have known that I was claustrophobic."

"It matters not. It was my wounded pride that made me punish you, a grievous sin that. I failed you and my King with my dishonorable behavior."

"You were angry, Cerebus. It was an understandable thing for you to do," Sam reassured him.

"Can you forgive me for wronging you, Sa-man-tha?"

Cerebus' dark eyes were soft with their regret and Sam couldn't have held a grudge if she'd wanted to. If there was one thing she'd learned about the people on this world it was that they were nearly incapable of harboring ill will towards each other. Rather, they enjoyed a peaceful harmony amongst themselves and all those who dwelled within the palace walls under their protection. Sam would not blame Cerebus for his punishment, no matter that it was brutal, for he hadn't known how it would affect her. "It's okay, Cerebus, I forgive you. I'm sorry for throwing the *phuq* dust at you and the others. I wasn't thinking straight."

"You are too kindhearted, Sa-man-tha. Worthy of our King in all ways." Cerebus bowed his head to them both.

"Don't banish him, my King. I'm all right now so there's no reason to be angry," she pleaded up at the man who held her.

"For you my Jewel, I will forgive anything if you but ask. But in the future," his voice hardened, "no one will have the duty of punishing you but myself."

"Master!" Cerebus gasped, surprised. "But that—"

"Later," he warned and Sam wondered what was passing between the two men for it seemed important. "My Jewel, let me take you now to your quarters. There I will heal your hands and heart and leave you to your rest."

Gently and carefully the King scooped her up in his arms and took her to her room as he'd promised. He laid her down into the sunken cushion of her bed and joined her, stretching out beside her. It was the first time he'd ever lain with her in her own bed.

"Lie still and relax. You'll feel a little warm but it will pass after a few moments if you ignore it." His voice was low and soothing.

The King ran his hand over the slopes and valleys of her body. Tenderly and with exquisite care he searched for any further injuries she might have sustained other than the bruises and cuts on her hands and arms. Her body did grow warm but it was a pleasant sensation, all the more so because Sam knew it was her lover's power that swam through her, heating her. When the King was satisfied that she had no serious bruises or wounds he directed his attention to her hands.

"I think you forgave Cerebus too soon, love. Perhaps you should have made him grovel for a while first." He softly kissed the wounds on her fists, but his eyes were hard as he took in the extent of the damage.

Sam laughed but her voice was so hoarse and ragged from her ordeal in the box that it sounded truly pitiful, even to her own ears. The King kissed her hands once more and the warmth in her body centered there, making her fingers tingle and her palms itch. There was a brief moment of intense heat and Sam gasped. Before her eyes the cuts and scrapes and swellings on her hands healed, leaving behind smooth and unblemished skin after but a few brief moments of the King's concentration.

"There. All better now." The King smiled gently into her widened eyes.

"Thank you." She was at a loss for more eloquent speech, too much in awe of the miracle she'd just witnessed.

"No more pain?"

"No more pain." She smiled.

The King leaned down and pressed a small electric kiss to her mouth. He stole her breath as he'd stolen her heart, but gave it back to her complete with all the magic of which he was capable. "You will never have to fear this claustrophobia again, Sam," he murmured. "I will let nothing harm you ever again. I vow it." He pressed his lips against hers again, softly worshipping her mouth with his.

"I love you." She spoke the words against his mouth before she could stop them.

The King's breath caught and he pulled away from her with a look she couldn't quite define. He cleared his throat but it took him two tries before he found his voice to speak.

"Rest now, Sam. When you wake up it will be time for the evening gathering in the throne room."

What had she expected? An undying declaration of love? No. It was enough that she didn't regret loving him. He was a man more than worthy of her heart, she was certain. Perhaps in time he would feel the same depth of emotion for her, but until that time she was content to have his devotion in the bedroom. He would always have that from her as well as the devotion of her heart.

The King rose from her bed and left her quarters, closing the jewel-handled door softly in his wake. Sam curled up in the downy softness of her bed and dozed, eager for the night to come so that she could be with her love again.

10

Sam gathered that night with the rest of the Collection before the throne and wondered idly which "mouths" the King would choose for the evening. Keln came to stand beside her as was their habit by now and Sam was almost afraid to look the centaur in the eyes after the *phuq* dust fiasco that afternoon. She needn't have fretted, as Keln was quick to reassure her.

"You should have seen the look on Cerebus' face when Faggia took him into her mouth and sucked him dry." She laughed. "I've never seen a look of horror, pleasure and guilt combined on one face at one time."

"I'm sorry you all got involved in that. I didn't really think that plan through rationally before I acted on it." Sam felt her face flush and gestured awkwardly, not knowing quite how to explain her motivations for causing the fiasco.

"Don't worry yourself over it, Sam. The Collector came

and explained everything to us while you rested this afternoon."

"The Collector?"

"Yes, he and Cerebus had a discussion with the Collection before you rose."

"Oh man," Sam wailed. "Then everyone knows what an idiot I was for acting out like that."

"We all thought it was sweetly romantic, Sam. You escaping your prison with such a coup. Rushing off to avenge your bruised pride against the King while the King was innocent of any wrongdoing. It is a story to tell your children one day."

"You're not angry then?"

"How could I be angry? I myself got a piece of Cerebus and let me tell you, that made everything worth it." Keln laughed again. "He has the most delicious cock. I wonder why it took an overdose of *phuq* dust for us to notice that."

"I can't believe you just said that. Cerebus of the delicious cock?" Sam laughed.

"You know, Sam, when you came here I wondered how well you would adapt to life with us. I feared for you, truth to tell. You seemed stubborn and prideful and those traits could have served you no purpose here. But you've become so much a part of our family that I find it hard to imagine how dull our lives were before you came and livened everything up. You've got the King and all of His attendants dancing a merry tune trying to keep up with you and it's a pleasure to witness. I'm glad you've found happiness with us, Sam. I'm glad you're here."

"Me too," Sam murmured in agreement.

On the raised throne the King motioned for silence. Sam's eyes drank in the sight of him, resplendent in his glittering forest green skirt, golden armbands, wrist cuffs and jewelry. He was truly the most magnificent man she'd ever known.

The King stepped down from the dais and approached the throng of women that always gathered in anticipation of his choosing. He pushed through their numbers, striding purposefully, erect and proud in his bearing as he went. He was a vision of regal grace and power if ever there was one. He came to a halt directly in front of Sam and stunned her by going down upon his knees before her. Their audience crowded around them, eager to witness the proceedings.

"My Jewel, my love, my Sam. My name is Valen-Illumai. I am 41 seasons old. I rule the planet of Valeo and all of its peoples. And I love you with all of my heart. Will you keep my heart close to yours and be my *chastity keeper* for all the days of our life?"

"W-what?" Sam breathed, too astonished to even hope she'd heard him correctly.

The King—Valen-Illumai—looked to the side where The Collector was standing and some unspoken message passed between them.

"Will you . . . marry me, as they say on your world, Sam?" He pronounced the word marry as mah-ri, causing a smile to break out on her face. "I promise you will never want or need for anything, ever."

It took her several tries before Sam found her voice, so overcome with emotion was she. "As long as you're with me I'll never need or want anything else," she vowed.

The King smiled and rose before her, capturing her hands in his. "Then will you say yes, Sam? Did you speak true earlier when you told me you loved me? Will you be my *chastity keeper?*"

"Y-yes. Yes I will. I will." Sam felt like a blubbering fool but was too happy to care. As soon as the words passed her lips she felt it appear on her hand—a golden glove not dissimilar in design to that of the King's.

With a whooping call of triumph the King gathered her in his arms and carried her back to the throne as swiftly as he could manage. He positioned her just so on his lap, pushing aside his skirt and spreading her legs on either side of him, quickly removing the Veil and chastity plugs that filled her. "You need never wear these again. I trust you not to need them."

"I kind of got used to being filled by the plugs. It felt good sometimes," she admitted with a smile.

"You need only grow used to being filled by me, now. And that will feel good at all times, I promise you." He stroked his hands down her breasts, making her sigh and stretch beneath them.

He reached beside them for a tureen of *phuq* dust but Sam stalled him with a firm hand on his, shaking her head. He looked at her questioningly and she kissed him gently on his smooth, straight nose. "I don't need it and neither do you." To prove her point she palmed his great length in her hands, pumping him until he gasped and gritted his teeth against the erotic torment.

"I need you so much, Sam," he breathed into her mouth.

"I need you too, Valen-Illumai."

The King moved her tighter astride him and filled her with one smooth thrust of his hips. "You feel so smooth. Like liquid fire."

Sam couldn't have cared less that they had an audience. Couldn't have cared that her body was exposed for all to see as the King palmed and squeezed her buttocks in his hands, bouncing her upon his cock again and again. It was heavenly just being there in his arms, knowing that he loved her and would for the rest of their lives together. It was pure magic and as he stretched her body with the invasion of his, her heart was stretched in a similar fashion as it swelled with love for him.

The King caught her lower lip between his teeth and suckled on it, moving his body even tighter against her, until her breasts were crushed between them. Their loving was almost soft compared to what she was used to from him, a gentle rocking of their bodies as he thrust his hard cock in and out of her welcoming heat. Her clit was swollen and wet with her arousal, rubbing silkily against the hairless flesh of his sex with every stroke until she was gasping and clutching at him with passionate abandon.

His cock was so thick and heavy it stretched her nearly to the point of pain with every movement they made. It was a delicious torment to the both of them, a perfect ecstasy in every way. Just before Sam found her way to the stars she heard the voice of Cerebus in her mind and knew that the King heard it as well when he smiled at her, boyishly handsome in his happiness and joy.

"It's a bit late but . . . happy Valentine's Day, Sam. And happy birthday to the both of you."

The two lovers laughed and flung themselves off passion's peak, shuddering in each other's arms as they found culmination together.

Learning to Live Again

S. L. CARPENTER

1

Michelle closed her eyes tightly, clutching the sheets. Her body jerked forward with the pounding thrusts as Keith's abdomen slapped against her ass. SMACK. SMACK. SMACK echoed through the dim room. She buried her face into the pillow, stifling a moan as Keith clamped one hand on her hip and grabbed a fistful of her blond hair in the other.

Loudly, Keith moaned, "Oh, baby, it's happening, ohhhh . . ."

She felt his hot bursts of air across her back. He grabbed her flesh with his rough hands. Squeezing hard, Keith pulled her against him with lustful intensity.

He pulled back on his knees and grasped hard on her butt cheeks, spreading them apart. Grunting, he plunged into her again, filling her with the burning syrup of his sex. His labored breathing slowed, his cock gliding back and forth inside her.

Satisfied, Keith smacked Michelle on her sore rear and

strutted into the bathroom, scratching at his hairy butt. Michelle lowered flat onto the bed, staring into the darkness with tear-filled eyes. *NO MORE!* She knew she couldn't live like this anymore. The tears trickled down her nose, falling to the pillow.

This life had become her prison.

Her torment.

She heard the shower start and Keith whistling. *WHAT AN ASSHOLE!* she thought. Michelle sat up, her muscles aching. *I need to get out of this.* She threw her legs over the side of the bed. Her underwear and dress were scattered on the floor.

She was sore because she hadn't been ready for sex and he hadn't cared to wait. Hissing, she muttered aloud, "Ouch! Damn, that is irritated. Dumb bastard." Standing up, she saw her reflection in the mirror.

"How did I end up like this?" Holding back her tears, she cried, "I deserve better."

Her body was slender and her blond hair fell along the slope of her neck and down her back. Looking hard into her own darkened, sad eyes, she saw her future. Looking around the apartment, she saw the memories of a miserable two-year relationship.

It made her feel disheartened.

Pulling her dress up her body, she saw red marks on her hip from Keith's hands. Her ass hurt from the slapping and her body ached. Reaching under the bed, she pulled out a suitcase. Michelle had made her decision long ago. She needed to get out of this nowhere, one-sided, fucked-up relationship. She stayed because of fear, not wanting to be alone and for some reason—she had thought she loved him. Michelle spoke quietly on the phone hearing Keith singing in the shower. "You mind if I come over? I need someone to talk to." *He can't hear me,* she thought. "Thanks, Marisha, I owe you."

Her past was all a bad dream, now it was her time to act. Grabbing her purse, she looked back into the room and noticed something. There was nothing in the apartment that she wanted. It reminded her of what was wrong in her life.

There weren't too many people she trusted. She went to her friend Marisha's house. Tears fell while she told Marisha about leaving Keith.

"I just can't take it. I dread going home every night and can't live like this. He takes me for granted and treats me like shit. I don't deserve that. I went to college for four years and I'm smarter than that dickhead! What should I do?" Michelle sobbed.

Marisha sat quietly listening to her friend's story of the way she felt and how she wanted to feel whole again.

"FUCK HIM!" Marisha said bluntly. "Good riddance. I always thought he was an asshole."

Michelle laughed through her tears, Marisha always made her smile. Even at times like this.

"I do have one thing to ask you, though." Marisha stared at her friend and asked, "Did he have a really little dick? I mean average or was it like a breakfast sausage? The way I look at it, if it doesn't fill my mouth then I don't even bother to see if it will fill my . . . well . . . you know."

They talked for the next few hours about men and their downfalls. Lack of commitment, no social graces, can't dress themselves to save their lives, believing that size doesn't matter. The wine helped wash away Michelle's heartache.

"Men are only good for a few things. Taking out the garbage, killing bugs and the occasional sex," Marisha laughed.

"I just wish I could find a man that knew how to . . . well . . . eat me out the right way. Keith acted like he was painting a fence. Up, down, up, down. Shit, I did a better job with my fingers."

Before taking over Marisha's couch, Michelle hugged her and could feel the first twinge of freedom. This was her new beginning.

Michelle told her boss she was leaving. With the layoffs, she saw it was time to go and figured it may be a sign. A good sign or bad sign, she didn't care. Michelle accepted a job offer in Vancouver, Canada, and wanted to get as far away from her past as possible. Irene from work lived there. She knew Michelle had talked about a change and was bugging her to move there. This great new job had opened up. Michelle could follow her dream, working with children.

She spent four years in college for it and Keith had held her back. He didn't want kids or a family. Well, no more holding back and no more Keith.

Michelle was already late heading to the station but wanted to make sure everything was all right at her mom's before getting there so she called her. The barrage of questions made her later than before.

"Yeah, Mom, I am on my way."

"Do you need anything, dear?" her mom asked.

"Of course not. I have everything I need, just relax. I'll see you in a few days. OH, CRAP! I have to get to the station. Love ya!"

Going home for a vacation was her first stop. Home to where things were a little easier. Her mom was alone, and it would be nice to spend time there and regroup. Maybe recapture some of that lost innocence of her youth.

She had so many great memories, the girls from the cheerleading squad, the football players, the freedom from responsibilities, the football players, the fresh air, the football players. She obviously had always had a weakness for football players. She had even lost her virginity to a football player. He was the tight end. She'd had a tight end until he loosened it up after homecoming. The memories made her long to return.

Michelle checked her bags one last time. She was meeting the girls before leaving. She would miss the weekly lunch meetings where they would talk about men. Especially that cute guy at the local coffee shop, she smiled, remembering. He really made her latte hot and steamy.

She boarded the train, happy to finally get some "Michelle" time, to think about her new dream job, to be alone. Wondering about what the future held for her and moving far away was a big step. She'd been so stupid. *You're stronger, smarter and better than what you had*, she thought while moving along the passageways.

Never again! She was determined, even if she knew there would be sacrifices to be made.

2

The dining car was full but Michelle found a table in the corner. She watched the crowd swell around the bar.

"What's going on at the bar?" she asked a waiter.

"It's some Valentine party thing. Most of the people over there are pretty wasted," he replied, and left to help another customer.

She felt out of place, but mostly, she felt lonely. For a moment, she remembered Keith. At least when he was with her she wasn't alone. She then remembered the way he made her feel cheap, took advantage of her and didn't show her any respect. She sighed, not hungry anymore, and motioned to the waiter for a check.

Michelle became shy when in unfamiliar surroundings, and the little party at the bar looked like fun. The people were all drinking and dressed like Cupid. All the couples kissing and laughing made her heart ache. Tomorrow was going to be

110

a depressing Valentine's Day. *Maybe I should go join the crowd,* she thought. She wanted to join the party, but it was late. Loneliness made her sad, so she left and headed back to her compartment.

She ran her keycard through the lock, not noticing the door being slightly open. Walking in, she jumped back.

"WHO THE FUC . . . !" she yelled when seeing a man lying on her bed. He was wearing only a bedsheet. She remembered the bar. A few guys were wearing something similar. This must be a cupid outfit or something.

"Oh, great. I get a drunk in my room the first night!"

She poked him and he mumbled, "I'm up, Mom, I'm up, just five more minutes." Then he started snoring again. What a way to start her trip.

She refused to try to fight the guy or have him thrown out. His large frame spread across the small bed against the wall. His feet hung off the edge. She noticed his two different sandals and different colored socks. One sock had a very fluffy cat on it and the other had a picture of a whip on it.

Her room was small. There was the small bed and a nice, red-cushioned chair in front of the window for sightseeing. She stepped into the tiny bathroom to dress for bed. All she wore was panties and a silk nightshirt that tied in front. She pulled a pillow and blanket from the small closet.

It was a beautiful night and the chair by the window seemed a nice place to sit and reflect until the deadbeat woke up. She felt safer in the chair anyway. Even if he woke up, she could kick him in the nuts if he tried anything. Outside, the dark scenery floated by like a dream. The soothing rhythm of the train gliding over the tracks helped Michelle drift off to sleep.

Her mind dreamed of better times. Romantic interludes,

feelings of undying passions, the caress of a lover's touch, and some strange dream about a bearded zookeeper, a boa constrictor and a koala bear. She was no longer trapped in the reality she left behind. She was now free to explore things. There was a great big world out there for her to find. Firstly, she needed to find the one person that had become lost in her younger years. The person so full of fun and was in total control of everything.

She needed to find herself again.

She awoke to a thump when her head bounced against the window while the train crossed a bridge. Glancing over to the bed, she saw the drunken man sprawled on his back. The light shone in from the occasional outside train lamps. They illuminated the bed with a deep yellow glimmer.

The man needed a shave but appeared like he kept himself in good shape. Tall and lean, he was actually very good-looking. He wore a nice Rolex watch and no wedding ring. That was a relief to Michelle. She'd hate to be found in her room with a married man. The local newspapers would have a field day.

The sheet slid up his torso and she saw he wasn't wearing anything under it. Michelle giggled, peeking under the sheet from the window seat. She tried to get a better look by leaning forward. Gently lifting the sheet, she saw a patch of black, curly hair and a long lump of flesh. The train bumped and she jerked her hand back, afraid of getting caught. The man rolled a little and she saw his cock fall along his thigh. He was well endowed and the fire within her began to warm at the sight of his shaft. She looked away and grinned wide. Licking her lips to moisten them, she debated on what to do.

A devilish little voice popped up in her head. *Don't be stupid, make sure your eyes weren't deceiving you. Take a closer* look! *That was at least ten inches long. Come on, don't be a chicken.*

Her rational voice replied, *It's not ladylike to look at a man's privates. Did you say ten inches? You should cover his penis and go back to sleep.*

Michelle never listened to the rational voice much.

She looked back and her mind swept with heat. Her body reacted to the needs of a lost passion within her. Being sexually deprived in a one-way relationship, she forgot the way she used to crave the taste of a man. Her eyes grew heavy and her body began to ache. She crossed her legs, closing them tightly, making the lips of her pussy press together. Biting her lip, she pulled the blanket up around her and sat back in the chair.

Her fingers shook when she untied the string on her nightshirt. Her bosom was heated with a flush of excitement. A small dampening of perspiration was between them. Michelle opened her top and kept herself hidden in the cocoon of the blanket. Her breasts were full and her nipples strained for attention.

She looked up staring at the strange man's body. His long, lean body was tanned and his legs looked strong, all three of his legs. Michelle tugged at her nipple, making herself squirm in excitement. This self-pleasure fulfilled a passion kept contained by her fears of letting go.

Michelle pulled her left leg against her chest and ran her long fingers up her inner thigh to the seam of her underwear. They were white with a pink, flowery band. The moistness of her panties made them stick to her swollen, seeping pussy. She pulled them away from her labia, trying to give her pussy breathing room. Her essence trickled between her ass cheeks when she slid her finger beneath the fabric. There was a silky feeling to her flesh as the juice from her sexual feelings awoke.

Running her finger over her pussy lips made her crazy with lust rushing through her hot blood.

She would glance up now and then to see the man's body and cock, and to be sure he hadn't seen her. His light snore was her sign to continue.

In the darkness, she felt the folds of skin open to her finger. She toyed with the thought of jumping the stranger but that wasn't her way. In her mind, she thought about it and slid her finger inside—her fantasy pictured the naked man's cock dancing inside of her. With her other hand, she massaged her breast letting it fill her hand. Her hand was his.

Falling into the fantasy, Michelle closed her eyes. This lover was toying with her. He caressed her clit while his cock slid between her sexual flesh. Over and over, he'd swivel his hips, spreading her pussy wider. The muscles stretched for his probing.

The blanket hid her from sight, but her soft moans were obviously those of deepened pleasure. She opened her legs wider and pulling her panties down to her lower thighs, continued her journey.

She breathed deeply, letting the night air fill her lungs. The cold glass of the window against the back of her head contrasted with the heat of her body. She glanced occasionally at the stranger's cock and slid two fingers inside her soaked pussy, imagining it was his hard, pulsing cock filling the void. Spreading her fingers caused her pussy lips to open wider and she sucked the fingertips of her other hand. She lowered them between her legs, massaging her clit in a circular motion. At first, it was gentle and noninvasive.

"Ohhhhhh, mmmmmmmmmmmmm," Michelle stifled the need to scream out.

Her fantasy took her to thoughts of the stranger feeding on

the succulent flavors within her. The direct stimuli to her tender clitoris made it firm and more sensitive. Like electric jolts, the nerve endings seemed centered on this erogenous switch. Her playful rubbing took more focus as her arm shook and her bottom lip fluttered. She was enclosed in a cocoon of heat which became an inferno from her body's temperature rising every second. Her breathing became more labored and she began to feel the crescendo from the symphony of desire building within her.

The blanket became a tent surrounding her while she slid her panties off. She lifted one leg up on the arm of the chair and set the other on the cold floor of the compartment.

This time her fantasy was right before her. Her mind's eye looked to see the man licking along the crease of her pussy. The hot saliva doused the fire inside. His tongue licked around her clit and her fingers followed the motions in her fantasy. She gasped and saw him thrust into her, grunting at the slippery feel of her vaginal walls. Even though her fingers felt differently, she pictured his long cock sinking in and out. Deeply stretching the wanton, hollow entryway to her passionate soul.

Cupping her pussy, she saw her lover was again pulsing into her with a fevered fury of need. He grasped her swelling breasts in his hands and pulled on a nipple with his teeth, making her swoon. Michelle looked out the window and watched the trees fly by as her fingers probed inside of her scorching pussy. A fog covered the window from the rising heat in the room. She closed her eyes and vigorously stroked and rubbed her clit. Michelle's fantasies flew through her mind.

Tears filled her eyes. She stifled pleasurable moans. Her hand tugged at her nipples pulling each one away from her body until it sprang back. Her teeth bit down and she closed her eyes tighter, tears cascading down her cheeks, and came.

The waves of her orgasm washed through her pussy. Her fingers were wet with the fluids of her sex.

There was a deep calming rhythm to the train as it flew across the tracks. This was her vessel to freedom. She was going home. To a better job, better life, better times and a new beginning.

She looked over and saw that the stranger had rolled onto his side. *Did he see her?* she wondered. What a way to make a first impression. Ignoring her wet underwear and crumpled nightshirt, she wrapped herself in the blanket, curled up in the fetal position and drifted off to sleep, relaxed, satisfied but not fulfilled.

Something was missing on this Valentine's Day. She needed a Valentine.

3

Michelle woke up as the train stopped. She looked out the window, seeing it was a bright, beautiful day. The bed was empty and straightened, and the door was closed. The stranger must have wakened and left during the night.

She got herself up and ready. There was a two-hour stop for new boarding and Michelle decided to go shopping. Maybe spend some time just taking in her newfound freedom. She decided to buy some new clothes, just because.

It was sunny out but a little cold. She watched couples laughing and holding each other. Feeling cold and alone, she pulled her thin sweater closed over her dress. She missed being held, jealous of the closeness of others while she window-shopped through the little stores. Looking through the window of a pet store, she saw a dopey-looking

Basset hound and thought of Keith. In the next window, she saw a stunning Boxer that was strong, proud, hung and drooled. He reminded her of the stranger in her room last night.

Feeling a gentle tap on her shoulder, she turned to see nothing. She shrugged and turned to look in the window and jumped back when the stranger laughed at her.

"I'm sorry, I didn't mean to scare you."

He stood next to her snickering at her reaction.

"It's okay, you just caught me off guard." She shook her head, blushed and stepped back. He smiled and she gazed into his stunning eyes. Suddenly, she wasn't cold and his body blocked the wind from chilling her.

He held his hand out to her. "I'm Josh. I apologize for falling asleep in your room last night. I was so drunk from the party and missed my room by two doors. Funny how the key opened your room, too."

Michelle stared at him. He was taller than she thought, lean but athletic-looking, and had a wicked smile that sent chills through her.

"Where are my manners? You're cold." Josh saw her shiver and took his jacket off wrapping it around her shoulders.

"Thanks, umm, my name is Michelle. I tried to wake you but you were OUT." She wasn't sure if he had seen anything last night and felt a little embarrassed.

"You should have kicked me and got me up. I am sorry, it was a long night and I was drinking all evening, and then always sleep like a rock when I do."

They continued their walk back to the train. She felt very comfortable with Josh. He had a mellow aura and it made her more playful and flirtatious. They joked and laughed all the while taking their time to get to the station. She breathed in the smell of his cologne on the jacket. Her chill lifted and warmth filled her from his jacket and his company. It also made other things warm and moist.

She told Josh, "I'm on my way back home to visit my mom. I already have my DREAM JOB in child development waiting for me in Vancouver. They are going to pay for me to finish my Master's and work at the same time. I couldn't pass it up. I love the thought of working with and helping kids. It's also the perfect reason to go back to where I grew up." Michelle looked back into his green eyes and smiled. Something about him made her feel at ease.

She didn't say anything about just leaving Keith. The last thing she wanted was to seem desperate. She was relieved but not ready to jump into another relationship.

"I'm going back to see my parents for their anniversary. I was away working in the city and finally finished. Took me two weeks to nail this promotional deal. I can't wait to get back home and relax."

Josh was concentrating on his career as the promotional manager for his parents' company. They laughed and talked about where they were living and the hustle-bustle of the rat race.

Josh was nervous and unsure if Michelle was married or attached but mustered up the courage to ask her to share dinner with him.

"Umm, Michelle . . . uh . . . would you like to have dinner tonight? It is Valentine's weekend and we won't be back in Maine until tomorrow morning."

"I'd love to," she said smiling.

They climbed back on the train and walked down the aisle to their rooms to get changed and ready. Josh fumbled with his keycard at his door with Michelle behind him, and waited to get by as a rather wide man filled the walkway. Josh stood in his doorway as she tried to get by and the man pushed her into Josh.

Michelle looked up and stared into his green eyes and, without hesitating, kissed him. She slid her tongue between his lips, tasting him. Michelle closed her eyes and Josh became lost in the sensuality of her mouth. Last night reminded her of emotions she missed having. Desire. Spontaneity—and a secret, carefree need.

He reached around and held the small of her back, pulling them together. Josh moaned quietly as he felt the softness of her lips against his.

The hallway was bright, and people passed by them, but they didn't care. Her body was a perfect fit against his. Michelle felt him starting to swell against her stomach as the intensity of their passions heated the kiss.

Michelle stepped back. Flustered by her actions and feelings, she placed her hand on her chest and gasped, trying to find the right words. "I am sorry. I just felt the need to kiss you." Embarrassed, she tried to muster a smile.

"I didn't mind at all!" Josh replied. "It felt great. You sure you don't want to—ummmm?"

Michelle smiled, "No, I got a little carried away. It must be those green eyes or something. Let's just have a nice dinner tonight."

She wanted to be careful and not fall for the next guy who showed interest in her. She had just left one relationship and didn't want to jump right into another one. Even if he smelled great, was a good kisser and had an ass to die for. His nice endowment was another plus . . . a BIG plus.

Finally ready for dinner, Michelle paused, taking a deep breath. The soft, silken blue dress caressed her skin when she moved. Her lace brassiere was thin and transparent, showing her rose-colored nipples through the fabric. She fiddled to get her thong on, feeling it ride up her rear end. She liked the tightness of the thongs and how they seemed to cup her pussy like a bowl of fruit, keeping the juices in. Michelle may have loved how they fit in front but she wasn't too keen on the way they acted like butt floss in the back.

She never wore them much. Keith would beg her to put them on and even though she liked the feel against her pussy, they became uncomfortable because he'd tug and pull them.

She looked in the mirror, admiring the person looking back. She hadn't dolled up in a while but figured, *why not? A good-looking man had asked her to dinner.* Her confidence was high and her freedom from Keith liberated her. She could do what she wanted with whomever she wanted and there was no guilt, no worries, no commitments, just fun. *Damn, I look soooo HOT! I'd even want to screw me!*

A knock at the door shook Michelle back to reality and nervousness set in. She opened the door, Josh stood in the hall looking strikingly handsome. He was in tight black Dockers that accentuated his lower torso and a long-sleeve white shirt. The shirt was unbuttoned a little revealing some chest hair poking out from the top. His green eyes stared at her, making her feel like she was melting. What was really melting was her thong. It became moist and warmth filled her. His stare undressed her and she liked how it made her feel.

Desired, admired, appreciated, but mostly she felt wanted. Michelle appreciated Josh being a gentleman.

"Let me get the door." Josh scooted in front of her, opening the glass door.

Josh had other motives—checking out her ass while she walked past and seeing the other men look at her. Making sure everything was taken care of, Josh held the chair for her, ordered her dinner. He even tipped the waiter to not bother them.

Their meals came to the table and they started to open up and talk. It was like old friends catching up. They jumped right into talking about everything. The weather, college, books they liked—Ellora's Cave Publishing—and the other necessities. Time just flew by.

Michelle was enthralled at how open Josh was about things.

"I really wish I could be a photographer. I would LOVE to take pictures of a woman nude."

"I bet you would."

"No, really, not sex stuff, just pictures accentuating the wondrous splendor of the female form. I could talk for hours about what I'd do with a camera, champagne, some strawberries and whipped cream."

"WHIPPED CREAM?????? You are so crazy! I'd be way too scared to ever do something like that. I'm basically a romantic nut. Julia Roberts movies and happy endings, that's me in a nutshell."

"I prefer movies with a little more action . . . like pornos."

They laughed and started talking about recent relationships.

"Well, she left me because I seemed to be more interested

in work than her." Josh finished telling her about his last relationship.

"I think that's wrong. She should have least talked to you about it first," Michelle replied, knowing how it must have felt.

"Well, I work for my parents and that makes it difficult to not try and work hard. I will end up with the business one day so I damned well want it to be successful." Josh paused, taking a drink then continued, "My work has me traveling a lot on business trips. I was away from her quite a bit. Of course, the four times I caught her cheating on me may have been part of the problem also. It wasn't the cheating so much as who she was with. I found her with this writer holding a rubber chicken. Another time she was in my office with my secretary."

Josh shook his head laughing at the embarrassment. "Cheating with her boss was bad but they took movies and I saw them online at a porn site. The last straw was these two guys at the library. She told me they were testing the *Joy of Sex* positions. Personally, I never saw that position before. Why'd they have an eggbeater there?" Josh hurt talking about it but still laughed.

"I just left a two-year relationship," she said, hanging her head. "I wasted all that time after college to be with a man who never cared about me. I was so stupid. I should have left long ago but was scared."

Looking at Josh, she didn't feel shy or restrained, she was just being honest. "I don't need to be a man's bitch. I just wanted to be loved and cared for. I guess I just got used to the dull day-to-day. He was a dickhead and treated me like a piece of property. I am free from him and feel good about myself. Now I just want to go back home and get my crap together then move up north. I want to start over. This dream job is going to be great. I just want some time to be ME."

Josh just sat, smiling at her.

"What?" she asked.

"That took a lot of courage. I admire that. I'm not sure I could move away from my home."

Josh sipped his drink and continued, "After I finished playing football in college I wasn't sure what to do. I had my degree and fell into my college relationship. I moved back home and started to live the standard family, kids, house lifestyle."

"You played football?" Michelle asked, feeling her weakness rise up. Something about those tight uniforms and the brutal force made her sigh.

"I played a little in high school. Played defensive back in college. Never made the pros. Loved playing though. You okay?"

Michelle parted her lips, sighing. Her mind wandered to a fantasy of Josh in his uniform. Wetness seeped between her legs and she became suddenly hot. She was aroused by Josh but needed to be careful. It was easy to become horny, but this trip was getting away from things.

"Sorry, got a little lightheaded."

"You done eating?" Josh asked.

"Are you?" Michelle answered.

"Not totally, I am looking at what I'd like to eat." His mischievous smile cut through her and made her even wetter.

"You know, if things were different, I'd give you a four-course meal."

"CHECK, PLEASE!"

Struggling with feelings and the awkward unknown situation, they walked back to her compartment. Josh leaned down and kissed Michelle. She placed her hand on his neck and let her lips move against his. God, he was so hot to her. Inside she was on fire, but she had to contain it.

"Goodnight, Josh, thank you for a wonderful evening."

"You sure? I mean I could . . ."

Michelle stopped Josh from continuing. "Let's not ruin this with a torrid night of incredible, hot, passionate, earth-shattering sex."

"Yeah, that would really be a bad thing," he sarcastically replied.

Josh looked down at Michelle. He kissed her forehead then raised her face with his hands and kissed her lips. His hands lowered along her sides, brushing the sensitive skin aside her breasts.

"Mmmmmmmm, oh, yes," she murmured.

Michelle's hands found his waist and her knees weakened at the affectionate way he kissed her. Her mouth dropped open and she lifted her head back when Josh blew hot air gently into her ear and squeezed her ass. She almost succumbed to his advances because she was already wet in anticipation for him.

"Josh, I ca-can't."

She hesitated before pushing him back. "I can't just jump into another relationship like this. It's too soon."

Looking down, Josh nodded but was obviously let down. He walked to his room and waved at Michelle but didn't turn towards her because his hard-on was making his pants poke out.

Michelle was being torn apart. What should she do?

Josh opened his door and Michelle pushed him in, closing it behind her.

"I thought you said . . ." Josh tried to talk, but Michelle

covered his mouth and pushed him against the closet door in the confining space of the entryway.

She smothered his mouth with her kisses and ripped at his shirt. She slid her hands inside and across his flexed abdomen. His skin was hot and she tore his shirt open to kiss his chest. Michelle's unquenched hunger was making her free from inhibitions and Josh would be her delicious treat.

"Mmm, you look yummy," she hissed through her teeth.

Placing her hand over his lips, she bit on his nipple, pulling at it with her teeth.

Josh moaned, "Damn, that feels good!"

Michelle dropped to her knees, kissing his muscular stomach. She tugged at his zipper then shoved her hand inside his pants. Grabbing his hard cock in her hand, she fumbled, trying to unfasten his belt.

"Damn belt, I hate these things!" He throbbed in her hand. She desperately wanted to set his cock free from his confining pants.

His pants fell to his knees and she yanked his underwear down. He was surprisingly large and rigid. She stroked down his length with her palm feeling the wrinkles of his flesh disappear. The glisten of fluid on the tip showed his desire. Looking up into his desperate green eyes, she consumed him in her mouth. The tip hit the back of her throat and almost gagged her.

Josh moaned and hit his head against the door. "Oh, shit, mmmmmmm . . ."

Michelle's hunger took over, and she devoured him like he was her last meal. Dragging her tongue along the vein pulsing in his cock she would let the tip pop out of her mouth then suck him back in. She had seen him from a distance the night before but now he was up close and personal.

He was glorious to her eyes, mouth and soon to her pussy. She kissed the tip as her hand stroked the length of his hardened cock.

"You are driving me fucking crazy!" Josh laughed. "This isn't fair."

"For whom? You or ME?"

A wicked look crossed Michelle's face. She stroked his shaft in her hand and watched the head flex as she pulled down the skin. She reached her other hand between her legs and felt the wetness seeping from inside. She gently rubbed her fiery pussy, making it burn hotter for Josh. The line was crossed and there was no going back.

She pulled her thong aside and the swelling lips of her pussy were damp and needy. Fingering herself, her passion became more voracious. She stroked Josh's cock in her hand and fingered herself. Gasping for air, she flicked her tongue on the tip, then swallowed the head of Josh's slick cock back in. She could taste the initial flavor of his seed. Her lips clamped around the tip, sucking in hard.

"Oh, damn, stop teasing me! You have to let me . . ."

Releasing his cock from her mouth with a "pop," Michelle stood up but held tight onto her prize. Slowly, she unfastened the buttons of her dress.

Josh breathed heavily, as he watched her reveal her bosom to his appreciative eyes. Josh reached up, cupping her breast through the lace fabric of her bra.

Michelle squeezed his cock in her hand, feeling her pussy tingling. "Mmmmmmm, that feels nice. You like these, Josh?"

Josh undid the clasp on the front of her bra, freeing her breasts. "Oh, yeah, you have wonderful breasts. Ouch! Don't squeeze so tight, you'll break it."

Her fleshy globes glowed pink and her nipples were a deep

burgundy color that begged to be sucked on. Josh obliged. He licked all around her nipples while cupping the fullness in his hands.

A deep moan of pleasure echoed from Michelle as he teased her supple breasts. Michelle breathed in his smell. The scent of his hair, his cologne and his body filled her lungs. Intoxicated by him, she let go all the inhibitions she possessed, daring to take him against her better judgment.

The devilish little voice popped up in her head again. *Don't stop. Look at this guy. He wants you so bad, can't you feel it in your hand? Just fuck him, who'll ever know?*

Her rational voice replied, too, *Yeah, just fuck him!*

"Josh, I haven't been with any other man in so long I don't know how to ask for . . . mmmmmmmmm," Michelle gasped.

"Just tell me what you want. I'll do anything to you," Josh said, nuzzling her breasts.

Teasing his eyes and mind, she slowly tossed aside each piece of clothing until she stood naked, and burning. Her fingers caressed his hot skin and while she stepped into him her fire began to rage. Grabbing Josh's thick hair she forced his head downward. She wanted to be ravaged—she wanted a man to treat her so wickedly with passion that he would get lost in her. "Ohhhhh, right there, ohhhhhhhhhhh . . ."

Josh slid his tongue along the length of her slit, feeling the heat from her engorged pussy boil from his tongue's movements. "You taste absolutely incredible, mmmmmmm . . ."

"I can't handle a lot of . . . of . . . OH, GOD!"

Josh spread her labia apart and flicked his tongue against her firm clit that begged for his attention.

His deep moaning vibrated through her body. She felt so damn hot that this wasn't enough. She needed to be filled. Michelle grabbed Josh's hair, pulling him up and pushing him against the closet door once again. She was soaking wet from her arousal by this virtual stranger.

"Damn, your pussy tasted sweet. I bet it feels better than it smells," Josh joked, almost asking for proof.

The entryway of the train compartment was about two and a half feet wide. Michelle leaned against the wall and spread her legs apart then pushed her right leg alongside Josh and against the closet door. Josh stared at her exposed pussy. It gleamed from wetness about six inches from his throbbing cock. Michelle smiled and motioned for Josh to move forward. "You wanna find out?"

Josh's face lit up and he leaned forward, kissing her. His cock rested against her pussy and the searing wet lips. Michelle reached down and pushed the tip against her hot opening, and felt the head of his cock spreading her labia apart. Josh put his hands on either side of her head. Michelle put her other leg against the wall and held herself up while holding Josh's shoulders. In a moment of obscene passion, Josh leaned into Michelle and sank his thickened shaft into her tight pussy.

Michelle screamed, "Oh, God, ohhhhhh, damn you feel so *FUCKING* good!" and dug her nails into his shoulders. Turning to kiss him, their tongues danced while his cock filled her. She tasted a trace of her own juices and it made her flutter and shake. She really did taste good. Michelle looked down at his stomach as he withdrew from her. She saw the glistening top of his shaft straining and it popped out. She grabbed the head of his cock and put its tip against her pussy saying, "You stay inside, no rest for you."

Josh grunted and plunged in again. His breath was hot against her neck and Michelle finally felt filled. She reached up and held the coat rack at the top of the wall, and let Josh grab her hips and thrust powerfully into her. She wrapped her legs around his hips flexing her legs with each stroke.

His furious thrusts rocked her body making her breasts jiggle. Shockwaves ripped through her while he slammed hard against her body, pushing her against the wall. The wall shook as the force of their sex mounted. Over and over he drove into her body, trying to get as deep as possible. She bit his collarbone and her vaginal muscles clenched his cock tightly.

"You are so beautiful, I . . . I just . . . you feel so damn good."

She clamped onto him, almost squealing in joy as she felt herself climbing higher. "Oh, Josh, you feel so mmmmmm incredible. Ohhhh, I can't take much more." Tightening her muscles around him, she kissed him again feeding her hunger.

Michelle licked the sweat on his chest. The salty taste made her want more.

Josh looked at her, admiring how her body was illuminated as she ground against him.

"Fuck, I am so close," Josh panted. He was relentless, like a jackhammer as he fucked her.

Michelle's pussy was so sensitive to Josh. She felt herself ready to explode. Suddenly everything got blurry and Michelle closed her eyes tightly and came. Her thickened vaginal walls gushed and spasmed. She felt the fluids trickle down her pussy to her ass.

"Ohhhhh, yesssssssss, mmmmm yessssss . . ." she hissed.

Josh was grunting and she felt his cock swelling. "I can feel your orgasm, fucking incredible, incred . . ." Josh firmly held her ass and sank his cock into her, and exploded his seed against her cervix.

It burned Michelle but felt so good. It was hot, wet and the next few thrusts seemed easier and made her feel absolutely wonderful. She hadn't felt like this in so long that she just sighed and smiled.

Josh let her ass go and she stood before him. She looked down at his cock, still dripping and slightly flaccid. "Hmm, well he looks tired," she giggled.

"He is happy now!" Josh said. "Ever since he saw you last night he has been thinking about you."

"Last night?" Michelle asked.

"Well, I woke up last night and saw you in the chair. Damn, you were beautiful. The moonlight across your face made me realize true beauty."

Michelle blushed then laughed when Josh drew two lines in the air, like counting brownie points. "I thought you looked familiar. Then I remembered I had seen you in my dreams and fantasies." Michelle was scared he had seen her in the blanket.

"That is by far the cheesiest line I have heard in quite some time. I love it." Michelle laughed, and they fell into the small bed. They both laughed as they peeled their clothes off—now in a crumpled pile on the floor. Thank goodness, they were wrinkle-free fabric. Josh was against the wall and Michelle in front of him. She was relaxed and while Josh stroked her hair, she drifted off to sleep in his arms.

The morning sun crept up over the mountains and shone in through the window. Michelle was warm and felt secure in Josh's arms. She didn't want to rush right back into belonging to someone else. She didn't really know Josh but loved how he made her feel. He ground his teeth when he slept, making her cringe. It sounded like nails across a blackboard. She could feel his naked flesh against hers and the body heat made her back hot.

She tried to get up out of the cramped bed without waking him. Sitting on the edge, she shivered from the chilly room. She was warm in bed but it was cold in the compartment. Josh's white shirt was on the floor, she grabbed it with her toes and pulled it to the bed and put it on. She couldn't button it because she ripped them off last night. The sleeve had a trace of Josh's cologne on it.

It was the beginning of a new day and it was beautiful outside. Michelle stepped toward the window. She leaned against it, watching the trees go by.

"You look beautiful," she heard Josh say.

"Thanks. Did you sleep well? You grind your teeth; damn, that is an annoying sound."

The shirt was big on her and he could see the outline of her body from the light shining through it. Josh grabbed his pants off the floor and pulled them on. Leaving them unfastened and open, he stood behind her looking out the window.

She leaned into him and their contours fit together perfectly. The curve of her ass nestled against his crotch. Josh breathed in the fragrance from her hair. He looked down her body and saw her breasts.

Michelle reached back and put her hand on his thigh. She sighed and breathed in deep making her chest expand. The sunlight cast an orange hue across her body as his baggy shirt she wore opened, exposing her skin.

Josh reached his hands around her and held her full breasts in his hands. Michelle moaned softly, "Last night was really wonderful, Josh. I hadn't felt like that in some time."

He kissed her ear, blowing hot air across her neck causing her to have chills.

Goose bumps rose across her body and her nipples popped to attention.

So did Josh's cock as it rose in his pants against Michelle's ass. Squeezing her breasts in his large hands, he molded Michelle to his frame. She pulled her head up resting against his collarbone and closed her eyes. Josh licked the back of her ear making her moan. "Oh, yes, you found a weak spot."

Michelle tried to turn around but Josh held her firmly. He pushed her forward, taking control of the situation. Her knees hit the edge of the chair in front of the window. Almost falling Michelle raised her hands in reflex and pressed them on the window.

"Mmmmmm, this is nice," Josh muttered feeling his excitement rise. She put her knees on the cushion and leaned forward pushing her ass against his stiffening cock.

"Now you found MY weakness," he said, kissing her lower back.

Josh let go of her breasts and slid his hands back to Michelle's hips. She looked behind her and saw Josh kneeling down. "Oh, please, I can't handle that, Josh." His hot mouth kissed the small of her back and followed the split of her ass. He reached his hand between her legs and dragged his thumb along the lips of her pussy. Her blond hair dangled, swaying with her movement. She looked back down between her breasts.

A stifled whimper crept from within her when Josh's finger spread her labia apart. He stroked the length to the perineum. Michelle threw her head back, moaning. Wanting more, Michelle rocked side-to-side, opening her legs wider.

Josh took the cue and grabbed her ass, spreading the cheeks apart. His finger darted in and out of her pussy making her squirm in delight. The gentle play made Michelle giggle.

Reaching her hand down between her legs, she rubbed her clitoral hood making it pull back to reveal her swollen bud.

Josh tapped against her clit with his finger. "Damn, you are so wet already." Josh held firmly onto the hardness in his pants. Doing this aroused him. He wanted to feel himself buried in her slippery flesh and extinguish the fire that burned inside. His thumb rested against her anus. She wasn't one for this kind of play but Michelle felt a tingling sensation and squirmed a little. His thumb was wet from her juices and pressed along the outer rim and when he pushed his finger into her pussy his thumb probed at her anal opening.

"You idiot, that tickles. Quit teasing me," she giggled. Michelle arched her back lower making her pussy more exposed to Josh's play. She was losing control and her muscles weakened, she had to hold her balance with her other hand against the window.

He spread her lips wide and fingered her, becoming frantic to have her. "Ohhhh, I love doing this to you. It makes me want you more," Josh groaned as he refrained from grabbing himself.

"You mind if I kiss your ass?" Josh joked running his tongue along the crease where her leg and ass met.

"I am so damn horny, let me feel you inside me," she moaned, almost begging for a release.

Without any more prompting, Josh stood up and pulled his stiff cock out, and rested it on Michelle's ass. He was toying with her needs and she loved every second of it. He held it in his hand and glided it along the crease of her ass to the wet opening of her pussy. "Damn, Michelle, you are so incredibly hot. You make me want nothing more than to . . ." His words cut through her as his shaft slid between her slick lips, spreading her pussy open again. A deep groan echoed from Josh as he felt her massage his cock inside her velvety pussy.

Michelle closed her eyes and began to spasm from the ecstasy.

She put both hands on the window as Josh's body pressed against her. His long slow strokes dragged against her clit filling her with elation. Her knees weakened and she realized she was climbing into a blissful orgasmic state. Josh groaned and his body was sweating as he tried to contain himself.

"Damn, you make me so nuts," he grunted.

His hot, wet hands moved up the soft bumps of her spine as she would rise and fall to his thrusts. His body started to become hot with passion.

She felt Josh trying to control himself. He would stop and breathe out, then hold his breath in and start again. Michelle closed her eyes letting the pleasure of his cock erase all her inhibitions and allow her to let go. She loved knowing she affected him like this. Michelle closed her eyes feeling every inch of him filling her. Josh sank his cock into her, becoming lost in his lust, succumbing to his natural, primal needs.

"I can't take this. You are so . . . oh, damn!"

"Make me come, Josh, make me come!"

With a brute force, Josh grabbed Michelle's hips and plunged into her. Bending his knees, he picked her up and filled her over and over.

"Oh, yes, I am ooooooooooooohh . . ." Michelle's body shook and she felt the abrupt ripple of her orgasm roll through her pussy and flow through her.

Josh whimpered and thrust into her again raising her body and engulfing her with the spewing of his seed. Michelle felt the hot juices melding with hers and she smiled happily. The fluid from their sex trickled down her inner thigh.

Josh leaned forward and kissed her back. The sweat was dripping from his forehead. At the same time, they both looked out the window. They heard a clapping sound as some people at the station had gathered outside and watched them having sex. From their reaction, they must have done a good job. Michelle recognized a face in the crowd who wasn't clapping. It was her uncle.

Josh grabbed the cord letting the blinds fall, covering the window. They looked at each other and burst into laughter. "I have never been so embarrassed in my life!"

Michelle was upset. Her stern frown struggled upwards as she started smiling and giggling, as Josh danced around the room. He shook his ass and swung his dick around singing some upbeat song by Garth Brooks. He sounded awful. She liked watching him dangling around while getting dressed though.

Michelle tried to think of a way to say goodbye. She hated goodbyes. It was always awkward.

Josh scribbled on a piece of paper by the bed then stood in front of her. Before she could speak, Josh started, "This is my cell phone number and email address. I live in town, in a cottage next door to my parents. I know you are struggling with a tough time right now."

He kissed her forehead and stared into her eyes and finished, "This trip has been a fantasy come true for me. You do what you have to do. If you decide you want to see me, call me. I'm leaving this open to you."

He held her hand and kissed her on the forehead. A last look and smile filled Michelle with hope as he grabbed his bags, stepping out the door. She looked at the paper seeing his phone number, email and Instant Messenger name . . . Sir-lix-alot.

4

The ride on the train was a good time for Michelle to regroup and figure out her life. She felt good about her decision to leave and move on. In a way, she was scared to be alone, but Josh had made her feel like a woman again. In the simplest way, he opened her up . . . in a few different areas. Her sore muscles were proof of that. Of course her uncle was quiet the entire ride home having seen his niece in a different light than he had before.

The scenery hadn't changed much since she'd left and Michelle was happy to be home again—even if it was only for a few weeks. The car pulled up in the driveway and her mom sprang from the house to see her.

"Ohhhh, you look so pretty. Come give Mom a hug. You need to tell me everything! How was work and the girls? How was your trip? Did you meet anybody interesting on the train?"

"Hey, tell your mom if you met anyone on the train ride."

Scowling back at her uncle, Michelle nodded and got her bags from the car. They went into the house chatting and her mom held her arm the whole way. Michelle went into her old room. It had been left it just like as had been before she moved out, except for a few craft boxes in the corner. She was home.

"Mom, I need to tell you some things, okay?"

"Of course, dear. What's going on?"

Taking a deep breath, she started, "Keith and I broke up. Actually, I left him. I took a job up north and that's where I am headed. It's what I always wanted to do." She stopped, seeing her mom wanted to ask something.

"Is this what you want, dear? Keith called saying you were going through some things."

"When did he call?"

"Yesterday. I thought it was odd. He never calls. To be blunt, I never really liked him. He acted like such an asshole."

"Why did everyone dislike him but never told me? I hate that he called here. I left him because he treated me like shit and . . . sorry, Mom. I did meet somebody on the train here, though." Michelle became warm talking of him.

"Wow, you're glowing, dear. He must be some man. So, umm, is he good at, ummm, well . . ." Blushing, Michelle's mom held her hands apart as if measuring a fish.

"MOM!!!" Flabbergasted, Michelle burst out laughing. She grabbed her mom's hands and opened them a little wider.

"Does he happen to have a single father?"

"His name is Josh and I know it was a simple fling but I really like him a lot."

They laughed and continued their girl talk for the rest of the evening. Feeling like a teenager again, Michelle showered then slipped into her pajamas. Standing in the bedroom doorway she scurried over and plopped on her bed. It was the same but everything seemed smaller. She had been away for six years and hadn't come back much.

Josh climbed out of the taxi and walked up the steps to his house. He saw his mom in the front window cleaning dishes in the sink. He picked up the newspaper on the doorstep and went in.

"Hello, honey, how was your trip?" his mom yelled while he hung his jacket on the rack and set his luggage down.

"It was fine, Ma. Where's Dad?"

"Oh, he's downstairs. Why did you buy that stupid satellite system? He's always watching TV."

He peeked in the kitchen, breathing in the scent of fresh bread baking. *Hmmmm, chocolate chip cookies, too*, he thought.

"Get out of here! Hey you brat, don't eat the cookies, they're for dessert." His mom swatted at him with a towel.

Josh went to his dad's basement office. Basically, it was a TV room. It was dimly lit but had a fifty-eight-inch TV, surround sound, DVD, satellite hookup and two recliners. Perfect for football.

Josh got to the bottom of the stairs and heard a deep moaning sound. "Mmmmm, aaahh, aaahhh, yeah, baby, ohhhhh, yeah, give it to me. Who's your daddy? Who's your daddy?"

"Dad? What are you doing?"

"Hey, son, come check this out."

Jumping into the other chair Josh raised an eyebrow and his jaw dropped.

"Uh, I am speechless. I didn't think a woman could bend like that." His dad was watching a porn movie from the satellite. They both tilted their heads to the right and became engrossed in the woman on the screen. Of course, the man in the movie was more INTO her.

"I saw a new movie. It was set in a circus. Never understood how they got that many clowns in a car. Now I understand. Did you know we get five channels of this stuff twenty-four hours a day? Son, I could kiss you for the satellite. Josh . . . JOSH!"

"Dad, after watching this I don't want you kissing me."

Muting the TV, his dad asked Josh about the trip.

"You get that contract? We really need that client. Our business will exponentially grow from it." Occasionally they'd stop and watch some porn. It was a pleasant distraction. They started talking about his train ride home and Josh told him about Michelle.

"You're kidding, THAT Michelle? Son, she is beautiful. Her brother is an asshole for the way he treated your sister, but she was always nice. Does she know who you are?"

"I don't think so. She probably doesn't remember me. I couldn't believe it was HER. Man, I had dreamed about her for years."

"Well? What happened? Did you guys . . . you know?"

Josh smiled, "Dad, that's personal. It's not right to talk about that."

"Okay, I respect that. I take that as a yes," he laughed.

"DAAAAMMMMMMMNNNNN!" they both yelled, as they saw a woman on the TV with a set of watermelon-sized breasts and a cucumber.

"Well, son, I'm gonna go jump your mother before dinner."

"Too much information, Dad. I'll go to my place before dinner." Josh joked. "Just make sure you clean the table when you're done."

While Michelle brushed her hair, she opened the drawer to her nightstand.

"Oh, look, my yearbook." She smiled remembering the past. She turned the pages reading the senseless notes from friends. *Have a great summer. Call me sometime. Thanks for the homecoming present.* "Mmmmm, I remember THAT home-cumming." She was seventeen again and didn't have any worries except going to college.

She turned to the dog-eared page, the football team photos. Her memories made her close her legs tightly together. She looked at the large varsity team photo looking at her old boyfriend. She stared intensely at number eighty-seven.

"Oh, my god! That's Josh." Franticly she turned to the senior pictures looking for him. She found his photo. "What a goober," was her first impression. She scanned the page to see if he left any notes.

"Have a nice summer. I know we didn't talk too much at school but I noticed you every day. You brightened my school experience, Josh."

Michelle fought back tears. It was so sweet. *He's really filled out nicely,* she thought and raised her eyebrow. Turning off her light, she lay back in her bed and held her favorite teddy bear. *I think I will call you now, Josh,* she thought, holding it against her chest. She stared up at the ceiling with the sprinkles of light reflecting off the stucco. She finally met someone who treated her nicely and seemed to be really respectful and caring. It pained her to know she had to leave him behind. Drifting to sleep, she thought of the train and her encounter with a mystery man she had been blind to before.

The next few days were quiet and Michelle found herself becoming more assured that this departure from Keith, her new revelation and the perfect job was the right thing to do. She called Irene in Canada, making sure everything was in line for her new job. Her flight information was confirmed. Everything was set to go.

Her mom wanted her to go to a friend's place with her. Michelle didn't mind. It was a beautiful day and they walked down the breezy street by the old houses of the neighborhood. It was refreshing and she could chat with her mom, woman-to-woman.

"So, this man you met on the train?

"It was nothing, just a fling."

"Sometimes a fling is a good thing," her mom mused. "As long as he has a long thing."

"His name is Josh Brinkman."

Her mom stopped and looked at her. "Josh? Uh-oh. You must not have heard?"

"What?" Michelle asked confused.

"Well, Josh's sister was your brother's fiancée. Right before the wedding, Josh caught your brother with Ellie McShaw in a car. You remember Ellie—she was the girl that got stuck on the gearshift of her dad's tractor. She does porno movies now. Well, to make a long story short, he told his sister about your brother and she called off the wedding. Your brother blames Josh for everything. Josh even took his position on the college football team his junior year. Your brother despises Josh! Never met the man myself."

"That was him? Oh, great, Mike would kill me if he knew I had a fling with Josh. Oh, well, I'll probably never see him because I'll be in Canada next week."

"Dear, I wanted some time to talk to you. Are you happy?"

"Why do you ask?"

"Well, I know leaving Keith must have been hard on you. He was a jerk and I should have paid more attention to you being down when you were together. When your dad passed, I was alone for quite a while. I never thought of anything except 'poor me.' You remember?"

"Yes, I remember. I wish I were here more for you. I had to stay with . . ."

"Stop," her mom interrupted. "I'm not asking you anything, I just want to tell you something. I am proud of you, Michelle. You are doing something I never did. You are taking a big step and following a dream. Four years of college and you take that crappy job, and let that man run your life."

Her mom stopped holding Michelle's hand and looked into her eyes. "Don't end up like me, dear. LIVE YOUR LIFE. Don't be like your brother, get the hell out of this town and see the world. Don't let someone change your dreams. I can tell there is something else. I'm your mother and I know. You'll be fine, dear." A tear filled her mom's eye and she hugged Michelle tight.

Michelle, her brother Mike and her mom sat at the kitchen table playing cards when the phone rang.

"Hello?" A smile widened across her face. "Nice to hear your voice, too." Excusing herself from the table, Michelle walked down the hall. She stopped and leaned against the wall.

"So what are you doing?" Josh asked.

"Talking to you. You lied to me. Why didn't you tell me we went to high school together?"

"I was different back then. We all were. I was sort of a geeky kid then. Played connect the dots with my pimples and couldn't get a girl to notice me much. That's why I took up football. I liked hitting people to take out my frustration. Really helped my confidence and got me into college."

Josh changed subjects. "Anyway, what color?"

"What color what?"

"What color underwear do you have on? And what are you doing this Saturday?"

"I'm not wearing any and I'm going to an anniversary party with my mom."

"Well this makes it easy. I was going to ask you if you'd like to go to my parents' anniversary party but I guess I'll see you there. I'm not wearing any underwear either, just got out of the shower."

"Hmmmm, wish I was there." Michelle really did wish it. Closing her eyes, she pictured him standing naked and talking on the phone. Dangling in all his glory with his broad chest, dark hair and . . .

"HELLO??? You there???"

"Sorry, distracted. I guess I'll see you there then. Thanks for calling."

She hung up the phone and went back to the table. "Who was that?" her brother asked.

"It was a friend." She winked at her mom. "Can't wait to go to the party tomorrow night!"

"Well, I'm not going, all those fuddy-duddies at an anniversary party. Sounds boring to me," her brother sarcastically replied.

5

The party was dull but Michelle was happy she went. Josh was talking football with a few guys sitting on the other side of him and would turn around and look at her with a smile. The knowledge that they knew each other made the game more fun. Michelle felt out of place but Josh made her feel okay. Her mom looked over and winked. Michelle blushed and winked back.

"So, Josh. I hear you and my daughter took the train home. How was the trip?"

"It was really pleasant. The scenery was beautiful. I drank a little too much the first night with friends but the rest of the trip was really fulfilling." He smiled and continued, "The compartments were pretty small but if you use some ingenuity, you can get into the tightest areas just fine."

Michelle jerked upright looking shocked when Josh slipped his hand up her thigh.

"Ummm, your hand must be lost. Shouldn't you be eating?" Michelle smiled, whispering into his ear.

"I'm looking for finger food." Josh finished the sentence as he pressed his finger up against her panties. His thumb rested along the top crease of her moistening pussy.

"Oh, they have some finger food on the table in the living room, dear," her mom piped in.

Not wanting to make a scene, Michelle reached under the table. Leaning over to Josh, she whispered, "Stop it, you are embarrassing me."

Josh pressed harder and looked away to talk to a neighbor sitting across from him. Michelle sat dumbfounded but suddenly became warm. Josh's thumb crept inside of her pussy with only the thin fabric stopping him from entering her deeper. Josh pulled his hand away and brought it to his nose, and breathed her scent in. Michelle sighed in relief then sat upright again, when he set his hand between her legs again.

Michelle couldn't take anymore. She got up to go the restroom to freshen up. "I'll be right back, Mom," she told her when she passed by. Lost, she went around the corner and looked down the hall trying to find the right door. She found the bathroom and went in.

"You need any help?" she heard the voice behind her ask.

"No, Josh, I'm fine. Don't you ever stop?"

Josh grabbed her arm and pulled her into his body, kissing her. His mouth was wet from the wine and the sweetness of the grapes seeped into Michelle's lips. Her knees buckled and she caught herself giving in.

"No, Josh, not here, you brat. Stop grabbing my ass, you goofball." She was determined to be strong even though he was being very persistent. "NO, now you go back to the table. NO. NO. NO," Michelle said as the door closed.

"Ohhhhh, yes, mmmmmmmm," was mumbled when the door locked. A loud thump hit the door. Josh had gotten his way.

Michelle's mom became worried about her. Since Michelle had been gone a while, she went down the hall to see if she was okay. She listened at the door hearing a soft muffled moan.

"Are you all right, dear?" her mom asked.

"I'll-I'll be there . . . in a few minutes," Michelle stammered back.

"Poor dear, she must be feeling bad. Probably the meat loaf. I hate it when the meat loaf is soft," her mom giggled and walked back to the table.

Michelle sat on the bathroom countertop, spread wide to Josh's forceful tongue as he kneeled before her. Michelle lost herself in the blur of her dark fantasy. "Oh, fuck, don't stop, Josh, this is incredible."

Michelle turned her head to the side against the wall-length vanity mirror watching her reflection. As Josh concentrated on her clitoris, he suckled hard and slid his thumb between her engorged labia. Michelle watched her face in the mirror and how blissfully enraptured she was in this heated moment of passion.

Her passionate juices dripped from her, mixing with his saliva. His thumb pressed on the flesh below her clit, forcing it upward. He flicked his tongue over the tip of her clitoris. Michelle smiled, seeing her reflection through half-open eyes. She loved being eaten and Josh knew her weakness.

The fear of being caught only heightened her intense arousal. She closed her eyes, grabbing Josh's head, begging him to continue. Josh slid his thumb into her pussy and stretched it open. Michelle came against his mouth when his tongue stroked the length of her clit with a long sweeping lick. Josh sucked and licked her pussy until she struggled to put her legs together. His hunger for her taste was unquenchable.

Josh fixed himself in the mirror and pinched her knee making her leg jerk. He licked his thumb and wiped his face on the washcloth. "You're a mess, you better straighten up, young lady!"

Michelle laughed and kicked him in the butt.

She tried to straighten and compose herself the best she could. She shook her head and giggled going back to the table. Josh was eating some cheesecake and talking to his neighbor again.

"Are you okay, dear?" her mom asked. "You look flushed and out of breath."

"I'm fine. It's just hot in here."

"You can say that again," Josh replied as they both smiled and she squeezed his knee.

Michelle looked uncomfortable while talking on the phone. "Yes, I left there a few weeks ago. That shouldn't be a problem, Irene. I can't believe that asshole ruined my credit like that. I am so happy to be out of there. Okay, okay, thanks and tell them I'll be there first thing Monday morning." She closed her eyes and shook her head mouthing the word FUCK.

"I appreciate you having all this set up for me, Irene, I owe you one." Pissed off and angry, Michelle hung up the phone and smoldered while sipping her coffee in the kitchen.

"Uh-oh, what's wrong, dear?" her mom asked, while pouring herself a cup.

"That prick Keith ran up my credit cards and never told me, then didn't pay the fees. Just once I'd like to . . ." She squeezed a donut in her hand. The cream filling plopped out and she squished it. "That's what I feel like doing to him."

Her mom grabbed a paper towel, wiping it up. "Men are so messy. I wish they were the sperm receptacle once and know what it feels like. I honestly believe they think with their penises. It's always getting them in trouble and doesn't make a bit of sense."

Taking deep breaths and calming herself with the warm coffee Michelle sat with her mom and asked, "Mom, have you, ummm, you know . . . since Dad died?"

Michelle could tell the question caught her mom off guard. "Wellllllllll, there was this one gentleman. Oh, boy, he was so nice to be around. We knew each other for a long time and one day, he asked me out. One date led to another date and eventually we, um, how do I put this so you'll understand what happened . . . we fucked like wild rabbits."

Spewing coffee, Michelle dribbled it down her chin. "MOM!?!?!"

"Well, you asked." Her mom giggled and continued, "I loved your father. Honestly, he was the love of my life. After he was gone, I was still only fifty. Then I met Ross. He was really nice. He taught me things I never knew about."

"Oh, my God, Ross Lassiter, the Biology teacher? He taught my Sex Ed class!"

"Yes, he was a GREAT teacher. I learned things about my body and about me that freed up all those fears of being alone and never feeling wanted again. He showed me I wasn't too old to still be a sexy woman."

"Mom, I am proud of you."

"Oh, quit it. It happened a few years back and not since. I must say it was liberating. There was a good reason he taught Sex Ed. Sure, it was a fling of passion, but it was something I needed to do for ME. My arthritis was making my hand hurt and I was using up all the batteries."

"Well, this thing with Josh has got to stop. He's a grrrrrreat lover . . . but . . . I don't know. I just left Keith and I'm not sure I can trust a man right now."

"That's up to you, dear. Take that job and find yourself. This is what you want so don't regret at least trying it. You'll look back and never forgive yourself. I never did. If Josh is for real he'll let you go and be here when you get back."

6

Josh and Michelle spent the next few days randomly meeting each other. It became obvious to Michelle that she had started to have feelings for him. She looked forward to his calls and the meetings. She was a teenager all over again and had a fickle crush on Josh. It couldn't last but she wanted to make the most out of the time at home.

Sometimes they would just go for walks. The park was beautiful. It was chilly but not too cold. Unusual springlike weather made the time there that much more special. They walked, holding hands and then sat down on a bench.

"So what do you think about kids and families?" Michelle asked.

"I like the idea of a family. A few kids, a nice house. Just not sure I'm ready yet. I don't know. If I met the right woman, who knows?"

"Shhhh, you hear that?" Michelle asked.

They stopped talking and heard a quiet moaning sound in the bushes behind their bench. Being typically curious, Josh and Michelle got up and wandered around the bushes, trying to be quiet. They peeked through the brush and saw a couple in a sleeping bag on the ground.

"Reminds me of a hotdog in a bun," Josh joked.

"Looks like she's the one getting the hotdog! I wonder if it's a foot-long?"

The young lady's black hair flowed from the opening of the sleeping bag and her long locks swept the grass below her. Josh and Michelle smiled at each other and watched the lovers. A deep-voiced moan from within the sleeping bag reverberated through the quiet park. A man's head popped from the opening. His face was covered with the black hair of the woman and he was gasping for air.

There was the sound of the side zipper opening and the woman sat up, exposing their semi-nude bodies. Josh's eyes opened wide as the woman threw her head back. Her large breasts sprang forward as she arched her back. She looked glorious and her large burgundy-colored nipples made Josh stutter. "Umm, uh, should we leave?"

"I can really see you want to go," Michelle grinned as she watched Josh drool.

Michelle raised her eyebrow when the man reached up and grabbed the woman's breast in his massive paw. Tattoos covered his arms. He sat up, burying his face in her breasts, sucking on her nipples one by one. The woman leaned forward to kiss the man. Their mouths opened and they seemed to swallow each other's tongues in a lustful kiss. Josh crossed his legs, trying to disguise his arousal in this live porno movie.

Michelle enjoyed watching the couple, the abandon of the

woman as she leaned back, stretching her breasts skyward as she rode atop this mammoth man.

His arms here huge and he was enthralled in her delight. The sleeping bag fell open and only the woman's miniskirt covered their bare bodies. The man reached down, raising her skirt and exposing her shaved pubis. A tattoo of a red arrow pointing down and reading "ENTER HERE" decorated her pubic bone area.

Michelle and Josh stared as the large man rolled the woman over and got atop her. He lifted up and rested his large, hardened cock on her tummy.

"Yep . . . a foot-long," Michelle smirked.

It throbbed as he slid it back and forth, teasing her. The woman grabbed a handful of his hair and pulled him down. Smiling, the man lowered back down to kiss her. Like two animals, they were lost in the instinct to mate. The woman's breasts flattened out, except for the raised tips of her nipples that she twisted between her fingers. The man grabbed her legs, holding one in each hand. He spread her open to his hungry gaze and gritted his teeth. Positioning himself, he plunged into the woman with one deliberate, hard stroke. The woman moaned and arched her back, squeezing her breasts together.

Michelle noticed the tattoo on the man's stomach of fire rising from his groin area. He relentlessly buried himself into this luscious, sexy, dark-haired vixen. Her moaning was that of dark pleasure and was making Josh crazy. Not able to stand anymore, Josh picked up his jacket and took Michelle's hand.

"I couldn't take any more. Damn, that was hot."

Michelle laughed as Josh walked fast, holding his jacket in front of himself to cover his protrusion. Josh opened her door and climbed behind the wheel of the car. Uncomfortably, Josh started the car.

"Take me home, Josh?" she asked.

Josh pulled out of the parking space and slowly caught his breath. Michelle leaned down and stroked his cock through his pants.

"Did that really get to you?" she whispered, as she licked the lobe of his ear, blowing gently.

"Not as much as this is."

Tugging at his zipper Michelle licked his neck and slid her hand inside the pant flap. Josh swerved the car when she grabbed his stiffened cock and squeezed the head. Unfastening his pants, she opened the front and saw a spot of anticipation staining his underwear. She moistened her lips and pulled his hard cock out.

"Just get me home," Michelle said, dropping into his lap. She licked a glisten of his pre-come with her tongue. Josh swerved again trying to remain composed.

"You want me to pull over?" he asked.

"Mmmmm, nope, you stop, I stop!

Speeding up, Josh fought with his focus on driving while Michelle slowly sucked his length into her mouth. The light turned red and Josh waited at the stoplight while she closed her eyes, moaning. The vibrations rocked through Josh making him shiver.

"Aw, the car stopped. I'll have to stop." Michelle kissed the tip of his cock and licked up and down the length waiting for the car to move. She teased Josh into a manic craze.

He looked over, blinking frantically, and the town minister was in the car next to him waiting for the light. Tapping his thumb on the steering wheel, the light seemed to take forever and he struggled to keep his eyes open. He waved and whispered, "Minister Jones is in the car next to us."

Michelle deep-throated his cock into her mouth making Josh strain to not stretch his legs. He curled his toes in his shoes and blasted a quick breath out.

Jamming on the gas pedal he shot through the light and hurried to her house. When Josh turned the corner Michelle ran her fingers along his inseam and sucked hard making Josh groan. "Oh, crap. You don't play fair." Josh slammed on the brakes and shot his seed into her mouth. Like she was taking nourishment, she swirled her lips along his stiff shaft milking him.

Michelle sat up, wiping her bottom lip and said, "Oh, look, we're here. I'll talk to you later." She tapped his sensitive cock and it flinched weakly. Hopping out of the car, Michelle turned back and blew Josh a kiss.

Laughing, Michelle threw her purse on the table by the door. There was some mail on the table and she saw her name on one. She opened the letter from Canada and read it.

Attn: Ms. Walker

We are happy you are joining us and have set up your training schedule to start in two weeks on the 14th.

Enclosed is your schedule and registration for the Academy for your schooling.

From our interview last month, I know you are a welcome addition. Your college records alone warranted us hiring you. This is a great opportunity for all of us here at the Institute for Child Development. Everyone is excited you are joining our winning team.

Sincerely,
Robert Carlson, PHD
Administrative Director

Michelle sighed. She felt bad knowing she'd thought about not going. This helped confirm her feelings to go. Everything was falling into place for her.

The next day she packed her things and set out to get on with her plan and not let anyone get hurt. Later that afternoon she called Josh.

"Josh, meet me at the Roadside Inn, tonight about seven. I don't want to go to your parents and can't stay here." Michelle held back her pain. She just needed to cut things off before they got out of hand.

"Nooo, nothing's wrong. Just . . . please. Just meet me there, okay?"

7

Michelle knocked on the hotel door. Meeting some-one like this seemed seedy and cheap. Her whole reason for coming home was to regroup and start her life anew with no ties. She was going to have to let go of Josh. He was everything she ever wanted in a man but she needed to be free from everything and everyone to find herself.

Michelle pushed herself inside when Josh answered the door.

Josh was upset by all the secrecy and his passion for Michelle was bubbling to the surface. "What are you doing? Who cares if someone sees you?"

"This is a small town, Josh. I just feel cheap coming to a hotel to meet you. You have no idea about . . . never mind." Michelle fidgeted with her hands trying to muster the strength to tell him goodbye. She was torn between her dream to grow and become free or take this opportunity to be with a man she truly felt joy with.

"Look at me. You asked me to get this hotel and then don't tell me why. Come on, look at me." Josh held her chin and made her look into his eyes. She felt a calmness within him. "What is it? Michelle, tell me . . . please."

"Hold me, Josh. Just hold me." Michelle couldn't tell him like this. She wanted him so badly but knew she had to leave. His big arms held her tight and she felt his heart beating in his chest. The loud thumping vibrated through her. What was it about him that made her care so much? She wasn't supposed to fall for the next guy, she was supposed to meet Mr. Right up north when she got her shit together and became independent. Now all she could think about was her need for Josh.

She pulled back, putting her hands on his chest. She stared into his green eyes and unbuttoned his top button, twisting the hair poking out. "Josh? Will you do anything I ask?"

"Yes, of course."

"Make love to me. Just be with me tonight and don't ask any questions." She wrapped her arms around his waist and held him tightly. "Hold me. Just hold me." For that single moment, everything was clear to her. But she was going to leave and couldn't bear telling him face-to-face. This would be her farewell.

Josh turned and picked Michelle up, carrying her to the bed. His strong arms made her feel secure and safe. He laid her atop the bed and she shivered from the cold and fright in her heart. There were candles on the nightstands by the bed. The perfumed scent filled the room.

His hands were slow as they moved over her clothes. She closed her eyes and a tear trickled down her cheek. Josh kissed her tear, saying, "Don't cry. There's only us here. No pain, no eyes watching what we do, just you, me and some chocolate syrup." Michelle couldn't help but smile.

Opening her eyes, she watched Josh's face light up when he unfastened the buttons on her blouse. The more he undid the more he grinned. He took the collar and spread her top open and away from her breasts. Her nipples were tight and strained against the bra. Josh licked his lips and unfastened the clasp, releasing her breasts.

"Mmmmmm, that feels better," Michelle moaned. She loved how he stared at her. Like he was looking past her flesh and seeing her soul. She beamed while he stroked her chest and the curves of her breasts. He scooped them in his hands and kissed each nipple so gently, it was like wind brushing them. Michelle was on a cloud. He licked across her nipples and they sprang up to meet his tongue.

"You are so beautiful," Josh replied to the moan of her body to continue.

He crawled down the bed. Pulling up Michelle's skirt, he rested his head on her pelvis. Stroking the skin of her legs, he felt her breathe deep, holding her breath whenever he brushed her pubis. She grasped her breast in her hand, squeezing it while she ran the fingers on her other hand through Josh's hair. This was ecstasy.

Painstakingly, he rubbed the waistband of her panties making it roll down her thighs. Each time she wished he would just rip them off and ravage her. But he was taking his time. He blew across her stomach making her twitch. Her soft patch of hair waved from his breath. His finger slid under the loosened band and pulled them down her legs, tossing them to the floor.

Josh's massive hands caressed her thighs and calves making Michelle fade into a blissful state. His hands were calloused and her skin soft and smooth. She spread her legs apart letting them fall open to his eyes and hands.

"Mmmmmmmm, that feels nice," Michelle whispered, as he drew along her inner thigh. She giggled when he wrote words on her legs. "What did you just write?"

"DINNER IS SERVED! Hmmmm, this is fun," he said, smirking.

Josh grasped her knees in his hands and opened her legs wider and nuzzled against her pussy with the bristles of his unshaven face. Josh took his finger and toyed with her labia. His tongue would divide the folds of skin and he'd press his finger into the small opening, barely piercing her pussy. He noticed her clit protruding and firm. Not to be ungentlemanly, he stroked it with his thumb.

Josh flicked his slippery tongue against Michelle's already throbbing clit. Her body tensed and relaxed in uncontrollable urges.

"Oh, please, don't stop," she moaned.

She wanted him so bad but knew this might be the last time she had him like this. Emotions filled her heart. More alive than ever, her body was brittle and about to break from a building tension of lust, passion and even love.

Josh slid his thumb into her and felt the juicy walls becoming hot as they filled with blood from her arousal. His mouth savored her taste. Grapes from the vine have a succulent bounty to them and she was his wine to drink. He slid in another finger and spread her walls wide to venture into the dark, wet cavern of her sex.

Josh mumbled while eating her out. The vibrations of his voice and the licking drove her crazy. "A, B, C, D, E . . ."

Josh rested his other hand between her breasts. Her chest expanded when she held her breath as Josh touched the perfect spot. The crest of a wave peaked close as he washed her in a bath of desire.

"Right there, right . . . oh, God, right there . . . mmmm-mmm . . ." Her moan echoed through the room.

Josh watched Michelle breathe and gasp, desperate to let go of this enormous weight filling her. Totally on the brink of rapture, she lost control and grabbed Josh's head pulling it into her.

Josh spread his fingers apart and rubbed them back and forth inside the most sensitive area of her pussy. He pulled his thumb out and suckled hard on her clit. She spurted her juices from the tortured desires built up in her.

"Mmmmm, just like candy. Damn, you taste sweet," he mumbled while suckling on her.

She felt exhilarated, but wanted him inside of her. Michelle's need became unbearable and she pulled his hair making him move above her. She grabbed his arms and rolled Josh onto his back. A frantic rage of desire swept through her. She threw her blouse onto the floor. Her mouth salivated and she was hungry to feed it.

Tearing at his clothes, Michelle was possessed. She yanked Josh's pants off and pulled his underwear down freeing his hardened cock. She growled and ravaged his cock in her mouth sucking hard when pulling up away from his torso. She couldn't get enough.

Popping him from her mouth, she moved up his body, dragging her breasts along his wet cock. It slid between the mounds. "Mmmmm, you feel so fucking hard . . . I could just . . . mmmmmm." She pushed her breasts together; making a valley of flesh that caressed his slippery cock.

"Now this is a different feeling, I have nev . . ." Josh stopped as Michelle pushed him through her breasts and rested her teeth below the head of his penis. "Shut up!"

"What got into you?" Josh growled.

Straddling him, Michelle grabbed his cock, angling it at her hot, damp opening. "Right now, you will get into me." A demonic groan came from Michelle as she lowered her pussy onto Josh's thick, straining shaft.

Holding in a deep breath, Josh felt the muscles inside of her pussy spasm and adjust to his penetration. She was always so tight.

He felt Michelle's juices trickling down the base of his cock to his balls. She was on fire. He reached up to fondle her breasts while she ground her pelvis against his. The rocking side-to-side was a lovely motion that reminded Josh of the train where they met.

Michelle's hair fell forward when she looked down at him and started a steady, deep pace. She rode on him and Josh closed his eyes. "No, look at me. I want to see you," she ordered. Grabbing her nipples, Josh flicked the pert tips and pulled at her breasts making her speed her rhythm.

Michelle looked between them at the juncture of their bodies and saw him vanish into her over and over. Her pubis swelled when he was completely buried into her.

"Ohhh, myyyyy, I can fe . . . eeeeeel your . . ." Michelle stammered when he thrust his hips up, making it seem he pushed against her womb. She couldn't control him, she wanted him too badly and needed to feel his fury. Falling on top of Josh, Michelle kissed him tenderly. "I want you on top," she mused.

A smile widened across Josh's face. "Yes, dear." He grabbed her hips and rolled over on top of her. He dropped all his weight onto her like a limp sleeping St. Bernard.

"OH, MY, you're smothering me, you screwball!" Michelle tickled his sides making Josh snicker.

Josh picked himself up off her on his strong arms and stared into her eyes, and lowered down to her, kissing her cheek. He brushed her lips with his and as his cock found its way into her, his tongue slid gently into her mouth. Michelle loved how he felt and moaned in pleasure as he pulled up and stretched her pussy open, dragging his shaft against her clit. Like an artist painting a picture, each stroke had purpose.

"If you only knew how incredible you feel," Josh said quietly.

"I can imagine." Michelle tightened around him when he withdrew and relaxed as he slid back in. She ran her fingers up his back, feeling the muscles ripple.

The slow, deliberate pace was more making love than desperate sex. The heat between them was scorching as they perspired and Josh sped up his rhythm. He was grunting and she felt him become desperate and thrust harder.

"Oh, shit, ohhhh, I can't hold it anymore." Josh erupted and the hot seed splashed within her. Over and over, he came inside, thrusting deeply in and out. She touched his mouth, brushing her fingers over his lips. She closed her eyes and came as he sucked the tip of her finger. The slow wave submerged her in warmth. Her body felt totally refreshed in her enlightened state.

"You made a mess. You get to sleep in the wet spot this time." Michelle joked, feeling the hot ooze of their sex within her wet pussy.

Josh lay next to her and wrapped his big arms around her. They fell asleep with the dim neon lights flickering from outside.

Michelle woke up a few hours later and she lay motionless in the bed, encased in Josh's arms, warm, safe and happy.

Michelle's eyes fluttered as they filled with her tears. Her heart was breaking. She wanted to stay but couldn't. Her new life was beginning somewhere else and even though her feelings for Josh were strong, she couldn't stay. This was her burden to bear.

Gently climbing out of the bed, she put her clothes back on. Michelle looked at the bed and Josh was lying there so peacefully. He was grinding his teeth again making her cringe. A smile crossed her face and she leaned over, kissing his cheek. This was her goodbye. She reached into her jacket pocket and pulled out a note she had written earlier. Michelle kissed the letter and placed it on the pillow beside Josh.

Opening the door, she stopped. *Was she doing the right thing? Maybe he was her destiny*, she wondered to herself. All of her second thoughts would haunt her. Torn, she shut the door and walked into the blustery night wind.

8

Josh awoke, quickly looking around the room.

"Michelle? Michelle? Where are . . . ?"

He lay back on the bed, stretching his sore muscles. The note fell from Michelle's pillow. Scared about what it said, Josh sat up, staring at the lipstick mark on the white paper.

> *Josh,*
> *You came into my life when I was troubled and scared.*
> *You showed me that there is more to a man than I*
>   *knew before.*
> *You showed me compassion, gentleness and desire.*
> *You woke feelings within me long thought gone.*
> *I can't see a train without thinking of you.*
> *I can't explain why I must go,*
> *I know in time you will understand.*
> *I know you can't leave, yet I can't stay.*

Forgive me for leaving like this.
Forgive me, for I couldn't face you to say goodbye.
Forgive my stupid pride because I need to find myself.
Forgive my love for you that begs me to stay.
Our paths crossed at the wrong time,
Our feelings took us by surprise and our passion was unbound.
Our lives are different but we want the same things.
Our journey will make our paths cross again, I promise you that.

XXOOXX
Michelle

Dumbfounded, Josh scratched himself while he sat on the bed. He set the note down and felt empty. His whole life he had looked at Michelle from afar wondering who she really was. He had wondered what she was like and now he had gotten to experience her joy. Like a dream, she was part of his life. Now he was waking and she was gone again.

Josh picked up the phone and started dialing.

Josh wasn't going to let her go without a fight. He was sitting in the living room of Michelle's house talking to her mother. "I know we haven't formally met and you must not have a really good impression of me from what happened with your son. I have to tell you, I love your daughter. She's an incredible woman."

"You know what?" her mom interrupted. "Michelle's my daughter, and I love her, but she's confused. She was in a bad relationship with that asshole and hasn't really found her feet yet. There are things you don't know about her, Josh. She just wants to become the best woman she knows she is."

Josh listened, but didn't want to hear what she said.

"This is hard for her. She just wants a new beginning for herself."

"I just wish she'd stay. I really don't want to lose her," Josh pleaded.

"Maybe because she's afraid of jumping into another relationship with a stranger. She just met you; she went from a beast to a pussycat. Well, a beefcake," her mom giggled. "He treated her so bad that she had to run away." Josh could see the mother trying to hold in her tears for her daughter.

The front door opened and Michelle tossed her keys on the entry table and hung her coat up. Walking into the living room, she saw Josh. "What are you doing here? Didn't you read my note?"

Josh stood up and walked toward Michelle. He reached to hold her hand and she pulled away.

"I just, I just didn't want it to end like this," Josh said looking into her eyes. "I won't just LET you leave. I can't."

"I'm going to leave you two alone to talk," her mom said, leaving the room.

"Michelle, I love you."

"Josh, don't do this to me! It isn't fair."

"Life isn't fair!" Josh barked back.

"I just left a relationship where I was treated like shit and never respected. You know how hard it was to leave my life there to get me here right now? Don't expect me to just drop everything I have worked for and sacrificed just to be here with you! I don't even KNOW you."

"But, I love you. I have wanted to be with you for as long

as I remember. Doesn't that mean anything to you? Why can't you stay? Just tell me why! Just be HONEST with me!"

Starting to cry, Michelle looked up. "Don't do this, Josh. Don't play these fucking games with my heart. I don't know what I feel anymore. I want to stay here but I won't live my entire life living for a man's dream and not at least following mine. I'm not going to end up stuck in this Goddamned town with four kids and a mortgage. I can't end up like this. Why can't you understand?"

Josh was holding back his pent-up emotions. He was being ripped in two and had no control. "I don't know what to say. I want you here with me and I can't leave."

"Then let me go! Please don't ruin these weeks of happiness for me. I left to find myself and I found you. You know how hard this is for me? I'll come back. I just can't stay NOW."

Upset and hurt, Josh said, "Then go find yourself. I found the one thing I was missing in you. I found love. AND WE'RE JUST STARTING! I haven't cared this much for anyone in my life. You hit me like a tornado and all my memories and feelings were brought out. I can't help it. I don't want you to go because I don't want to lose the best thing that's happened to me."

"I can't win." Michelle put her face in her hands, crying tears of pain. "Why must things be so complicated? I just wanted to move on. I wasn't looking for any more burdens."

Red-faced and wailing, Michelle lashed out, "Why are you making me feel like this? If I ask you to leave you say, *No I can't, my life is here*, but it's okay for you to ask me to give up my dreams. You have no fucking idea what is going on inside of me! You're just like Keith."

"DON'T FUCKING COMPARE ME TO HIM! I am not HIM! Get that through your head." Josh stood up, his face enraged and glared at Michelle. "You do what you have to. I am here. I will still be here when you need me. Don't forget that." Josh walked out, slamming the door behind him.

Michelle dropped her face into her hands, ripped apart for having to do this.

Standing in the shower, Michelle cried. She was leaving and saddened by what had happened and the situation she had created. She calmed a little and let the water wash away her tears. The hot water rinsed over her, cleansing her body. Depressed and hurt, she put her hand on her chest, aching inside for Josh. The void he left in her was more than just the hole in her heart.

Her rational voice popped into her head, *I know, I know. He's a great guy. But you're following your dream. You need this. It's everything you've worked for.*

The devilish little voice didn't say much. *WHAT? Can't I be quiet for once?*

I just figured you'd have a smartass remark, her rational voice replied.

She doesn't want my opinion, the devilish voice barked back.

"Yes I do," Michelle answered, "Really, I want to know."

Her devilish voice shrugged her shoulders. *I think you should stay with him. He treats you good. He adores you. And honestly tell me the last time you had an orgasm that strong. Hell, you rolled your eyes so hard you could see the back of your head!*

"Well, that's true. Stop confusing me. I'm doing the right thing. Just let me . . ."

Looking around the bedroom, Michelle's mom asked, "Who are you talking to?"

"Nobody, just myself."

"You know your Uncle Frank talks to himself. They gave him some BIG blue pills for it. Now he sees little blue people running around his room playing hockey with flamingos." Her mom smiled, thinking how stupid that sounded.

Michelle's mom helped her pack, knowing her baby was in anguish. "Dear, are you okay with this?"

"Yes, I've worked a long time to get an opportunity like this."

"I'm not talking about the job. You know what I'm talking about."

"He can't leave and I can't stay. Who knows, maybe later . . . I don't want to regret what I am doing. Keith held me back and look where I ended up, miserable and feeling worthless."

"Josh isn't Keith, dear. He'd take care of you. It's none of my business, but I like him. He's not bad-looking either," her mom teased.

She held her mom, not wanting to go. For the first time in way too long, she could tell her mom knew what she was feeling. Michelle sighed and carried her bag to the door. Looking back into the room, she saw her teddy bear. She dropped her bag and went to the bed to pick it up.

Josh sat in his office mindlessly fiddling with his paperwork. He leaned back and stared out the window at the trees blowing in the breeze. It was a beautiful day. But he knew it wasn't perfect. Inside he knew she was gone and he already missed her desperately. The phone rang, jerking him back to reality.

"Yes, Dad, I know. I made my decision."

The plane terminal was busy and Michelle stood ready to check in. Dazed from confusion and doubt, she mindlessly went through the motions of checking in. Her thoughts were elsewhere. At any minute, she thought she'd see Josh bolt through the airport and take her away in his arms. She knew it was just a fantasy. Life wasn't that simple.

Taking her seat, Michelle just stared out the window. She was beginning her new life and couldn't look back at woulda, coulda, shoulda situations. She was moving on.

Oblivious to everything except the sight of her small town where she grew up, and a man she thought was "the one," Michelle didn't notice someone sitting next to her.

"This is my first trip to Canada, what about you?" she heard from the man sitting next to her.

"Me, too," Michelle answered, staring outside. Scared to fly, she closed her eyes waiting for the plane to liftoff. The rumbling of the jets and the bump of the turbulence shook through the plane. Tears trickled down her cheeks as the plane steadied. She knew it was over. The turbulence and her relationship with Josh had come to an end. Looking forward, she wiped her tears, laughing at how silly she felt.

The man next to her handed her a handkerchief.

"I'm sorry," Michelle started, "I just left home and the one man who made me truly happy."

"Maybe you left home but the man is right here." Josh spoke, knowing his words were true.

Michele looked out the window, then back at Josh, then back out the window in a befuddled state. "How did . . . I thought . . . What are you doing here?"

"It became a simple choice between staying without you, or going with you," Josh said, grabbing her hand. "If you don't mind supporting an out of work promotional manager, I'll make sure to do my best. At least you won't have to pay for a maid. We can work out a payment schedule. I'm not a great cook, don't mind doing housework except toilets and will try not to mix our underwear up in the drawers."

Kissing her cheek he whispered, "I can't promise I won't try your underwear on though. However, those thongs are a bitch. They make my balls look like coconuts hanging from a tree."

As the plane pushed through the clouds, they held hands tightly. Michelle leaned over to Josh, looked in his eyes and asked, "You ever heard of the Mile-High Club?"

Fantasy Bar

TRISTA ANN
MICHAELS

This story is dedicated to four wonderful ladies. First, Lydia, who came up with the name Fantasy Bar, the two words that started a firestorm of inspiration. To Ester, our lady bartender and inspiration behind the interesting idea of ordering your sexual fantasy by ordering a drink. To Sarah, for her input on plot and for always reminding me to rate my chapters, so she has a heads-up to the content, even though most of the time I forget. And Sharon, my partner in crime, for letting me "borrow" some of her outrageous sayings and continually keeping me in stitches. You guys are the best and I love each and every one of you.

1

Oh, my God, Kira! What happened?"

Kira Vordak stumbled into the room and slumped onto the edge of Mirage's velvet settee. Her back burned and needles of pain shot through her limbs. Her shirt clung to her bloody flesh, but she was pretty sure the wounds had stopped bleeding. With trembling hands, she removed her overcoat and swallowed back a sob.

"Oh, shit, Kira." Mirage tugged at the blouse and hissed as the material broke away from the dried blood. The shirt slid down her arms and fell to the Oriental rug. "You stay right here. I'm going for the doctor."

"No!"

"No? Forget it, girl. Your back is a mess and needs to be stitched. It's way beyond my capabilities. But the second the doctor leaves the room, I want to know who did this to you."

The door slammed and Kira laid her head in her hands, the fatigue and pain finally catching up with her. The rush of adrenaline she'd been relying on had vanished, leaving her weak and trembling. For the first time in hours, she felt safe. She knew no one could find her here. No one knew of her connection to Mirage and the Fantasy Bar on the small planet of Klindor.

She'd made sure to remain well hidden in the back of the transport from Meenus Prime, hoping and praying no one recognized her. She still couldn't believe her stupidity. How in the hell had she gotten into this mess and more importantly, how the hell was she going to get out of it?

The door opened and she sat up straight then winced. Lightheadedness overtook her and she leaned precariously to the side, no longer able to keep herself upright. Mirage caught her, offering her shoulder for support.

"Help me get her to the bed," the doctor ordered after a brief inspection. "It looks like she's lost a lot of blood and we need to get these cuts closed."

Kira wearily watched the doctor as he opened his bag. His eyes were shadowed, but his hair was thick and black, just brushing over wide shoulders corded with muscles that flexed as he moved. His face was masculine and tinged with a hint of Mediterranean. Certainly not someone she would consider a doctor. She always pictured them with glasses and thin builds.

He moved to touch her and she closed her eyes, bracing herself. His warm fingers brushed across her shoulder, reassuring her. "I'll be as gentle as I can."

She nodded and waited, her shoulders tense with nerves.

"Oh, God, there's so many," Mirage sighed. "Kira, what did this?"

She was so tired, so weak, she couldn't open her mouth to speak. Instead, she remained silent while the doctor cleaned and sealed her wounds.

"Looks like a whip," the doctor replied quietly. "See the jagged edges?"

"Oh, God," Mirage sniffed and placed her hand over Kira's when she flinched at the doctor's gentle probing.

"She'll be sore for a few days but she should be fine."

"Thank you, Jaimee," Mirage said as she walked the doctor to the door.

"You're welcome. Call me if you need me."

Kira watched as the handsome doctor touched her friend's cheek with such tenderness it made her heart ache. To have someone touch her like that was her deepest wish, but she doubted it would ever come true. Especially now.

"How are you feeling?" Mirage sat on the edge of the bed and gently ran her fingers along the red and swollen tears.

"I've been better." Kira tried to smile but it quickly faded. Her eyes drooped heavily and her words were sluggish. "I feel strange."

"Jaimee gave you something to take care of the pain and to help you sleep. What happened?"

"I was leaving the university. I had a late class in intergalactic business trades and I stayed to grade papers. When I was heading home someone caught me from behind. He bound my hands and feet, gagged my mouth. I was so out of it from the hit to my head, I couldn't put up a fight. I never even saw his face, Mirage, never knew who he was until . . ."

"Until?"

Kira swallowed her sob and squeezed her eyes closed, trying to block out the images, the pain. "Until I killed him."

Jerrod Scollin stalked back into the brightly lit bedroom after stepping outside for some fresh air and a few much needed moments to collect himself. The stench of dried blood and death permeated the small space. He'd been an investigator for the high regent of Meenus Prime for almost ten years and he'd never become accustomed to that smell. Even now, it rolled his stomach.

Trying to turn his mind to other things, his trained eye took in the scene. Clothes and linens lay scattered about in disarray. Blood splattered the bedsheets and headboard. The lifeless body of his best friend Micas Lordakin lay across the foot of the bed.

He'd been informed of his death prior to his arrival, but that didn't prepare him for actually seeing it for himself. He'd been shot in the chest four times at point-blank range. His eyes still stared at the ceiling, focusing on nothing. Wasn't it just last weekend they had been planning their yearly trip to Vingosa?

Think about your job, Jerrod, he scolded himself and pushed his grief aside.

There had been no forced entry, and as far as Jerrod knew, Micas didn't have any enemies. Considering he was shot in the bedroom, he would bet Micas knew his killer.

"Find anything, Simas?"

Simas turned from his study of the blood-soaked bed linens. A lock of blond hair fell across his forehead and he brushed it back in aggravation. "It's not his blood. It's female."

Jerrod frowned. "Female?"

"Yes."

What the hell were you doing, Micas? "Can you determine what happened?"

"Not from what little there is here. I've run a scan. Whoever it belongs to isn't in the system."

"That just means she's not a criminal." Jerrod wandered around the room, looking for something, anything that would answer the questions running through his mind. What had gone on here? Had Micas been involved in something illegal? Had he brought home a prostitute that later turned on him? Had she been injured and was that why her blood was all over the room?

With a tired sigh, he dragged his hand down his face. So many fucking questions!

"Sir?"

Jerrod spun and looked at the young investigator standing behind him. Daniel. He stood a good three inches shorter than Jerrod and had to crane his neck slightly to look at him. He was new to the force, just out of the academy, but Jerrod heard he had excellent potential as a profiler. "Did you find out anything?"

"Yes, sir. The doorman said he saw the same woman Micas arrived with two days ago leave last night. She seemed upset so he followed her to the transport dock. She boarded a ship bound for Klindor."

"Klindor?" Simas mused from his position kneeling by the bed. "Interesting destination."

Jerrod nodded. "Especially for a woman alone. She was alone?"

"Yes, sir. As far as the doorman knows."

"Now why do you suppose the doorman would follow her?" Simas stood and placed his hands on his hips.

"The guy said she was hot. He wanted to get her alone and sample her wares, if you know what I mean."

"Her wares?" Jerrod asked.

"Yes, sir. He said Micas indicated the woman was a prostitute when he arrived with her the other night. He brought her in through the back entrance. She was slung over his shoulder and bound. Micas told him it was 'all part of the S&M package.'"

Simas swore softly and Jerrod glanced at him. Immediately, a veil dropped over Simas' expression. For a second, Jerrod wondered what the outburst was about, but he returned to the investigation. "Thank you, Daniel," Jerrod mumbled then turned to sit on the only clean spot at the foot of the mattress.

"Micas was into S&M?" Simas whispered. "Did you know about this?"

Jerrod shook his head, his mind reeling from the possibilities. He'd known Micas since they were kids. They'd grown up together, playing in the same abandoned mines and flying the same spaceports. His friend had a wild side and sometimes even a cruel streak, but Jerrod had had no idea it ran to this extreme. S&M was one thing—and sometimes quite fun—but it was obvious from the amount of the woman's blood on the bed it had gone beyond fun and turned quite deadly.

"What are you thinking?" Simas asked.

"Daniel." Jerrod raised a hand and waved the young man over. "I need a physical description of the woman. Did you get one?"

Daniel related what the doorman had told him while Jerrod quickly recorded it in his mini-computer. "Blond, green eyes. About five feet, seven inches tall, maybe one hundred and twenty pounds. He also said she had nice legs."

"Nice legs?" Simas smirked. "That'll narrow it down."

Jerrod flipped his computer closed in aggravation. "That will be all, thank you."

"Yes, sir."

Jerrod headed to the main living area, Simas following close on his heels. "You didn't answer my question."

Jerrod frowned. "What question?"

"I asked what you were thinking."

"I'm thinking of going to Klindor to try and find the woman."

Simas pointed to the computer. "Based on that description?"

"It's all we have, Simas. You got any better ideas?"

"Not at the moment."

"Besides, how many women arrive alone on Klindor? She shouldn't be too difficult to track down."

"Why don't you let me go?"

"Why?" Jerrod asked. Simas never wanted to go out in the field. He preferred to work the scene, handle the evidence. What had brought about the sudden change?

Simas shrugged, not meeting his stare. "I thought since you'd just returned, you might want to stay here."

"No. I'll go. I have a higher clearance than you. I can get into places you can't by flashing my badge as an employee of the Planetary Senate."

"True, but Klindor isn't officially a member of the Senate."

Jerrod's frown stopped Simas' argument. "I said I'd handle it, Simas. Klindor may not officially be on the voting roster, but they try to stay on the good side of the regent. They won't be a problem. Besides, I need you here. I want you to search this apartment from top to bottom. Find me something." With a pointed look that brooked no argument, Jerrod pulled his coat collar around his ears to ward off the winter chill in preparation of stepping onto the private landing pad just outside Micas' apartment.

"Even if we don't like what we come across? Micas was your best friend, my mentor and possibly the next regent elect. What if this was self-defense, Jerrod? Do you have any idea what kind of a scandal that will raise? How do you explain the next leader of the Senate being shot because he was trying to kill a prostitute?"

"That's why we need to find the woman."

2

⁘

"On your knees, whore," the man hissed out, the words followed immediately by the sting of the whip slashed across her back.

She bit her lip, the metallic taste of blood filling her mouth. Again the whip landed across her flesh and she cried out, bending her body to escape the harsh leather.

She lay facedown in the same position she'd been in for what seemed like days, her hands shackled to the bedposts. Black material covered her eyes, preventing her from seeing her attacker, but she could smell him. His nasty, evil scent invaded her nostrils, making her want to vomit.

"On your knees!"

She couldn't get on her knees. Not the way she was lying and he knew it. He only wanted to yell at her, scream demands he knew she couldn't possibly meet just so he would have a reason to beat her again. She couldn't take much more. Blood trickled *down her back and onto the sheets. She had to find a way out of here.*

"Kira?"

She awoke with a start and couldn't seem to pull enough air into her lungs. Grasping her throat, she tried to relax, tried to take a few deep breaths to slow her frantic heartbeat.

Sitting up, her nervous gaze darted around the suite, checking dark corners. The maroon walls reflected the soft light coming from the fireplace and created flickering shadows. A human form appeared amidst the dancing designs and she gasped as fear trickled down her spine. With growing trepidation, she jerked her head toward the door.

"It's just me." Mirage stepped farther into the room. Her blue silk dress clung to her petite curves and gave her gray eyes a turquoise hue. "You okay?"

"Yeah." Kira sighed and placed a trembling hand against her chest. Relief surged through her and she sagged against the pillows. "Just nightmares."

Mirage sat on the mattress, her tiny hand resting on Kira's thigh. "They'll pass soon. It was self-defense, honey. You didn't have a choice."

"I know. That's what I keep telling myself. But the nightmares continue."

"It'll get better, I promise. After all, no one knows that nightmares fade better than I do. Have you let the university know you're okay? I'm sure, since you didn't return to your classes, they're wondering where you are."

"It doesn't do for the professor to miss class, does it? No. I haven't contacted them. I'm not even sure what to say. I'm sorry I brought this here."

Mirage shook her head with a frown. "Don't be. We're friends. No matter what. You'll stay here as long as you need to."

"I can't just sit up here, though. I could tend bar."

Mirage bit her lower lip in a move Kira recognized as uncertainty. "Are you sure that's a good idea?"

"No. But I am half-owner, so it wouldn't be unreasonable that I would be here. It should be safe enough. It's been a long time since I've tended bar. I hope I remember how."

"I know. Not since the last time you were here, which was what? About four years ago?"

"Yeah." Had it really been that long?

Mirage smiled. "I remember where we first came up with the idea for this place."

Kira chuckled at the memory. The whole thing had started out as a joke, a silly idea from four drunk women who were bored out of their minds. But with Mirage's imagination and Kira's business savvy, it soon took off and developed a life of its own.

Fantasy Bar was now the most popular and profitable business on Klindor.

It was the only bar where you could order a drink and have it become your sexual fantasy.

Mirage patted Kira's thigh. "Let me take a look at your back."

Kira sat forward, allowing her friend to exam the quickly healing slashes.

"Jaimee said they would remain red and sore for a while longer, but you can move around and do whatever you feel comfortable doing. Have you kept up with your birth control injections?"

With a start, Kira realized that no, she hadn't kept up with them, but it might not be a bad idea. Fantasy would be a great place to exorcise some demons. She shook her head. "It's been at least a year. I wasn't seeing anyone so I just didn't see a point."

"I'll have Jaimee give you one. The injection he uses takes effect immediately." Kira tensed as Mirage gently ran her fingers over the welts, checking for any sign of infection. "They look as though they're healing nicely. Still a little red though, so be careful," Mirage said.

Mirage stood and walked over to the lounge chair by the fireplace and picked up the outfit that was lying across the arm. "I laid out some clothes for you. I thought the green would go exceptionally well with your eyes."

"Thanks," Kira said with a slight smile. After Mirage studied her for what seemed like forever, Kira frowned. "What?"

"Should we color your hair?"

Kira ran her hand down her long blond locks. She hated the idea of changing the color, but it might not be a bad idea, just in case. She'd killed a prominent man, well known in high society and government circles. She'd never kept track of the news, but she'd seen enough to know who the man was.

She still didn't know if she should turn herself in or not. Would they believe her story or would they hang her from the tallest tree after the joke of a trial? Changing her looks might be smart, at least until she decided what to do. "What do you think of red?"

Mirage titled her head to the side, her lips pursed in concentration. "Just a little red, I think. Not too much."

"Well," she sighed and threw the purple satin sheets aside. "Let's get this over with."

Jerrod strolled into Fantasy Bar, his eyes scanning the dark interior. He'd heard of this place as far away as the Neptune Moon. If you ordered a Blowjob, you not only received the drink but an actual blowjob. Same with Slow Screw, which he could see going on in the far corner.

A male patron had the barmaid bent over, her hands resting against the deep red wall, her hips moving in rhythm with his as he pumped his cock into her pussy. Another couple off to the left was engaged in the same fantasy, only positioned differently. With this couple, the woman's back was against the wall and her legs wrapped around the man's waist.

Jerrod's cock twitched at the erotic displays around him. He'd come in here for a drink and to check the place out, not to participate in the hedonistic activities. He'd had enough of one-night stands. He'd wanted something more for quite a while now. Something deeper than just sex. He seriously doubted he'd find it in a place like this, though.

As he made his way farther into the room, he took in the French influence throughout the two-story bar. Whoever decorated had been to Earth. His mother had loved the Napoleonic era and had redone her whole house with pieces from that time period. He recognized much of the furniture as replicas. A smart move. It would be foolhardy to decorate a bar such as this with actual antiques.

Along the wall to the right was the long mahogany bar. It was packed save for a few open stools here and there. At the table to his right, two blowjobs were taking place. It was quite a show, a dark-haired woman taking every inch of a man into her mouth and down her throat. Beside them, two men licked at the large cock of another man. He just shook his head and moved on.

Stepping through the mass of bodies laughing and undulating against one another, he moved toward the bar and sat down at one of the stools. He was tired and this would be his last stop for the night. So far, he hadn't had much luck. A woman had arrived here alone, but where she'd gone once she exited the transport was a mystery.

"Can I help you?"

Raising his gaze, he found himself staring into the most beautiful pair of green eyes he'd ever seen. They were fathomless, turned up slightly at the corners, holding just a hint of amusement. Could she help him? Is that what she'd asked? He wasn't sure he'd heard her right over the pounding of his heart roaring through his ears.

She was a beauty, and he couldn't stop staring at her, which probably accounted for the adorable grin now gracing her china-doll face. What the hell was she doing in a place like this?

She raised an eyebrow. "Need time to think about it?"

He shook his head, trying to clear the fog that had settled in his brain. He smiled, slowly letting his gaze memorize every inch of her oval face and full lips. "No. I think I know exactly what I want."

"And that would be?" she asked with a soft chuckle.

Something in the sound tugged at a part of his chest that had been long buried, waiting for the right girl to come along and uncover it. For a second, it startled him. How could a laugh do that? A smile? "Your name, for starters."

Her head tilted to the side as she laid her hand against her hip. "Sorry, not on the menu."

"Not even a hint?"

She slowly shook her head, her lips twitching ever so slightly. He could stare into those eyes all day, and all night for that matter. They were deep green, like the summer grass of Earth, framed with long, elegant lashes.

"How about I just call you Gorgeous then?"

"Flattery will get you—"

"Everywhere?" he asked, raising an eyebrow.

She chuckled. "Nowhere."

He clucked his tongue. "My loss."

"What can I get you to drink, charmer?"

"I'll take a Vegan Ale."

She nodded. "Vegan Ale it is."

Turning, she sashayed to the other end of the bar. The soft sway of her hips caught his attention, and he couldn't seem to look away. The green material clung to her, outlining her perfect curves. Not chubby, but not too skinny either. She had hills and valleys his hands itched to explore. But would one night with this gorgeous woman be enough? Something deep inside told him no, he didn't think it would be.

He hadn't had that kind of reaction to a woman in a while. Matter of fact, he wasn't sure when he'd ever had that kind of reaction. He wanted her body, yes, but for some reason he wanted her name more. He wanted to talk to her, find out why she was here, for she certainly didn't fit.

Glancing around the bar, he tried to block out the erotic images all around him. Coming into this place had been one hell of a bad idea. But then he locked gazes with his gorgeous redhead again and realized maybe it wasn't a bad idea at all. Maybe it was the first thing he'd done right in years.

Kira drew in a steadying breath and tried to concentrate on pouring the Vegan Ale. The man was sexy as hell. He certainly didn't look like the type that would need to come to a place like this for sex. He could probably get any woman he wanted. If circumstances were different, he could certainly get her.

From the second she'd seen him cross the floor, she'd known in her gut there was something different about him. Something she couldn't put her finger on. Normally the atmosphere of the bar didn't affect her. She could ignore it or participate if she chose, but ever since this man had smiled at her, participating was all she could seem to think about—or at least participating with him only. No one else she'd seen tonight—or the past several years for that matter—interested her.

Glancing to her left, she caught him watching her. His intelligent, sapphire gaze held hers hostage. Her whole body tingled from the current skimming through her, making her heart race. What was it about him that did this to her? Turned her normal self-control into nothing but a jumbled mass of nerves?

He looked to be about thirty-six, just three years older than her. He had short black hair with just a hint of wave to the thick locks. A day's worth of stubble completed his masculine face. She loved a man with stubble, especially when he would scrape the rough hairs against her flesh.

Long fingers rubbed his chin and she admired them, wondering what they would feel like against her skin. He had strong hands. Masculine hands, and for a second she tried to imagine if they would be gentle or firm. From out of nowhere fear and uncertainty traveled up her spine before she trampled it down. She didn't want what had happened to her to make her skittish of men. They weren't all that way.

She doubted he would be cruel. He held a look of gentleness in his eyes, a playful look. As she stared like a fool, thinking about his lips, ale spilled over the side of the glass and over her fingers. "Damn," she mumbled, shaking the liquid from her hand and searching the bar for a dry towel.

Dax, their oldest bartender, handed her his. "First rule of bartending here at Fantasy," he whispered in her ear. "When a customer affects you that badly, you fuck him."

"Real cute, Dax."

She tossed the towel at his chest and he caught it with a

grin. Taking a deep breath, she grabbed the glass and turned back to her gorgeous customer. She'd have to face him sooner or later. Might as well be now.

His eyes twinkled with laughter as she walked toward him. Inwardly, she cringed, the heat of a blush spreading up her cheeks. Why did he have to see that?

"Here you go," she said with as steady a voice as she could muster.

"Thank you." He smiled and a dimple formed in his cheek.

Ah God. A man with a dimple. Those adorable indentions were her weakness.

"You're welcome. Anything else?" Like an Oral Sex, perhaps? A Screaming Orgasm? What was she thinking? She was here to bartend, not participate in the hedonistic activities.

"I could try again for your name. On the menu yet?"

Her name? She shouldn't give him the name she normally went by and racked her brain for an alternative. "Tired of 'Gorgeous' already?" she teased.

He grinned behind his glass, his eyes crinkling in mischief and smoldering desire. "I don't think I would ever get tired of gorgeous."

She bit at her lip. There was an underlying meaning to that but she ignored it. "I don't recall seeing you here before," she said. For all she knew he could be a regular. After all, it had been four years since she'd been here.

He swallowed a sip of his ale. "I haven't. It's my first time."

"Ah," she sighed with a nod. "A Fantasy virgin."

He smirked and glanced around the room. "A virgin wouldn't remain a virgin for long in this place."

"Yeah, if you're not used to it the atmosphere can be a bit . . ." She waved her hand, mentally searching for the right word. "Arousing."

"All this doesn't affect you?" he asked, his eyes widening in slight surprise.

She shrugged. "Not anymore."

"So if this doesn't affect you, what does?"

Her heart jumped at the dimple in his cheek and the way his eyes seemed to devour her. She must be out of her mind. The last thing she needed to do was stand here and flirt with someone she didn't know. She was here to hide, not get into something she wouldn't be able to finish. But for some reason she couldn't make herself walk away from him. "Fishing for information?"

"Fishing is what I do best. Have I caught a bite or am I just dangling in the water?"

Taking a deep breath, she glanced over his shoulder to the far corner. There were two new couples engaging in a sexual fantasy there now, the four of them huddled together, pleasing each other in ways even Kira hadn't seen in a while.

What would it hurt to have a little fun? Maybe if she stayed with her gorgeous customer a while longer, she might figure out what it was about him that made her so frazzled.

Meeting his gaze dead on, she grinned. "It takes a lot to affect me. I'm very hard to please."

God, I am such a liar. The man's sapphire gaze affected her. The way he tilted his head and studied her, amusement dancing in his eyes, affected her. The way he licked his lips just then affected her.

"Hard to please, huh? Sounds like a challenge to me." His lips spread into a devilish grin that made her heart lodge in her throat. "And I love a challenge."

She just smiled. The sultry look in his gaze made moisture gather between her legs. It would be so easy to lose herself to this man. Even in here. She didn't care. She'd done the whole public sex thing before. Just the thought of him pleasing her made her nipples tingle, and she could tell by the look in his eyes that he knew exactly what she was thinking.

A man behind her yelled, trying to get her attention. Damn. She glanced over her shoulder to the waving customer. "Excuse me, I need to get back to work."

"I'll be right here. Just in case you want me to take you up on that challenge."

"You wish," she replied devilishly.

Jerrod sipped on his drink, his gaze studying her as she moved up and down the bar. *Hell yeah, I wish.* Occasionally, she looked in his direction and he winked. She immediately turned away, her cheeks deepening to an adorable shade of red. It seemed odd that a woman who worked in the midst of all this sex would blush, but he loved it.

With an aggravated sigh, he realized he'd forgotten to ask her about the female fugitive he was searching for. Oh, well. He had all night and at the moment he was perfectly content to just sit there and watch her.

Suddenly, he wasn't so tired and he began to plot out an idea to get her interested in more than just bartending. Maybe he should do a body search. He grinned at the idea.

It was getting late—too late to roam the streets questioning people. Tomorrow he would continue his search. Tonight, he'd pursue the nameless minx.

3

Kira didn't know how much more of the erotic scenes she could tolerate. Everywhere she looked couples were having sex. She'd forgotten just how arousing working here could be.

Her mystery man wasn't helping matters either. He kept staring at her like he knew exactly what she was thinking. And wanting. Turning back toward the crowded floor, she put her back against the edge of the bar and surveyed the dark room. Slow, sexy music played in the background while couples danced and swayed against one another.

Two tables away, one of the male customers grabbed Lyanne, their youngest and most popular barmaid, and pulled her down on his lap. She leaned her head back and giggled while the man buried his face in her neck.

"Seron," Lyanne moaned and wiggled on his lap. "I've missed you. Where have you been?"

"All that matters, my sweet, is that I'm here now and I want you."

Kira smiled slightly at the two of them. From what she'd heard, Seron was a regular here and always went for Lyanne.

With a growl, Seron stood and laid Lyanne back across the table, lifting her short, pleated skirt around her waist. Lyanne liked to dress like a young girl in a private-school uniform and apparently Seron liked it as well. He freed his engorged shaft, letting his pants drop around his knees before plunging deep between her legs. Her scream of pleasure could be heard above the usual chatter of the bar patrons and several of the customers stopped what they were doing to watch. Including her dream guy.

If the couple having sex did so in the open, it was nothing unusual for other customers to join in and most did in one way or another. Kira stared as her mystery man stood and made his way over to the couple. His brown pants clung to his firm ass and accentuated his trim waist. His white shirt opened partially, giving just a hint of the hard chest beneath.

Never taking his eyes off Kira's, Jerrod popped the buttons of Lyanne's shirt and slid his large palm over her breast. With a groan, she thrust it further into the air.

Kira frowned, unsure how she felt about him putting his hands on another woman. It didn't feel right to her, and she wanted to tell him to stop, but at the same time, she couldn't look away.

His sapphire eyes met hers, silently challenging her as he leaned down to circle Lyanne's nipple with his tongue. Kira's breathing hitched, her nipples beading into hard pebbles. He sucked Lyanne's breast further into his mouth, his daring gaze never leaving Kira's.

He was doing it on purpose, trying to arouse her, daring her to join in the play. She could tell by the way he watched her, the way he held her stare and wouldn't let go. Kira's gut told her he wanted her, but did she dare go to him?

Seron lifted Lyanne's legs over his shoulders, and she moaned her pleasure, her hips moving in time with Seron's. Kira gasped, mesmerized, as her dream man unzipped his slacks and removed his magnificent shaft.

Oh, jeez.

Her gaze remained glued to his fingers as they worked up and down his thick length. She swallowed hard, fighting the urge to take it into her mouth, to swallow every last drop of cum he spewed forth. Her eyes moved back to his. They smoldered, boring into hers with intensity that stole her breath. There was that challenge again, that dare she was finding harder and harder to resist.

"Give it to me," Lyanne sighed, her eyes locked on his cock. "Put it in my mouth." Seron grunted his approval, his eyes glazing over in pure animal lust.

No!

Possessiveness raced through her, sending a jolt of shock through her veins. For some reason, Kira didn't want Lyanne touching him. Any part of him. Pushing away from the bar, she walked toward him, choosing to act on the feeling instead of trying to analyze it. Grabbing his arm, she turned him away from Lyanne and dropped to her knees.

Jerrod inwardly smiled in triumph as he watched her walk toward him and turn him from the other couple. Her eyes glowed with the same possessive passion and need that gripped him and his heart beat a hard, excited rhythm. He'd hoped his silent challenge would work—that she felt the same tug in her chest that he did. There was something between them, something he couldn't explain but wanted desperately to explore.

Deep down, he knew now wasn't really the time for this. He was here on business, investigating, but all thoughts of his job left his mind as her tiny hands gripped his shaft. Damn, he'd never been so hard in his life. He knew he'd explode the second her succulent lips enveloped him, and he ground his teeth to keep from losing control.

"I was hoping you would join me," he rasped.

She glanced up at him, her small hand circling, teasing the head of his cock until he thought he would scream.

"So all that was just for show? To get me interested?" Slowly, her hand moved up and down, her fingers squeezing just under the purple head.

He sighed, fighting the pleasure that skimmed through him with every movement of her hand. "Did it work? Are you interested, Gorgeous?"

In answer, she closed her lips around his cock, and Jerrod sucked in a breath. Her mouth was hot and wet and felt so damn good. In one swift move, she took him deep in her throat. He groaned, his hips jerking forward.

Through heavy-lidded eyes, he watched her take his shaft deep in her mouth, her cheeks sunken in from the sucking motion. He touched the side of her face, brushing the soft skin of her cheeks with the back of his fingers. Her surprised gaze met his and for a fleeting second he wondered why such a move would shock her. Had she never experienced tenderness before?

He supposed in a place like this, she probably wouldn't and that bothered him, more than he wanted to admit. Backing away from her, he pulled his cock from her mouth and reached down to grab her shoulders, tugging her to her feet.

She watched him questioningly as he grabbed a chair and sat down. With a hard jerk, he ripped her pants down in one swift motion. She gasped and for a second, he thought she might shy away. Fear clouded her eyes, and he reached up to touch the side of her face. "I won't hurt you."

A small smile lit up her face. "I know. Dax wouldn't let you."

She nodded her head toward the bar. The massively built Dax kept a close eye on the small group, making sure nothing got out of hand. She kicked her slacks aside and straddled his lap, her wet pussy rubbing along his raging hard-on.

"Damn, I want you," he growled against her lips. "What is it about you, Gorgeous? Did you put something in my drink?" He grinned slightly. "Put a spell on me, perhaps?"

"Maybe you did that to me. This place doesn't affect me, remember?"

His palms gripped her hips, moving her in a slow rhythm along his shaft. "Haven't you figured out yet, this place has nothing to do with it."

He tried to kiss her, but she jerked away at the last second and wagged a finger before his nose. His brow creased in a frown as he stared at her. "No kissing. That's not what this is about."

"What's it about then, Gorgeous?"

"Sex. Pure and simple."

He grinned. "Woman, you are so in denial."

Kira lifted her hips and slid down his length, effectively silencing any other argument he might have. She knew she was in denial, but she couldn't let it get that personal. She just couldn't. Not now.

She groaned as his thick cock stretched and filled her. Slowly, she began to move back and forth, each rock of her hips taking him deeper. This would be quick. She'd been so turned on when he entered her, she knew she wouldn't be able to last for long.

His palms cupped her breasts through her top and a ragged sigh escaped her lips. It had been so long since a man had touched her like this. It almost made her forget the last week of torture.

There had been no sex. The man hadn't raped her, just hurt her. It had seemed the louder she screamed and the more blood there was, the more excited he'd become. But he'd never fucked her, just masturbated and shot his cum all over her, while in the background someone laughed.

Someone laughed? Who had laughed? Had there been someone else there? The memory was just beyond her consciousness, just out of her reach, and she couldn't grab it.

Closing her eyes, she tried to block the memories and concentrate on what was happening now. She would figure everything out later. The feel of this well-endowed man deep inside her, his lips warm and wet against the flesh of her neck, made her forget it all. She whimpered and arched her back, her fingers gripping his shoulders through his shirt.

She lifted herself, dragging his cock almost completely out of her, then slowly slid back down his length, teasing them both. He growled, his fingers digging into the flesh of her hip. Again, she teased him, and he threw his head back, his hips lifting off the seat. "Damn it, Gorgeous!"

His palm slapped the cheek of her ass, not hard, but enough to heighten her already out of control passion. It had been years since she'd done this—let herself go in the middle of the crowded Fantasy Bar. The people watching only turned her on, made her hotter, bolder.

Oh, God.

She was so close. She could feel the walls of her pussy squeeze him, dragging him deeper. His grunts and groans mingled with hers as her whole body tensed then exploded into a wave of pleasure so strong she screamed.

She had no idea how much time passed before she felt him yell and jerk, his own body lost in the bliss of release. Laying her head against his shoulder, she sighed, her muscles relaxing as she slowly came down from the high. A high she never dreamed she could reach. Was it him or was it because she'd been without for too long?

It has to be the abstinence. I refuse to let it be anything else.

His arms tightened, held her closer and for a moment she allowed herself to curl into him. She felt safe in his arms—protected—and after the last few days she wanted to hold onto that feeling. If only for a little while.

Out of breath, he buried his face in her neck and mumbled, "There's no way in hell I'm leaving this bar without your name."

Kira stiffened. Oh, God. The name again. "I don't know yours either," she whispered, stalling for time.

She sat straight and met his gaze. His sapphire eyes were almost black with fading passion. "It's Jerrod," he said with a smile, making his dimple deepen.

His hand was buried in her hair, sifting through its thickness. She closed her eyes, the gentle motions of his hand relaxing her. He placed a soft kiss on the sensitive spot behind her ear. "Name, Gorgeous. I'll figure it out one way or another. You might as well tell me."

"I see Kira hasn't lost her touch," Dax snickered from behind her, and she tensed, turning to glare at him. For the first time since she'd known him she felt like slapping the smirk from his face.

Jerrod chuckled, a smile of satisfaction spreading his lips. "Thanks, Dax."

So much for coming up with an alias.

4

Jerrod rolled over and tried to block out the high-pitched beep of his communicator. *It's too damn early for this.* The incessant beeping continued, and he buried his head deeper under the covers. For several minutes he remained there, trying to ignore it.

Sunshine streamed in through the crack in the blinds, sending streaks of yellow across the hardwood floor. Vaguely, he wondered what time it was and peeked at the clock on the bedside table. Damn. Didn't he just get into bed?

The beeping continued, and he ground his teeth. Rolling to his back, he threw his arm over his eyes and sighed. Whoever was calling wasn't going to stop.

With a growl, he threw the covers off and rolled out of bed. The streams of sunlight warmed the floor and it felt good against his bare feet. Stepping to his portable computer, he lifted the screen and punched in his code before sitting down. Instantly, Simas' face appeared.

"Damn, Jerrod. You look like hell."

Jerrod snorted. After only about two hours of sleep how the hell else was he supposed to look? "Good morning to you as well, sunshine."

Simas chuckled. "Sorry."

"Have you found anything yet?"

"You mean besides a diversity of sex toys and bondage paraphernalia?"

"Shit," Jerrod sighed and rubbed his forehead.

"You know, everyone is entitled to their little quirks and tastes, but this," Simas held up a belt, complete with handcuffs and two dildos. Jerrod quirked an eyebrow at the erotic images the toy brought to mind. "This is just a tad bit strange, even for Micas. I'm not even sure I know what the hell this is."

Jerrod grinned. "Think about it for a minute or two, Simas, and you'll figure it out."

Simas tossed the handcuffs aside. "That's all right. I think I'll remain ignorant."

Jerrod chuckled and shook his head. Thinking about sex toys brought his mind to Kira. There were a few toys he wouldn't mind using on her, as well as his mouth and hands. She'd disappeared last night after their little foray into exhibitionism. He'd tried to find out from Dax where she'd gone, but he'd gotten nowhere with the tall giant. If nothing else, he was protective of the women who worked there.

He'd hung around for a couple of hours in the hopes that she would come back out. While he waited he questioned some of the waitresses. As far as they knew, no one new had been around looking for a job, but if they heard of anyone, they'd let him know.

"Jerrod!"

At the sound of his name, he snapped his head up and stared at the screen. "I'm sorry. Did you say something?"

Simas frowned. "Yeah. I asked if you'd found out anything about the woman?"

Squeezing his nose to try and relieve the banger of a headache he felt coming on, he nodded. "The transport pilot said there was a woman who matched our description who disembarked, but he has no idea where she went. He thought she might have been hurt, but she refused his help."

"All that blood on the bed was hers. I'm shocked she was able to walk out of here at all."

"You'd be amazed what people would do to survive."

"So you think that's what this was? An S&M session that got out of hand?" Simas asked.

"Maybe."

"Sure you don't want me to come up there? You look awfully tired, Jerrod."

Jerrod frowned. Something wasn't right here, but he couldn't put his finger on what. Maybe he was too tired to do this right.

"No," Jerrod said with a sigh. "Stay there and continue looking and keep me informed."

"Will do."

Jerrod flipped his screen down and stared at the wall. How was it that he'd been best friends with Micas but had had no idea of this fetish of his? Light bondage could be fun sometimes, Jerrod had even dabbled a little in it himself, but to physically hurt a woman was something else entirely. That was just sick and certainly not the type of behavior befitting a future candidate for high regent.

Maybe that was why he'd kept it hidden from him. Micas

must have known he'd never approve and would certainly never have let him get away with violence against a woman. Apparently, there had been more to his friend than met the eye. The only thing that concerned him was what else he would discover.

Kira made her way through the streets of Klindor, Dax close behind. He'd refused to let her go out alone. Even in broad daylight, crime was high. Klindor hadn't been this bad when they'd first opened the bar, but with all the gaming halls and bars that had opened since, the planet had deteriorated fast.

Dragging in a deep breath, she grimaced. The thick air was damp and moldy. She hated the smell of this place, but scenery-wise, it reminded her of the swamps of Louisiana back home on Earth.

It was terribly hot and muggy. She tugged at her damp shirt and perspiration slid down her back and between her breasts. She needed clothes. Unfortunately, there weren't many places here to get them. They would have to be ordered, so she headed to the only shop in town where she could take care of that.

Mirage had said to bill everything to the bar, that way Kira could keep her name off the order. She was glad she'd thought to open herself an account under another name when they first started the bar.

She'd done it that way to keep the university from finding out one of their professors was half-owner of a hedonistic bar. It would be even worse if they knew she sometimes worked there as well.

She enjoyed it. The exhibitionist in her loved the thrill,

the excitement of having sex within a crowd. All her life she'd been fascinated with the idea, but she never actually went through with it until the first night the bar was opened.

She'd become hooked and always spent her summers here, until she was offered the job as assistant professor at the university on Meenus Prime four years ago.

It was affiliated with Harvard, an extremely old university from Earth, and it had been an incredible opportunity. She'd jumped at the chance to finally be recognized for her business knowledge. Last night was her first time back in several years. And she'd certainly jumped right back into things.

She sighed and shook her head, thinking about the gorgeous man who'd driven her crazy. Just remembering the feel of his hands on her, the look in his beautiful sapphire eyes, made her skin tingle. Never in her life had a man affected her like he did. Scowling, she realized she'd even become jealous. Jealous? Why on Earth would she be jealous?

This is so not the time for this.

Finally spotting the store she needed, she put her hand out to open the door, but a firm, tan arm snaked out to block her way. She gasped and came to a complete stop.

"Good afternoon, Kira."

Jerrod.

She'd recognize that voice anywhere if for no other reason than the immediate surge of desire that ran through her veins. Turning her head to her left, she caught his stare and was held hostage by his twinkling eyes. Warm sunlight beamed down and highlighted the streaks of gray within his hair. She loved that salt-and-pepper look. It had been so dark in the bar last night she hadn't noticed it. She'd been too enthralled with his thick shaft and how good it had felt buried deep within her.

Clearing her throat, she moved back a step and stood ramrod straight. "Jerrod." It was the first time she'd been approached by a customer outside the bar and she wasn't quite sure how to act. The patrons knew what happened in the bar stayed in the bar.

He raised an eyebrow in amusement. "I was just thinking about you and then suddenly, there you were."

She swallowed and glanced around uncomfortably. "Really?"

He took a step toward her, bringing his body close. Too close. She could smell his musky scent, feel the heat radiating off his skin and her whole body sparked with unseen energy. Sexual energy.

Damn. What the hell is the matter with me? I'm a fugitive. "It's nice to see you again. But if you'll excuse me, I have errands I need to take care of."

"It's nice seeing you again?" His eyes narrowed slightly, and she got the impression he didn't care for her cold attitude. Well, neither did she if the truth were known. She desperately wished she wasn't in trouble and could pursue something with this man. He tugged at her heart in ways no one else ever had. And she'd only just met him.

"So that's it?" he asked. "We have incredible sex and then I get the cold brush-off?"

Kira sighed. "What happens in the bar stays there. I don't have relationships with patrons outside Fantasy."

He shrugged. "I'm not asking for a relationship, just a drink. This Klindor sun is killer, so I thought you could use something cold."

"Oh." She licked her lips nervously. "I'm sorry. I'm a little on edge today."

"Perfectly understandable." His lips spread into a charming smile that made her insides melt. "It's just a glass of Earth tea, Kira. I promise I won't jump your bones."

His hand touched her back and sharp pain slammed through her. She gasped and shrank away from him. Immediately, her gaze met his worried one.

She mentally scrambled for something to say. "I leaned too close to the furnace last night and burned my back. It's still very sore."

"Did you have someone look at it?" he asked.

Nodding her head, she glanced toward Dax who stood off to the side, watching her closely. With a trembling hand, she pushed a curl behind her ear. Physically, she wanted to touch Jerrod, run her fingers through his hair, kiss his lips. Kissing was definitely out. It made the sex at the bar too personal—it needed to be kept on a strictly physical level.

Emotionally, she was terrified. In reality she was on the run and shouldn't trust anyone she didn't know. And that included this man, no matter how badly she wanted to.

He brought the back of her hand to his lips, sending a shot of awareness straight to her stomach. "Come on, Gorgeous. Take pity on me."

She gave a very unladylike snort then watched his eyes crinkle in amusement. "I can assure you, pity is the very last thing I would feel."

Actually what she felt was heat, radiating up her arm on a wave. His fingers held hers as he watched her over his knuckles. "You know you want to," he taunted with a grin.

She couldn't help the chuckle that escaped. She was making a huge mistake. She just knew it. "Why is having tea with me so important?"

His gaze never wavered. "I don't know. But I'd like to find out."

Oh, God. She gulped. *I am in such deep shit.* She pulled her fingers from his grasp and sent him a firm look. "Tea only."

He smiled, deepening his dimples, and her resolve chipped away a little more. He held his elbow out, inviting her to slip her hand inside. She did then glanced at Dax over her shoulder. He nodded and continued with them down the street.

Jerrod looked behind him as well and shot her a look of amusement. "Will it be the three of us then?"

She grinned back. "Afraid so."

"Do you really think you need protection from me?"

Jerrod's blood pounded in his ears when she sent him a playful look out of the corner of her eye. "Maybe he's here to protect you."

"Now there's a thought."

She laughed and the sound floated through his senses, again tugging at that spot long buried. How the hell did this happen? He'd never dreamed he'd meet a woman like this here.

"What are you doing here?" he asked without thinking.

He felt the muscles in her arm tense and wondered what brought it on. He knew her story about the furnace had been a lie. What would they need a furnace for in this heat? The investigator side of him knew she was hiding something, but he couldn't imagine what.

She pointed to a table beneath a large, overhanging tree. It sat on the edge of the dock, just outside the tiny restaurant. "This looks like a good spot."

She grabbed a seat, Dax close by at the table behind them. At least he wouldn't be sitting at the same table. As he sat across from her, images of the night before flashed through his mind. She'd felt so perfect in his arms. So right. Was he out of his mind? Was everything moving too fast?

"You never answered me," he said.

Her eyes widened and her face paled just a hair, but before she could reply a waiter came over to take their order.

"I'll have the orange tea," she replied with a smile.

"Same here," Jerrod said. "And one for that gentleman there."

"Yes, sir."

He turned back to Kira and watched her fiddle with the napkin. "Well?"

"Oh, sorry. I'm from Earth."

A small smile tugged at his lips. That wasn't what he'd asked her. "Where on Earth?"

"Louisiana."

"That explains your accent."

She stared at him in surprise. "I have an accent?"

He nodded with a smile. "It's faint, but it's there."

"I thought I had gotten rid of it. Are you from Earth also?" she asked.

"I was born there, in England."

Her eyes filled with censure. "You don't have an English accent."

He grinned. "I wasn't raised there. My father moved us to Vorhala when I was three."

She nodded and resumed fiddling with her napkin. Jerrod reached across and placed his hand over hers, stilling it. "Why are you so nervous, Kira?"

Her gaze remained glued to his hand over hers. He felt the slight tremble in her fingers and frowned. What had happened to her to make her so jittery?

She jerked her hand away and looked out toward the swampland next to them. Turning back to him, her eyes held mischief, and he knew in his gut that she was about to lie.

"You're mistaking an inability to keep still for nervousness."

His lips quirked at her ability to quickly cover herself. "I thought they were one and the same."

"No." Her eyes narrowed slightly. "They're not."

Okay, Kira. I'll give you that one. "You know, you never answered my original question."

She frowned. "You asked me where I was from."

He shook his head. "No, Gorgeous. I asked why you were here."

She reached out and straightened the fork and spoon to her right. "Same reason as everyone else. I'm here to a make a little money." At his look of disbelief, she shrugged. "Okay. A lot of money."

Jerrod laughed and held up his hands. "Okay, I give. If you don't want to tell me that's fine."

"What about you? Why are you here?"

He took a moment to think about his answer, unsure he wanted to tell her the truth just yet. Although for the life of him he wasn't certain why it really mattered. Just something in his gut that told him to tread slowly with her. "I'm looking for something."

She snorted. "Aren't we all."

5

Later that evening, Kira made her rounds about the bar, stocking shelves and putting everything in order. With a mumbled curse, she stopped dead in her tracks, causing Mirage to run into her back.

Kira hissed at the pain but kept her eyes on Jerrod as he walked in. His T-shirt hugged his chest, outlining his pecs and firm abs, and her heart raced at the powerful grace of his movements as he made his way over to a dark corner table. The bar had just opened. What was he doing here so early? Hadn't they just had tea a couple of hours ago? God, the man was going to be a thorn in her side.

"Oh, God, sweetie, I'm so sorry. You okay?"

She turned to face her friend, trying to block out the way Jerrod's bronzed skin glowed like gold under the bar lights. "I'm okay. It was my fault."

Brushing past Mirage, she stomped back to the bar. Her friend's softly spoken "oh" made her turn with a frown.

"What?"

"Well, I was about to ask what made you stop so quickly, then I saw him."

Mirage's face spread into a saucy grin and Kira scowled. "I don't know what you're talking about."

"Yes you do." Mirage glanced over her shoulder at Jerrod. "He's gorgeous and I understand the two of you put on quite a show last night."

Kira shrugged, the heat of a blush spreading across her cheeks. "It had been awhile since I'd had a good fuck. Where did you run off to last night?" She spun and continued on to the bar, Mirage fast on her heels.

"I had something I needed to take care of."

Kira shot her a grin. "Like the doctor?"

This time it was Mirage's turn to blush and Kira's grin widened. "I knew it!"

Mirage shook her head. "It's not what you think."

"Mirage. Would it be so bad if it was?"

"Yes. It would."

Kira's eyes widened. Her friend's blue eyes were downcast, studying something on the bar. Tonight she had her hair piled on her head, a few tiny ringlets framing her face, and Kira saw the love bite just below her ear. When was Mirage going to just admit she loved Jaimee? "Please tell me you don't still have that love-and-marriage hang-up."

Mirage narrowed her eyes. "Stop trying to change the subject. I believe we were talking about you and hot stuff over there." She pointed over her shoulder with her thumb and Kira quickly grabbed it, pulling it down before he saw her.

"Would you stop that?"

"What on Earth has gotten into you?"

"You know what," Kira sighed. "He could be anybody and right now attracting attention is the last thing I need to do. Regardless of how gorgeous the man is." *Or how I feel when I'm with him.*

"I could find out who he is."

"People never use their real names here. You know that."

"You did," Mirage teased with a smirk.

"That was Dax's doing! Which reminds me, I haven't chewed him out for that yet."

"Like that will bother Dax." Mirage studied Jerrod for several minutes. "You know. He looks really familiar."

Kira raised an eyebrow, her nerves jumping. "Familiar how?"

Mirage shrugged. "I'm not sure, but it'll come to me sooner or later." She turned and moved to lean her hips against the back of the bar. Kira shifted to face her, putting her back to Jerrod and the corner table. Which was fine by her. The more she looked at him, the more unnerved she became. Unfortunately, Mirage continued to study him, her brow creased in thought.

"Would you stop staring at him like that? You're going to bring him over here."

"Honey, I've got news for you. If he comes over here it won't be because of me."

"I'm supposed to be hiding out, remember?" Kira hissed in exasperation. What was her friend doing?

Mirage's expression softened. "I know, sweetie. But I also know that sex like that, well . . ."

"What do you mean 'sex like that'?"

"Dax saw the two of you. He saw the connection that you have, whether the two of you realize it or not."

Kira frowned, determined to turn this conversation away

from her and Jerrod. "Like the connection between you and Jaimee? I saw the way he looked at you the night I arrived." Mirage rolled her eyes and Kira grinned. "It's not so fun being on the receiving end, is it?"

Mirage pointed to the bar behind Kira. "You have a customer."

With an amused shake of her head, Kira spun around and found herself not two feet from the man she most wanted to avoid. Jerrod. She glanced at her friend and caught the devilish smirk on her face.

Damn you, Mirage.

"Hello, Jerrod. What can I get you?"

"You mean besides you? Alone?"

The grin on his face made her skin tingle. Erotic images of her flat on her back and him buried between her thighs ran through her mind, and she swallowed back a groan. All it took was that smile and she melted, desperate to be in his arms.

"Hmmm, I don't believe I have a drink called 'you alone,' " she replied with a cheeky grin.

"I wasn't talking about a drink, Gorgeous."

"I am."

Jerrod chuckled. "Okay, I get the hint."

"It's a good thing. I would hate to have to get Dax after you."

He tilted his head to the side, studying her. "Would you really do that?"

"Do you really want to know?"

His grin widened and her heart skipped a beat.

"I'll take a Buttery Nipple, preferably yours." When she shot him a glare he winked. "But in the glass is fine for now."

She strolled to the far end of the bar to fix his drink and he followed her, taking a seat at one of the stools close by. Uneasiness swept through her at the way he studied her, his eyes ever watchful, curious.

"It's awfully quiet here tonight."

His softly spoken words almost made her jump, and she took a deep breath to steady her shaking hands. "It's early yet. It'll pick up before too much longer."

She slid the glass across the bar, causing the drink to slosh over the side and onto the deep cherry wood. "Sorry," she mumbled.

"It's okay, Gorgeous."

It made her uncomfortable when he called her that. It wasn't that she didn't like it—she did. Which was a bad thing. "My name's Kira."

A look of startled confusion crossed his features. "I know. But I like calling you 'Gorgeous.' It suits you."

His gaze held hers, seeming to reach clear through to her soul. She glanced away and surveyed the small crowd gathering around the pool table on the far side. Later, she was sure, the table would be used for something other than pool. Bodies would cover the green felt top. Men and women alike would undulate against each other, moan and scream their pleasure.

Kira swallowed as a wave of lust slammed through her. She could see her and Jerrod making use of that table. On her back, her legs hooked over his shoulders as he pushed his thick cock into her over and over.

"Kira?"

"What?" Her startled gaze jerked back to Jerrod, and she blushed at his knowing grin.

"You all right?"

"Yeah, fine." *Kira, you are such a liar.* "I better get back to work."

Grabbing the towel lying on the counter, she quickly wove

her way through the growing throng of people to the other side of the bar.

Jerrod's lips twitched in amusement. He wondered what she'd been thinking about while she stared at the pool table. He certainly knew what he'd been imagining. He hadn't been able to stop thinking about her all damn day. Nothing felt right until he came in here and saw her. Just the sight of her, the knowledge she was close by, put him at ease and that more than anything startled him.

One of the other waitresses walked over and with a seductive smile introduced herself as Sky. She was pretty in a young, perky kind of way. Not the classic beauty that Kira possessed. Sky's black hair looked blue under the lights, her brown eyes were framed by black lashes, long and curling upward. He returned her smile then took a sip of his drink.

"Would you like anything other than your drink?"

"Not at the moment, maybe later."

His gaze wandered back toward Kira, who now stood at the pool table talking with a couple of younger men. Something tugged in his chest. Something he didn't like. Why would he care if she talked with other men?

"Got the hots for Kira, huh?"

Startled, he returned his attention back to Sky. "What do you know about her?"

"I'm fairly new, so I don't know her that well. I just know she's half-owner."

Jerrod choked on his sip. "Half-owner?"

"Yeah. Her and Mirage started this bar about six years ago. She's not here much."

"Not here much?" His curiosity was piqued. "What does she do when she's not here?"

"I think she's a professor or something." She shrugged her

dainty shoulders. "She just returned a couple of days ago, so I haven't had a chance to really talk to her."

Jerrod's drink froze halfway to his mouth, his heart pounded in his chest. A couple of days ago? He remembered how she'd acted when he'd touched her back earlier in the day. Was Kira the woman he was looking for? The woman who killed Micas?

Ah, hell!

6

Slowly strolling around the dark bar, Kira nursed her fourth Sexual Frustration. An apt drink for how she felt at the moment. Every time she glanced toward the far end of the long bar, Jerrod was watching her. His gaze raked over her body, sending sparks of awareness to every pore on her flesh.

This is insane!

Avoiding his sensual gaze, she turned her back to him and gulped down the rest of the drink. The alcohol burned her throat, making her wince, but she welcomed the heat. Anything to keep from attacking Jerrod, throwing him on the pool table and having her way with him, running her hands over his tight, hard flesh, inhaling his masculine scent. Just like the threesome there now.

A group had gathered, watching the two women and one man pleasure each other. Threesomes were one of the more popular fantasies. Although she'd never participated in one with two women, observing never failed to turn her on.

Her whole body was on fire and all she could think about was Jerrod's face between her legs, doing to her what the man was doing to the woman spread before him now. The other woman was positioned below and between his legs, his cock moving in and out of her mouth.

Two more women came up, one on each side of the woman on the pool table, their mouths suckling the girl's breasts. A man came behind each of them, lifting their skirts and exposing their wet pussies. One man unzipped his slacks and fucked the woman before him with quick, deep strokes. The other was more patient, taking his time to prepare the woman before slowly sliding deep into her ass.

There were now seven and more joined in. The scent of sex permeated the air, making her nostrils flare. She should turn away but she couldn't. It was like a train wreck, and she wanted desperately to participate. She shook her head. No she didn't. She wanted Jerrod and only Jerrod.

Despite her desire, she remained frozen, unwilling to encourage him. She couldn't shake the feeling she should stay away from him. He was dangerous. Unfortunately, she couldn't put her finger on why.

She caught him, out of the corner of her eye, slowly stalking toward where she stood, like a lion stalking his prey. She didn't look at him. She couldn't. She knew if she did he would see the obvious longing in her eyes, the desire to have something she knew she couldn't.

He came to a stop next to her and she could feel his heat, his breath on the side of her neck. "Do you like watching them?" His whisper sent a shiver down her spine.

She shrugged. "I see this kind of thing every day. It doesn't affect me one way or the other," she lied.

"Liar." His finger brushed over her extended nipple, and she sucked in a breath. "Your reaction gives you away, Kira. Why do you fight it?"

Jerrod was dying. He wanted her so bad he could taste it. It wasn't just physically though. He wanted her in his arms, in his life. He wanted to know everything about her—her likes, her dislikes. But most of all, he wanted her to trust him enough to tell him the truth. Her arrival on Klindor, coupled with a sore back she lied about, was too much of a coincidence. The investigator in him knew something was up, but the man wanted desperately to ignore the mounting evidence.

Leaning over, he buried his face in her long hair and inhaled her vanilla scent. "Do you taste as sweet as you smell, Kira?"

His palm slid up her thigh and under her short skirt, cupping her mound. She wasn't wearing any underwear and her wetness coated his palm. Brushing his finger along her slit, he smiled at her soft moan.

"Jerrod, we . . ."

He pushed a finger into her dripping pussy and her knees buckled. He caught her around the waist, holding her close. "You're a woman of many secrets, aren't you, Gorgeous?"

She nodded then shook her head no. He didn't want to believe this woman was the one he was looking for. Surely a coincidence. Please let it be a coincidence.

He slowly moved his finger in and out, stretching her as he went deeper. "Oh, yes, Jerrod," she whimpered and he almost lost it. To hell with the investigation. At the moment, he just needed to taste her.

Finding a free spot on the other side of the table, he sat her on the edge then lifted her skirt. Her long legs were the color of cappuccino, firm and muscular. He'd never liked women with reed-thin thighs and Kira's were just perfect. Exactly the way he liked them.

She fell to her back and he grabbed her hips, pulling her closer. With her skirt around her waist she was open to him, to anything he desired. And he desired her.

Leaning down, he spread her labia with his fingers and circled her clit with his tongue. He inhaled, dragging her scent into his lungs. Damn, she did taste as good as she smelled. Her hips undulated against his face, her hands sank into his hair, pulling him closer. He was about to burst. His cock throbbed to be buried inside her delectable pussy. She was so wet, so hot. And so damn good.

Another man came forward and lifted her shirt, putting his mouth on her breasts. She arched her back and moaned.

Jerrod wasn't sure he liked another man touching her, though for the life of him, he wasn't sure why. He'd never been jealous in his life, but damn if the emotion didn't suddenly almost bring him to his knees.

Grabbing her hands, he tugged her away from the other man. Jerrod scowled at him over her shoulder and the man lifted his hands in surrender, shifting to horn in on someone else.

He turned back to Kira and caught her startled expression. "I didn't like him touching you," he said simply.

Her lips lifted in a slight smile, and she touched the side of his face with her palm. He turned his head and kissed it, letting out a ragged sigh.

"Are you running, Kira?" His gut clenched, waiting for her

answer. Her eyes widened in fear then clouded over, a brick wall firmly in place.

She licked her lips. "Why do you ask that?"

He shrugged. The middle of a bar, his cock rock hard and aching to be inside her was not the right time or place for this—he knew better. He needed to get her alone. "Just a sixth sense." A long silence passed between them. "I can help you," he whispered.

Kira stared at him, her insides waging a war. She had no idea who he was. She couldn't tell him, but she wanted to so badly. There was something about him that made him seem like he would be easy to talk to, easy to trust.

What would he do if he knew she had killed someone? Would he stare at her in disgust or fear? Or would he turn her in? She couldn't risk it. She wouldn't. Until she decided what she was going to do, she couldn't get attached to this man. There was no point.

He moved his lips close to hers, his hands gently framed her face. She still sat on the pool table, his hips sandwiched between her thighs. His tenderness and the . . . was that love in his eyes? Fear? "Let's get out of here. Go somewhere and talk. Whatever it is, Kira, I can help you."

"No." She shook her head, her lower lip trembling. "You can't help me."

"Why don't you give me the chance to try? Damn it, Kira. You can't keep running."

Her stomach rolled with nausea. *Oh, God. What did he know?* "I'm not running."

"Kira," he sighed in exasperation.

"Let me down." She shoved at his chest, hard, but he didn't move.

"No."

"I'm not running, Jerrod. I'm here to help Mirage. Now let me down."

When he continued to stare at her, she shoved again. "Do I have to yell for Dax?"

With a sigh, he stepped back, allowing her down. Without looking back, she fled up the stairs to the office level. She heard Jerrod behind her, yelling for her to stop. She glanced over her shoulder and saw Dax step between him and the bottom of the stairs. Jerrod ran a hand through his hair and scowled. "Damn it, Dax!" he snapped.

Shutting the door behind her, she wobbled to the desk and sank into the chair. Her lower lip quivered, and she swallowed down the tears that threatened. She had to get out of here. It was the only thing to do.

She thought back to his comment about not liking the other man touching her, the jealousy shining in his eyes. In some ways, the idea of belonging to only him sent a wave of warmth through her, but she quickly pushed that nonsense aside. She didn't have a clue what tomorrow would bring. For all she knew, she could lose her freedom in the snap of a finger. She had to get a grip on her emotions and forget Jerrod.

Mirage burst through the door and Kira jumped, placing her hand over her chest. "Jeez, Mirage. You scared the crap out of me." Mirage was pale, her eyes wide with fear. "You all right?"

"I just remembered where I know him from."

"Who?" Kira asked, dread gripping her heart.

"Jerrod."

Kira sat straighter, every hair standing on end. She had a feeling she wasn't going to like what Mirage was about to say.

"I've seen his picture in the papers. Don't you read the papers, Kira?"

She shook her head. "No, you know I never read the news. Why? Who is he?"

"He's Meenus Prime's lead investigator and best friend to the man you killed."

"What?" she croaked. *Oh, fuck!*

"We've got to get you out of here. Now."

7

Jerrod strolled along the dock, his hands clenching and un-clenching at his sides. Kira had once again gone into hiding. He'd tried to get into Fantasy and see her that morning, but Dax had said she was still sleeping.

He'd actually thought about using his position, flashing his badge and demanding to be let in, but changed his mind. If Kira was the woman he was searching for, the last thing he wanted to do was scare her off—if he hadn't already.

Once he realized he wasn't getting in to see Kira, he went back to his room at the local hotel and sent Simas a message to contact him as soon as possible.

Five minutes later Simas called him back. "You want me to research Fantasy Bar? What the hell for?"

"Just do it, Simas. I have my reasons. I'm particularly interested in a woman by the name of Kira."

"All this for a woman?"

"Possibly the woman we're looking for," Jerrod growled, and Simas immediately nodded his head, agreeing to get started right away.

So now here he was, walking along the dock, staring at the swampland that bordered Klindor City. This town was a lot like the old city of Earth called Las Vegas, but gambling had been outlawed there, which had put the city and several more like it out of business.

Some of Earth's gamblers and casino owners had moved here, building even larger casinos and brothels atop floating docks. Klindor had flourished, but it had also become home to some dangerous people.

A hot wind blew, and Jerrod adjusted the sunglasses on his face. It was almost time to call Simas back. Hopefully, he'd found something. Jerrod just hoped it wasn't what he thought it might be. He'd become attached to Kira and the last thing he wanted to do was arrest her for murder.

Kira threw a few more outfits and a couple of sweaters in the bag then zipped it closed.

"Do you think you have enough?" Mirage asked.

"For a couple of days. Once I get there I'll get more clothes."

"I slipped some extra money in the hidden compartment underneath."

"Mirage," Kira said, shaking her head. "I'm fine. I have enough money. Besides, you've already given me most of your clothes."

Mirage frowned and handed her the green sweater that went with the slacks Kira wore. "You won't be able to touch your account on Earth, so you'll need some extra 'just in case' money. Don't argue with me."

"Yes, mother," Kira sighed.

"It's not funny. I'm terrified for you. It's not a coincidence that he's here."

"I know it's not. But maybe I should tell him what happened." If he'd found her here, he would find her wherever she went. But if he knew she was guilty, wouldn't he have already arrested her?

"You killed Micas Lordakin, right-hand man to the high regent, not to mention candidate for the next election. They would never believe he almost killed you. He's Meenus Prime's quintessential golden child."

Kira sighed. "You're probably right."

Mirage walked over and placed something in her hand. "Here's the key to my house on Portaka 3. It's right on the beach and secluded. You should be safe there until we figure out what to do."

"You really shouldn't know where I'm going."

Mirage waved her hand. "Don't worry. I'll be fine. And so will you. Now hurry, the transport leaves in twenty minutes."

Kira hugged her friend, her eyes closing against the tears that threatened. How in the hell had her life become such a mess?

"I'll see you soon," she whispered.

Jerrod had no sooner walked into his room than his communicator began to beep. He flipped his computer screen open and hit the enter key. Immediately, Simas' image appeared.

"What did you find?" Jerrod demanded.

"I've got two things I need to discuss with you. Neither one you're going to like."

"First things first. Did you find out anything about Kira?"

"Yes. I checked into the bar, but neither of the women that own it is named Kira. After some digging, I found out that your Kira used an alias on the deed."

"Wonder why?" Jerrod mumbled.

"I can almost guess. Kira is none other than Kiranda Vorkin. Professor Kiranda Vorkin."

Jerrod sat straighter, trying to think. "Why does that name sound familiar?"

"She's the newly promoted, youngest, I might add, head professor of the Intergalactic Trade Department at the university on Meenus Prime."

Jerrod nodded, inwardly impressed. He'd heard of her. She was considered a brilliant mind when it came to business. "Sounds like she used an alias so the university wouldn't know about it."

"That's my guess. I also contacted her department. They said she hasn't been to work in almost two weeks, which would put her disappearance at about the time Micas took the woman to his apartment."

Jerrod sighed. This wasn't looking good.

"Before we go any further, there's something you need to see."

"What?" Jerrod asked with trepidation.

"I'm sending it through now."

Jerrod made the window with Simas' real-time image smaller to allow room for the digital video coming through. As the file downloaded, Simas continued to talk. "We found a hidden camera in the ceiling of Micas' bedroom. Everything he did to the woman is on there, including his death. You were right, Jerrod. It was self-defense."

Jerrod remained silent and hit the play button. With growing dread, he watched as Micas beat a woman repeatedly. He never raped her but took her blood and coated his cock, then masturbated until he came all over her bloody back. Bitter bile rose in his throat, and he grimaced. How in the hell had he missed this?

"You all right, Jerrod?"

"Yeah," he croaked, unable to take his eyes from the sick images.

"There's five more of these videos. All the women but this one died."

He'd heard Simas, but he'd stopped listening, paying more attention to the woman on the screen. She was fiddling with her bindings and was almost loose.

Finally one hand was free, and she lifted the black cloth from her eyes. Her nervous glances kept straying toward the door, watching for her captor to return. There was no sound on the tape but he could imagine her anxious whimpers, her frightened sobs. He gritted his teeth, trying to block the sound.

She was free, and he gripped the arm of the chair as she searched frantically for something to use as a weapon. Opening a drawer, she pulled out a gun then pointed it at Micas the second he walked in the room. When Micas stepped toward her to take it away, she fired, knocking him back onto the foot of the bed. Just like Jerrod had found him. Her hands were shaking so badly he was amazed she'd even hit him.

He still hadn't seen her face. She hadn't looked up fully

to the ceiling, but there were other parts of her body he recognized. The thighs in particular. His instincts screamed it was Kira, but he needed to see her face to be sure. Finally, she glanced toward the ceiling and the hidden camera. His gut clenched at the frightened look on her face, the tears streaming down her cheeks. To him there was no doubt. Even though the image was slightly blurred, he knew it was Kira.

Damn it all to hell!

"Have you shown this to anyone else?" Jerrod demanded.

"No. There were two other investigators there when videos were discovered, but I'm the only one who knows what's on them."

"Sit on them for a couple of days." Jerrod stood and started to close the lid to his computer.

"Not until you tell me why."

Jerrod sighed. How the hell did he explain this? He wasn't even sure what he was going to do. "If this were to get out, Simas, whether it was self-defense or not, the woman would be ruined. She doesn't deserve this."

"It's Kira, isn't it?"

"Yeah. I won't let Micas destroy everything Kira has worked for. Not like this."

Simas scowled. "Damn it, Jerrod. What the hell were you thinking falling in love with her?"

Jerrod frowned at his friend's image. "I didn't say I had." Had he?

Taking a deep breath, Simas ran his hand down his face.

"Look, Simas. I honestly don't have a clue how I feel. I only know I need to talk to Kira before I go any further. I need two days. Not because I'm your boss, but because I'm your friend."

Simas nodded, although his eyes shone with reluctance. "You've got them."

"I need to see Kira," Jerrod demanded as Dax tried to block him from entering. This time, he wasn't going to take no for an answer.

"Sir, I told you . . ."

"I know what you told me, damn it." Jerrod opened his wallet and showed his badge. Dax's eyes widened, but his resolve to keep him out remained if his stiffening body was any indication. "I want to see Kira, Dax. Now. You can't keep me out and you know it."

"She's not here," a soft voice replied from behind Dax.

Jerrod peered around the tall giant and scowled at Mirage. She wrung her hands but her chin was high, her stance determined. "Where is she, Mirage?"

She nodded to Dax and he stepped aside, letting Jerrod enter.

"She left. She had business to attend to somewhere else. I don't know when she'll be back."

"I need to know where she went and I think you know why."

Her chin went up another notch. "I told you, I don't know."

He stepped closer and placed a hand on her shoulder, his voice soft as a whisper. "I know what happened, Mirage."

"How?"

"We found a hidden video. He'd recorded the whole thing. I know it was self-defense."

Her shoulders sagged and she glanced at him with uncertainty. Desire to help her friend and desire to keep her safe were more than likely waging a war within her. "She almost didn't make it here," she whispered. "He beat her so badly—her back will never be the same."

"I know."

"How do I know that you're not going to cover up his activities and put this all on her?"

Jerrod sighed. He didn't have a clue how he would convince her. "I'm not going to let anything happen to her, Mirage. I promise. I'll make sure the high regent knows what happened. But it's imperative I talk with her now."

8

Kira walked along the beach. The deep blue ocean lapped onto the sand, covering her bare feet. The water was warm, more so than the oceans of Earth. The thermal core of the planet kept the liquid heated to perfect bath temperature.

An offshore breeze blew, whipping her hair into her face. She brushed it back and glanced over her shoulder toward the house embedded in the cliff.

Mirage had incredible taste and had designed her house to blend into the scenery. And blend it did. If you didn't know what to look for, you'd never know it was there.

It became one with the cliff face—only the glass was visible and then you had to really look for it. The roof was dirt and grass with a small path down the side of the hill to the entrance.

Once inside, one was greeted with a six-foot waterfall that fell from the rock wall into a small pool surrounded by tropical plants indigenous to both here and Earth. Gray metal lights hung from the stone ceilings, casting a soft glow against the tile floor. Colorful rugs were thrown about to add color and warmth. To the right were the two bedrooms, each with large windows that overlooked the surf below.

The glass lightened to a soft gray during the day but darkened to black at night so the light from inside wouldn't be visible to someone on the beach.

The perfect hideaway.

Turning back toward the ocean, she inhaled the salty air and closed her eyes. The waves crashing against the shore relaxed her and she smiled as the warm water slapped against her calves.

She felt safe here, but she couldn't keep her mind off Jerrod. Last night she'd dreamt of him. His hands caressing her skin, his lips nibbling at the sensitive spot behind her ear. Their bodies fit so well together and she'd awoken with a need she came nowhere near to appeasing. Just thinking about it made tingles run along her flesh, and she shivered.

She never should have had sex with him. She would compare every man from now on with his gentleness, his passion. She knew in her heart no one would ever measure up.

What men? I'll spend the rest of my life hiding.

She spent a couple of hours that morning investigating Jerrod. The Galactic Net was quite a source of information. Anything and everything you could ever want was right there at your fingertips. It turned out Jerrod was quite the investigator, several times receiving the Golden Star for capturing galactic fugitives no one else seemed to be able to catch. It had even been rumored he might run for regent elect himself. If there was ever a man out of her league it was Jerrod Scollin.

Taking a deep breath, she made the decision that she

couldn't live like this. She had to do something. Maybe she should just suck it up, turn herself in and pray for the best.

"Penny for your thoughts."

She stiffened, her breath catching in her chest at the softly spoken words. Her eyes opened to stare out at the waves. A storm loomed just beyond the horizon, but the electricity in the air was nothing compared to the fear that snaked down her spine.

Please let me be hearing things.

Slowly, she turned and almost fell to the sand in a heap. *Jerrod.*

"I think you and I need to have a talk, don't you?"

An overwhelming desire to run gripped her, and she stumbled back a step.

Jerrod shook his head, his mouth set in a firm line. "Don't, Kira." He took a small step toward her, his outstretched hand a lifeline she wanted desperately to grab. "I can help you, sweetheart. Just trust me."

Could she trust him? She wanted to so badly but was still so afraid. "Why should I? You were his friend."

His hand dropped and guilt clouded his eyes, making them darken to navy. "He may have been my friend but I would never have condoned his actions."

She swallowed. "How did you find out it was me?"

"There was a video camera in the ceiling. It caught the whole thing."

"Oh, God." She felt sick. Jerrod had been witness to her humiliation, her shame and desperation. She took a deep breath, trying to calm her stomach.

"Kira," he whispered and took a step closer.

She shook her head and jumped back. How did she know he wasn't just like him? "Don't. How did you find me?"

"Mirage."

A muscle jerked in her cheek and she clenched her hands. Had Mirage sent her here on purpose, knowing Jerrod would only be a few hours behind? Why would her friend do that?

"She just told you?"

The corners of his mouth lifted in a slight smile. "She tried to keep your whereabouts from me, but I assured her I could help."

"And she believed you?" she asked incredulously.

"Yes." He nodded. "She only wants what's best for you, Kira."

"And she thinks you're what's best for me?" Anger now rolled through her. She felt as though she was on a roller coaster—emotions up and down, uncontrollable. She felt helpless.

"Right now I'm all you've got, kiddo. Whether I'm best or not, I'm it."

She stared at him, her eyes pleading for him to understand. "How do I know I can trust you? I don't even know you. How do I know you won't do the same sick things?"

He raised an eyebrow. "We've had sex, Kira. Did I hurt you at all then?"

"We were in public. In a damn bar!"

He opened his mouth then closed it, his eyes narrowing, his forehead crinkling into a frown. "I want to help you out of this mess." He spread his arms and sighed. "I don't know what to do to convince you of that. You just have to take a chance."

"Here, sweetheart."

Jerrod handed Kira a cup of hot coffee. His chest tightened

when her small, trembling hands gripped the mug. Right now he could kill Micas with his bare hands if he weren't already dead. What the hell had made him do those things, and more importantly, why the hell hadn't Jerrod seen it?

"How are you holding up, kiddo?" He sat on the sofa beside her. Lightning flashed, illuminating the living room and the uncertainty in her eyes.

"I've been better." She gave him a faint smile and took a sip of her coffee. She grimaced, making Jerrod smile apologetically.

"Sorry," he said. "My assistant usually makes the coffee."

"I can see why." She chuckled softly and set the cup on the table.

She was so beautiful, so fragile. He hadn't stopped thinking about her since the first time he saw her. It wasn't just the sex. There was something about her, something that drew him to her, gave him peace. He wanted to know everything about her, but even more than that, he wanted her to trust him, open up to him.

"How in the world did you and Mirage come up with a place like Fantasy Bar?"

She eyed him in surprise then her brow creased in thought. She was so cute when she did that. He wanted to smooth out the tiny lines with the tip of his finger.

"It started out as a joke. We were laughing over some of the crazy names of drinks and wondered what it would be like to have a place where sex was based on your drink order. Mirage and I made the idea a reality." She shrugged. "There's really not a whole lot more to tell. We just hit the market with something fresh and new that took off."

"It was a brilliant idea. Have you thought about opening more of them? The small planet of Eden would be a good place. Or even Sincta 5."

"We've talked about it. We believe Dax would be the perfect person to open the next one, but he's a little reluctant. He doesn't want to leave us."

"Can't say I blame him." Jerrod grinned and a blush spread up her cheeks. He took a sip of his coffee. She chuckled when he grimaced and set the cup back down. "Maybe you should make the coffee next time."

"Definitely." Her smile faded and she wrung her hands, nervously twisting the small pearl ring on her finger. "Why me? Why did he do this to me? He didn't know me from Adam." Her eyes widened as an idea dawned. "Do you think he knew me from the bar?"

"No." Jerrod shook his head. "I checked. Micas had never been to Klindor."

"What makes you think he didn't use an alias?"

"He had plans to run for regent. He wouldn't have risked going there. It was too public." The second he said it, he realized how lame that was. "What the hell am I saying? He made every mistake there is with you, an alias wouldn't have been out of the question."

"What mistakes and why would he have made them?"

Jerrod wasn't sure what to tell her. He had a theory, but they would probably never know if he was right. "I have an idea."

"Want to share?"

Taking a deep breath, he stood and paced to the counter separating the kitchen and living room. He leaned on the waist-high tile countertop and stared at the bowl of Portakin fruit. Picking up a small purple berry, he twisted it between his fingers. "I believe Micas wanted to get caught."

"Why? Because of the mistakes?"

"Yeah."

"Maybe he just didn't know what he was doing."

"No." Jerrod dropped the berry and ran a hand through his hair. Guilt once again slammed through him. "He knew what he was doing. His first mistake was that you're high profile. You would have been missed. Micas watched the news daily, so he would have known who you were."

"You didn't."

He grinned sheepishly. "I've been out of the loop, so to speak. I'd been on Earth for several months and hadn't kept track of what was happening on Meenus Prime. But I know Micas would have and he would have known who you were."

She shook her head, confusion creasing her brow. "I still don't understand."

Jerrod began to pace. "He kidnapped you at the university, right?"

"Yeah, how did you know that?"

"Your car is still there and Micas' fingerprints are all over it."

"Oh." Her eyes widened in surprise. "I'd forgotten all about my car."

"I think he left it there on purpose. Micas isn't . . . or wasn't, stupid. He knew a lot about my job and how I did things. What I looked for. Your car would have been something I'd have investigated and he would have known I would have dusted for prints. What do you remember about that night?"

"Not much. He hit me from behind, tied me up. Most of the two days are still a blur. I do remember that we passed a doorman on the way in. He actually stopped to talk with him."

Jerrod raised an eyebrow. "Don't you think that's a little strange? That was his second mistake. Once someone noticed you were missing, your picture would be all over the news. I think he was counting on the doorman remembering you and reporting it."

"I don't know, Jerrod." She shook her head with a frown. "How do you know he would have reported it?"

"I don't. But there are other slips he made. Your fingerprints were all over his house, his car. My assistant found your purse in the trash bin in the basement. You were also the only one he kept alive for more than a day."

Her face paled and she swallowed, raising her shaking fingers to her chest. "Oh, my God! There were more?"

"Yeah, five that we know of for sure. All died the same day he brought them home. My guess is he wanted to keep you alive so we would find you there."

"But I killed him before any of that could happen."

"Yes. When Micas didn't show up for his appointments that morning his assistant went to his apartment and found the body. I was the first one they called. The doorman had followed you and saw you board the transport for Klindor. That's how I tracked you, but I wasn't sure it was you until I saw the video."

She closed her eyes and covered her mouth. Her face paled and protectiveness swept through him. He hated to see her like this, all the spunk gone, defeated.

Jerrod grabbed her hand, pulling it away from her trembling lips. "I'm so sorry he did this to you, Kira. In some way I feel responsible."

She opened her watery eyes and stared at him. "Why? You didn't make him pick up the whip."

"No. But I didn't see this side of him. I should have. What kind of investigator am I that I can't even see the signs in my best friend?"

"Because he was your best friend," she whispered.

How had it gone from him comforting her, to the other way around? Leaning forward, he kissed her cheek and inhaled the scent of salty sea air on her flesh. She stiffened and pulled away, confusion and wariness darkening her gaze.

"What now?" she asked hesitantly.

A wry smile tugged at his lips as he brushed a stray curl behind her ear. "I'm going to do my best to keep your name out of this. I don't want your life ruined because of him."

"Why would you do that?"

He ran his thumb along her bottom lip, thinking about his next words and just how much he would tell her. "Because you did what you had to do and shouldn't be punished for it. There's something about you that touches me somewhere I haven't been touched in a long time. I can't stop thinking about you and I want us to have the opportunity to see where this goes."

She bit her lower lip and his cock tightened. This was the wrong time for sex. They had things they needed to talk about, but the lure of her full lips tugged at him, made his pulse quicken with the need to feel her mouth against his.

"I'm scared," she whispered. "What if they don't agree? Because of the bar, what if they think I went with him willingly?"

"It's all on the tape, sweetheart. It's obvious you were fighting him. I'll take care of this," he whispered as he took her face between his palms. "I promise."

A single tear slipped free and he kissed it away. The salty taste lingered in his mouth. When she didn't back away he placed another kiss on her cheek, her skin soft and warm beneath his lips. Slowly, he worked his way to the corner of her mouth. Her lips parted in response and the smell of mint and coffee floated across his cheek.

"I want to kiss you, Kira. This isn't the bar, and this is a hell of a lot more than just sex."

Her gaze met his. Her green eyes were filled with passion and just a hint of fear.

"I'm not Micas," he whispered. "I would never do what he did."

"I know."

She licked her lips and he closed his eyes, swallowing his groan. He'd spent his whole adult life jumping from one woman to another. Not one of them had made him feel the things Kira did. He wanted to protect her, take care of her.

He wanted more than just sex. He wanted to hold her and watch the surf play across the sand, talk about her ideas, her desires. He just wanted to be with her and he'd do whatever it took to keep her safe.

He waited, their gazes locked. The indecision slowly faded from her eyes and she leaned forward, gently touching her lips to his.

9

His lips were soft against hers, coaxing, and she shuddered, wanting so much more. For days she'd wondered what his kiss would be like. His tongue touched her lower lip, encouraging her to open for him, to allow him entrance into her mouth.

With a sigh, she parted her lips and welcomed the onslaught of his kiss. The soft texture of his tongue glided around hers, teasing, stroking, sending a stream of desire coursing through her veins. His mouth molded to hers, his taste all consuming. She sagged against his chest, her fingers fisting in the soft cotton of his shirt.

His groan rumbled in his chest, vibrating against her hands, and she answered with a moan of her own. One hand buried itself in her hair, holding her steady while his tongue plundered her mouth, exploring every crevice.

Pulling away, he laid his forehead against hers and brushed his fingers across her cheek.

"I want to do it right this time," he whispered. "Where's a bed?"

She let out a small laugh. "Down the hall on the other side of the center fountain."

He stood and grasped her hand, pulling her down the hall. She followed him into the massive suite and jumped as a flash of lightning lit up the room. She wasn't afraid of storms, but the ferocity of the ones here made her jittery.

Trying to take her mind off the weather, she glanced around the room. She had actually been staying in the smaller one. This room just seemed too big for one person.

A king-size bed took up the far wall opposite the massive window, its deep blue satin sheets and comforter a stark contrast to the dark rock of the wall behind it. Other than a dresser, there wasn't much here.

Another flash of lightning flickered and she glanced outside. The sky was almost black, the clouds a menacing swirl of dark cotton. The ocean waves were angrily slapping the shore, the foam breaking against the rocks.

She hugged her arms around her chest while Jerrod lit the candles on the dresser, bathing the room in soft light. "Does the storm frighten you?" he asked softly as his arms encircled her waist from behind.

She leaned back, the warmth of his chest seeping into her. He rested his chin on her shoulder and she smiled.

"For the most part I like them, but sometimes the sudden crack of thunder can startle me."

"You're safe here." The back of his fingers brushed her neck and she wanted to purr like a contented kitten. "Right here in my arms."

For a moment they remained by the window, each lost in their own thoughts. Her fingertips trailed along his forearm.

The scent of jasmine-scented candles filled the room, mixing with Jerrod's masculine, woodsy smell. Closing her eyes, she inhaled the erotic combination.

"You're so beautiful when you smile."

She opened her eyes and caught his reflection in the glass as he watched over her shoulder. His fingers tugged on the buttons at the hem of her shirt, slowly releasing one then working his way to the next. His hand skimmed across the flesh of her stomach, making her muscles twitch. Finally, the last button was free and he parted her shirt, revealing her bare breasts. His palms brushed over her nipples in small circles and they hardened beneath his touch.

With a soft moan, she rested her head against his shoulder. His teeth grazed the sensitive spot behind her ear, setting her body on fire.

"I want you, Kira." His hot breath brushed along her flesh and she sighed, arching her back, putting her breasts more fully into his hands.

He squeezed and she moaned softly. His hands moved to her shoulders to push her shirt down and she stiffened. "Jerrod."

"Shh," he whispered as he slid the shirt down her arms. She closed her eyes, waiting for the shocked gasp to escape his lips, but it never came. His fingers trailed along her scars, soothing her heated skin.

"Oh, baby. I'm so sorry he did this to you." He kissed one of the scars and she melted at his tenderness. "But in some ways, I'm not." His lips moved higher, skimming across her shoulder. "I would have never met you if he hadn't."

The backs of his fingers brushed the side of her neck, sending goose bumps along her flesh. "So gorgeous," he groaned before turning her chin with his fingers and capturing her lips in a kiss she felt clear to her toes.

She wanted him so much. Her pussy throbbed and juices flowed, coating her panties. She moaned and turned to face him, her arms wrapping around his neck, pulling him closer. His strong arms circled the small of her back, pressing her stomach against his thick cock. Every pore in her body hummed with need. She knew how good he would feel and she was desperate to get him inside her. She wanted him filling her, stretching her.

She shifted, rubbing herself along his length and he moaned deep in his chest. "Damn, Gorgeous, you're killing me."

She chuckled seductively and pulled him with her to the bed. With a light shove, he pushed her to the middle then fell on top of her, his warm weight pressing her into the cool comforter.

Spreading her legs, she moaned into his kiss when he ground his hips against her throbbing pussy, teasing her, making her hungry for more.

Moving his lips lower, he cupped her breast. His tongue slowly circled her nipple and she fisted her hands into the blanket, trying not to scream in frustration. "Jerrod."

"Patience, Gorgeous."

With deliberate slowness he covered the hard nipple and sucked it into his hot mouth. She squealed, the pleasure bordering on pain.

The fingers of his other hand worked lower, unbuttoning her slacks before slipping inside her panties to fondle her sensitive clit.

"You're wet, Kira," he whispered against the skin of her neck. "But I want you wetter."

She groaned, wondering how in the hell she could get any hornier than she already was.

Rising up, he pulled her slacks and underwear off, dropping them to the floor with a playful grin that set her heart racing wildly.

"You're still dressed," she pouted playfully.

He crooked a finger. "Then come undress me."

She sat up with a smile, anxious to finally see his naked flesh. Her fingers trembled in impatience as she pulled at the buttons of his shirt. In aggravation, she tugged, popping the buttons free in her haste. They pinged against the rock and floor tile, sounding loud in the silent room.

Biting her lower lip, she trailed her hands along his massive chest, tan from the sun, hard and bulging with muscle. His skin was smooth, hairless, and his chocolate brown nipples hardened beneath her touch. Moving lower, she grinned when his washboard abs jerked beneath her fingers.

Grabbing the button of his slacks, she worked it loose then slid the pants down his hips while he removed his shirt and tossed it across the room. His hard cock sprang free and she encircled him with her hand just below the purple head. He put his hand over hers, moving it up and down in a slow pumping motion. A drop of pre-cum escaped and she rubbed it around his head of his cock. She put her finger in her mouth and licked it off, meeting his heated gaze.

Jerrod dragged in a ragged breath. Her finger in her mouth, licking his cum, was almost his undoing. Damn, he wanted her.

"Lie back," he instructed, his voice rough with need.

She smiled seductively, stretching her body out along the bed. The woman had one hell of a body. All soft curves, smooth skin, and those breasts. He could play with those things all day. He dropped his gaze between her legs and smiled at the patch of hair just above her pussy. She was definitely a true blonde. The golden curls glistened with her juices. Juices he wanted to taste again.

Settling on his knees in the middle of her splayed thighs, he lifted her knees and bent to lick along her slit. She hissed and bucked her hips toward his face.

"Like that, Gorgeous?"

"Yes," she groaned as he pushed one finger deep into her dripping pussy. Removing it, he placed it in his mouth, licking her juices from his knuckle.

"You are such a tease," she admonished.

"Tease, huh?" He chuckled and once again lowered his head. "I'll show you a tease."

With infinite slowness, he separated the lips of her sex and gently licked, barely touching her swollen clit before re-treating. Her hips undulated in silent invitation. Her whimpers spurred him on. She was so sweet, so fucking hot. It took every bit of willpower he had not to plunge into her and bury himself deep. He knew from experience it would be pure heaven. Her tight walls would squeeze him, milking his cock dry.

He rose up partially and watched her face as he pushed two fingers into her wet passage. Her lips parted as she gulped in air, her face flushed pink in her rising passion.

He switched to the tight bud of her anus and gently slid his fingers in while his tongue circled her clit.

"Jerrod, damn it," she groaned. "Please."

It was all he could take. Removing his fingers, he settled between her thighs. He toyed with the opening of her pussy with the head of his shaft, teasing her and himself. Her hips pushed forward, taking him part of the way inside her.

"Oh, fuck!" he shouted, then plunged balls deep.

She screamed and lifted her legs higher, dragging him deeper. Immediately, he began to move, grinding against her clit on the downward thrust. She moved with him, met every thrust with one of her own. They fit together so perfectly he never wanted it to end.

Pausing, he lifted her legs over his shoulders and drove deeper. She whimpered, her fingers fisting in the sheet by her head. He kept his movements slow, gentle, until he felt the beginning throbs of her climax. Her muscles rippled along his shaft and he couldn't hold it any longer. With a growl, he increased his rhythm, plunging harder, faster.

"Yes, oh yes," Kira yelled. Her whole body tensed beneath him.

With one final plunge, he came with her, emptying his seed deep within her. Every muscle in his body quaked with the intensity of his release. He'd never felt anything like it.

Her legs lowered to cradle his hips within the warm cocoon of her thighs, her hands feathered along his back. With a sigh, he rested his forehead against hers.

"I could stay like this forever." His eyes opened with a start. *Did I just say that out loud?* Meeting her gaze, he grinned sheepishly. "You're one hell of a woman, Miss Kira."

She smiled. "It's the afterglow talking."

He chuckled. "That's one hell of an afterglow."

Rolling to his side, he pulled her with him, wrapping his arms around her in a protective embrace. They had so much they needed to talk about, feelings they needed to explore. Or at least ones he needed to explore. She'd given no real indication she had any feelings for him at all, other than passion.

Tomorrow, he thought as his eyes closed and he drifted into sleep.

10

Kira awoke with a start, her frightened gaze roaming around the still-dark room. Small, quick images from her dream floated through her mind, but never close enough to catch or see clearly. Someone else had been in the room with Micas. She'd thought it before but she was certain now. She didn't know who but she'd heard his voice. Clear, deep and evil.

She shivered and tried to push the sound from her mind. Jerrod lay beside her, still asleep. Deciding not to wake him, she headed to the kitchen to start coffee and breakfast. She'd had no idea if what she had dreamt had been what actually happened. She still remembered so little of those two days. Maybe someday it would all come back, but what if the other man was still out there, looking for her?

Stopping in the doorway, her heart leapt at the sudden thought that came to mind. Jerrod? She stared at him in the bed. He lay on his back, the sheet around his waist. She watched the slow rise and fall of his chest in sleep, one arm thrown over his forehead, the other across his waist.

No. It wasn't Jerrod. It couldn't be Jerrod. The voice wasn't the same. Trying to steady her racing heart, she continued to the kitchen.

Standing at the counter, cutting fruit and watching the sunrise over the ocean, she hit the knife blade against the cutting board a little harder than necessary. The bang echoed through the room and she froze, waiting to see if Jerrod had heard it. When it remained silent, she continued making breakfast, her heart heavy with confusion.

She couldn't stop thinking about last night, about the things he made her feel. Was she in love with him? She didn't know. She'd never been in love. She'd spent her whole adult life worrying about her career. Men were on the backburner, unless it was sex. Then it was get in, get some then get out. Which is what made the bar such an incredible idea. No one expected anything out of you beyond the moment.

But Jerrod had changed everything. For the first time in her life she wanted more than just the moment. She wanted what they'd shared last night. It had been sweet, tender and so hot.

Jerrod came up behind her and wrapped his arms around her waist. His body was warm and she sagged against him, melting into his embrace.

"Good morning, Gorgeous." He buried his face in her neck and inhaled. "Mmmm, you smell good. I missed you in my arms when I awoke."

A small smile curved her lips. "I couldn't sleep so I thought I would make us some breakfast. Are you hungry?"

"I'm starving," he drawled, sleep making his deep voice

sexy. His palms slid up and cupped her breasts. A shot of desire went straight to the pit of her stomach. Taking a steadying breath, she brushed his hands away and turned to face him. "I meant for food, Romeo."

"Darn." His lips spread into a sexy grin, making her want to sink to the floor in a puddle. "And here I thought you were making a pass at me."

"Making a pass, huh?" She held up a piece of pineapple and placed it on his tongue. "What on Earth would give you the impression I would want to make a pass at you?"

He chewed, his eyes crinkling with mischief. "Maybe," he mumbled as his arms wrapped around the small of her back, pulling her close, "it was all the begging you did last night."

She stiffened with an indignant frown. "I did not beg."

He chuckled and kissed her forehead. "We'll call it a . . . soft pleading."

She halfheartedly swatted his chest, making him chuckle. "I have coffee made if you'd like some."

"I'd love coffee."

She pointed to the counter on the other side of the room. "There are cups by the pot."

While his back was to her, she took a moment to admire his tight butt in the slacks he wore. He'd left his chest bare and the muscles of his back rippled as he moved. The early morning sunlight landed across his shoulders, making them appear golden and absolutely perfect. Swallowing a wave of lust, she turned back to the fruit just in time for him to face her.

"So what's with the hidden house?" he asked.

She glanced at him over her shoulder. He stood with his hips leaning against the counter, one arm holding the coffee cup to his lips, the other tucked under his biceps. God, he looked good. His slacks hung just below his belly button, showing off one hell of a muscled stomach. Her gaze met his and he raised an eyebrow in amusement.

She quickly cleared her throat and kept cutting the fruit. "It's Mirage's. When she was a little girl her dad used to beat her and her mother. Everywhere they ran, he found them. As an adult, she tried a relationship one time and ended up with someone like her dad. Thank God, she got away from him. Once the bar was successful, she had this house built. It's her safety blanket. The one place she can run to when she feels trapped or afraid." Kira smiled slightly. "She hasn't used it in a while so I'm hoping she's getting over some of her fears."

"It's interesting she would open a place like Fantasy Bar, not to mention work in it."

Kira shrugged. "It's public, in the open. I think it's the only place she feels safe enough to have sex with someone."

"That's a shame. I hate that there are men out there that abuse women."

"Did you and Micas ever talk about stuff like that? Did he know your view?"

Jerrod frowned. "You know, now that I think about it, he always changed the subject or just remained silent. I don't think he ever expressed an opinion."

"I guess now you know why."

She set two plates on the table overlooking the beach. Between them, she placed a bowl of fruit and a platter of croissants.

"Breakfast looks great." Jerrod took a seat and immediately dug in.

"I hope it's okay. I'm not a big breakfast person, so I didn't have the usual 'hungry man' food in the house."

Jerrod grinned. "It's fine. After all, I'm certain you didn't expect me on your doorstep."

"True," she replied with a chuckle and took a bite of her croissant.

"Why did you run?"

The question startled her and for a second she just stared. "Which time?"

"This time."

She glanced down at her plate and pushed her fruit around with her fork. "Mirage remembered who you were. I knew you would eventually figure out who I was, if you hadn't already. I should have turned myself in, but I panicked."

She hated that about herself. Normally she was a strong person. She'd had to be to make it in the business industry. Despite strides women had taken, there were still planets where they were considered weak and inferior.

"Panicking is natural, Kira."

She shook her head. "Not for me." She sighed and waved her hand. "Let's change the subject."

"All right." Jerrod stabbed at a strawberry. "Let's talk about us."

Kira's startled gaze met his. She certainly hadn't expected that and her heart lodged in her throat. "I . . . umm . . . what about us?"

"First off. Do you agree that there is an us?" His intense gaze bored into hers and her mouth went dry.

Do I? "Yes, I agree we have . . . something."

"So do I. And it's something I want to explore."

She lifted one shoulder. "How?"

"Spending time together for one." He grinned. "What are you doing after all this is over?"

"I was thinking about that." She smiled and placed a strawberry in her mouth.

"Well, let's hear it."

"I want to open a resort."

He raised an eyebrow in interest. "A resort?"

"Yeah. Fantasy Resort, and at the center will be Fantasy Bar. Same principle just on a much bigger scale. We could even offer classes or a group setting for an orgy-type environment."

"Classes in what?"

She shrugged. "Masturbation, oral sex." For a moment she paused, unsure she even wanted to include this one, but also knew it would be popular. "Sensual spanking. It doesn't have to be classes, it could be a club setting, where people with similar interests come to experience things together."

"Sounds interesting." He wiggled his eyebrows, making her giggle. "Where would you put it?"

"Here."

He pointed to the beach. "Right here?"

"Well, in this general area. Mirage owns this. Ten acres on each of the three sides, but I own some beachfront property further to the south. It's more tropical than here and definitely more level."

"How much land do you own?"

She grinned. "Over fifteen thousand acres."

He choked on his coffee and grabbed a napkin to wipe his mouth. "How much?"

She leaned forward, enunciating her words. "Fifteen thousand acres. Not too shabby for a girl on her own, huh?"

He raised his cup in salute, his lips lifting in a smile.

"It's the perfect spot. It's right by the ocean and close enough to Vorkin City that getting guests there would be relatively easy."

"Sounds like you've really thought this out."

She nodded, her excitement building. "I probably have

about fifty percent of what it would take to do this. The rest I can borrow." She bit her lip. "What do you think?"

"I think it's a great idea."

"You'll be on Meenus Prime though. I don't know how often we'll see each other."

He pushed his fruit around and remained silent, studying his plate. "The big question is . . ." He raised his gaze to meet hers. "Do you want to see each other?"

For the first time, she saw uncertainty in his eyes. It made him appear vulnerable and she wanted to relieve him, let him know she felt the same as he did. "Yes. Can we make it work?"

"We can make anything work if we want it bad enough." He pursed his lips and waved his fork in the air. "Maybe I'll retire from investigation and become a partner in this little venture."

"A partner?" Her heart warmed at the idea. The two of them running the resort, working side by side, together always.

"Yeah. Think you could handle me underfoot all the time?"

"Of course. I like having people to walk on."

He snorted. "Cute. What about the university?"

She drew in a deep breath then let it out slowly. She'd decided this morning that she wanted to close that part of her life. "I don't want to go back." She shrugged. "Too many bad memories, I guess. Of course all this is contingent on your idea working." She frowned. "What is your idea exactly?"

"Let's just say the high regent owes me one."

"Owes you one?"

Jerrod reached across the table and took her hand in his. "Trust me. I promise, a year from now we'll be overlooking the new Fantasy, hand in hand, jumping from one of your clubs to another."

She chuckled. "I would hope that some of those times we'll be alone."

He brought the back of her fingers to his lips, the warmth of the soft kiss sending electric shocks up her arm. Tingling warmth settled between her legs and she squirmed in her seat, fighting the rising passion that blazed hot and unrelenting.

"You can have me whenever or wherever you want, Gorgeous."

"Oh." She glanced out the window, toward the beach and the beautiful blue sky. "How about there?"

"Now?" he asked, his lips tilting upward into an adorable grin.

"Right now."

11

Jerrod couldn't take his eyes off Kira as she strolled along the beach, shedding her clothes as she went. Completely naked, she smiled seductively at him over her shoulder. His whole body heated beneath her emerald gaze. Her eyes sparkled with devilment. He was beginning to see a side of her she'd only hinted at before—playful, mischievous and absolutely delectable.

Her firm ass swayed as she sauntered toward the waves and he swallowed his lust, determined to not rush things. Unfortunately, his cock had other intentions.

"Are you coming?" she called over her shoulder before diving into the sparkling water.

She emerged on the other side of the wave and he stood mesmerized by the water glistening on skin. Damn. He put his hand over his bulging shaft and squeezed. Would she always affect him this way? He hoped so. He looked forward to a lifetime of being turned on by this woman.

He'd awakened that morning knowing exactly how he felt about her. He was in love. For the first time in his life he was actually in love with a woman.

At first, the idea shocked him, that he would have these feelings for someone. Especially this quickly. But no longer than he'd known her, he couldn't imagine his life without her.

"Jerrod?" He mentally shook himself and smiled at her as she waved to him from the water. "The water's great. Are you going to stand there all day or are you going to join me?"

He unbuttoned his pants, his chest tightening at the thought of being next to her. "Have a little patience, minx."

She grinned. "But I want you," she purred.

That was all he needed to hear. In a rush, he dropped his pants in the sand and took off toward the surf. Once in the water, he dove under and grabbed her legs, pulling her down. They both emerged laughing, and Kira splashed water in his face. "You brute."

"I may be a brute," he growled playfully, grabbing her around the waist. "But you want me."

"Who says?" she teased back.

"You just said."

"Well, okay." She slid her palms up his chest and around his neck. Her eyes narrowed seductively. "I guess I did say that."

"You guess?" He bent down and bit the side of her neck, relishing the tremor that skimmed through her.

"Okay, I did."

He bit harder, and she erupted in a peal of giggles. Palming the cheeks of her ass, he lifted her. Her warm pussy settled against his hard cock and he groaned deep in his chest. "Feel what you do to me, Gorgeous?"

She ground her hips along his length and his whole body shivered in anticipation of sinking inside her tight walls.

"Is all that for me?"

"Every last inch."

He covered her lips with his, the waves crashing around them, rocking their bodies against each other. She tasted of melon and coffee, rich and sweet. One hell of a heady combination and he couldn't get enough of her. Grabbing the back of her head, he anchored her and deepened the kiss. Their tongues battled for control, their bodies clamoring for fulfillment.

"Jeez, Kira," he murmured between kisses. "I want you. Now."

Lifting her hips, he set her at the tip of his cock and drove deep. She threw her head back, her yell scaring a flock of ocean birds searching for food on the shore. They flew over, their high-pitched squawks drowning out Kira's moans.

Her walls encased him like a glove, squeezing him, dragging him deeper. Never in his life had a woman made him this out of control, this hot. God help him, he never wanted it to end.

Her mouth descended on his, her tongue delved and teased. He met her demanding kiss and made a few demands of his own. Not only with his mouth but with his cock. She sighed as he relentlessly thrust deeper, hitting her womb.

"Jerrod," she whimpered, then screamed as her release gripped her. Every throb of her pussy pulled him closer to his own bliss and with a shout, he burst deep inside her.

A strong wave hit them and his legs wobbled, causing him to almost lose his balance. "Whoa," he laughed and held her tighter against him, spreading his feet wider to keep them balanced.

Kira slid down his body, her feet coming to rest unsteadily on the sand beneath them. She grabbed his forearms for support, her tiny hands gripping his muscles. She looked so adorable, her face still flushed from their passion. A breeze blew her hair into her eyes and he brushed it back, his heart in his throat. She had all the power. She could crush him if she wanted to and the very idea threw him for a loop.

"Nice show."

Jerrod turned and stared at Simas in surprise. "What the hell are you doing here?"

Simas stood on the beach, his hand behind his back. "Just checking. Making sure you found her."

"Of course I found her. I told you I knew where she was."

Something didn't feel right. Kira's whole body went rigid and her hands trembled. He glanced down at her pale face, concern racing through him. She didn't look well at all. "You all right? What's wrong?"

"It's his voice. I've heard it before."

He glanced at Simas, still on the beach, watching them with interest. Kira's lower lip began to tremble and his concern intensified. "Where, Kira?"

"At Micas' apartment. He was there. He was with him."

Kira's stomach rolled with nausea. Missing images and sounds from those two days came rushing back. She'd never seen his face but she'd heard him encouraging Micas, telling him to hit her harder. His teeth had bitten into the flesh of her back, drawing blood. She cringed at the remembered pain.

Jerrod touched the side of her face and leaned in close. "Are you sure?"

"Yes," she whispered.

He turned to face Simas and pushed her behind him. "Stay behind me, understand?"

She nodded. "Yes."

She glanced around his shoulder. Simas still stood on the beach, his leer making her shiver in dread.

"We're not dressed, Simas. At least turn your fucking back," Jerrod snapped.

Simas smirked but turned.

"What the hell are you really doing here?" Jerrod asked.

"I told you. I wanted to make sure you found her."

They slowly made their way out of the water and Jerrod handed her shirt to her. As quickly as possible, she put it on, covering herself as best she could.

"Why? So she wouldn't point her finger at you and let everyone know you were at Micas' apartment egging him on?"

Simas spun around and faced them. His face contorted into an evil scowl. "So you know."

"Not until just now."

Kira stood behind Jerrod, looking around the beach for anything she could use as a weapon. There was nothing and her heart sank. They were in real trouble.

"How long have the two of you been doing this?"

"Micas caught me years ago with a woman. He was fascinated with what I'd done, turned on by the blood and the screams." Simas shrugged. "We began to do it together. Until he developed a fascination with her."

"Why me? I'd never met him," Kira screamed in frustration.

"Yes you had. You just don't remember. He was at the university party, the one that introduced you as the new head of the department. I told him not to take you, but once he did, there was nothing I could do. It had to be played out."

"But why did he keep her alive when he killed the others so quickly?" Jerrod asked.

"He was playing a game. He wanted to prove he could do

it and not get caught. He was flaunting it in your face, Jerrod. Granted, he wasn't supposed to show her to the fucking doorman!"

Jerrod shook his head. "Why? What kind of sick thrill do you get out of doing this?"

Simas' lips spread into a nasty grin. "It's all about control, friend."

"That's bullshit and you know it."

Simas shrugged and took a step closer. "It's all in your perception."

Jerrod reached behind himself and pushed Kira back, making sure to keep a safe distance between them and a man he'd considered a friend. A friend he'd apparently never known at all.

Damn, they'd hid it well. He hadn't had a clue either of them were crazy.

"How did you find me? I didn't tell you where I was going."

Simas held up a small device and smiled. "Tracking device. Ingenious invention. I put it on your ship before you left Meenus."

"Son of a bitch," Jerrod mumbled.

"You might as well move aside, Jerrod. I'm here for the woman and I won't leave without her."

"What do you want with her?" He knew, he just needed to keep Simas talking until he could figure a way out of this mess.

Simas rolled his eyes. "She can identify me, but then you know that. Stop trying to stall. Both of you have to die."

He pulled a gun from behind his back and Jerrod swore.

"How will you explain it, Simas?"

"She killed you in her attempt to escape and I had no choice but to shoot her. Sad really. She's such a beauty, so hot and delectable. Do you remember, Kira? Do you remember the feel of my mouth on you, the pain as my teeth sank into your tender flesh?"

Kira whimpered behind Jerrod, her hands balling into fists against his back. He had no doubt she was remembering and it probably terrified her.

"Stop it!" Jerrod snapped. "I'm not going to let you do this, Simas."

"And how do you think you're going to stop me?"

Jerrod lunged forward, grabbing the gun. "Kira, move," he yelled, hoping like hell she followed his instructions.

They struggled, his heart in his throat. The gun was facing upward and Jerrod fought, trying to point it toward Simas. Time seemed to stand still then move in slow motion. Simas' face was red with his exertion, his determination to keep the upper hand. He was stronger than he looked, and Jerrod's arms began to shake with his efforts.

Suddenly, he became angry. Angry with himself for not seeing what they really were, angry that they'd pulled the wool over his eyes. Jerrod brought up his knee, slamming it into Simas' groin. Simas fell to the ground, his howl of pain echoing off the rock cliffs behind him.

"Damn you, Jerrod."

Jerrod stood over him, his chest heaving, his disgust for the man he considered a friend eating at him. "Damn *you*, Simas. You'll pay for what you did."

"How?" Simas sneered up at him, his expression triumphant. "How am I to pay and keep her out of it? Huh?"

"Oh, I assure you. I'll figure a way." He moved the gun to his other hand and glanced to his left, looking for Kira. She stood by the cliff, just below the path that led to the house. What the hell was she still doing there?

"Kira, go to the house."

She nodded then a shot rang out. Jerrod watched in anguish as she fell to the ground, motionless. "Kira!"

Spinning around, he caught Simas on his knees, gun in hand. He must have had another one hidden on him somewhere. Without thought, he aimed, shooting Simas between the eyes. He didn't even wait for his body to hit the ground before he took off toward Kira's lifeless body.

Kira groaned. Hot searing pain shot through her. She tried to open her eyes and see Jerrod, but the pain made even that small movement nearly impossible.

She'd heard the second shot but she had no idea who'd fired.

"Kira. Kira, baby, answer me."

Jerrod's hands touched her face and tugged at her shirt. Relief washed over her and she bit her lip to stop the sobs. "Simas?" she croaked.

"He's dead. He won't bother you again."

He applied pressure to her seeping shoulder wound, and she winced.

"You're going to be fine," he soothed.

"I don't feel like it at the moment."

She opened her eyes and caught him smiling at her. Love. It was the only word that came to mind. She loved him. She knew it now without a doubt.

"Let's get you some help."

She nodded and closed her eyes, falling into the relief of unconsciousness.

12

Jerrod watched anger crease the brow of High Regent Kimpak, then disgust. Kimpak's gray hair was pulled tight into a ponytail, making him look older than his one hundred and twenty years, but his green eyes still sparkled with intelligence. He was a good regent. A kind one. Hopefully that kindness would be present today.

"I've seen enough," Kimpak groaned then turned away.

Jerrod stepped forward and closed the computer screen. The click was loud in the silent room. Simas had been under the false impression he'd covered all the angles. Edit himself out of the films, make sure everyone knew it was Kira who had killed Micas, then frame Kira for Jerrod's death as well. The whole incident would have ended in her *supposed* suicide. He shuddered every time he thought of how close Simas came to succeeding. "It was self-defense, your Excellency."

"Is that why you hid her face?"

Jerrod nodded. He knew the regent would notice—he'd just hoped Kimpak would choose not to say anything. "Yes."

"You know her identity?"

"Yes."

"Well."

Jerrod met Kimpak's level stare with determination. He would not give up Kira. "With all due respect, your—"

Kimpak held up his hand and scowled. "You would give your career to keep this woman's identity a secret?"

"Yes. She's a highly educated, highly respected woman who was at the wrong place at the wrong time. To reveal her identity, even if it was self-defense, would ruin her. I refuse to allow that to happen." Taking a deep breath, he continued. "Micas was my best friend, but I had no idea what he was into or how sick he was. Simas being involved was another shock, and I feel responsible for the deaths of those women. I'm a better investigator than this. I should have seen it."

Kimpak shook his head. "You were too close, Jerrod. Sometimes it's most difficult to see what's directly in front of you."

"Regardless, I won't let you or anyone else take this woman to hell and back just because she was trying to save herself."

"I saw the video, Jerrod. I know what happened to her and why she did it."

"Then I see no need to reveal her to the public. We can say the woman died of her injuries."

Kimpak appeared surprised. "So you're going to reveal Micas and Simas' activities?"

"Yes. My only request is that you allow me to speak with their families first. I want their parents to hear it from me and not the press."

Kimpak sat silent for several minutes. Jerrod's nerves screamed with unease and he felt like a caged animal. He needed to pace, move, something. Finally, Kimpak spoke and Jerrod prepared himself for the worst.

"I never would have thought Micas, or Simas for that matter, could do those things. It makes me ill to think how many others there might have been."

Jerrod swallowed. He'd thought the same thing numerous times since seeing this video. "There are five others that we know of because of the hidden videos we found. They were unable to escape Micas and died of their injuries. Simas edited out his involvement, but his work was hurried and sloppy. It's obvious where the edits were made. Those videos are in there as well if you'd like to see them."

Kimpak help up his hand and actually paled. "No."

Jerrod nodded but said nothing more. He just waited.

"Tell the woman I commend her bravery and determination to survive." Jerrod's heart soared. Was Kimpak going to let him keep her a secret? "I will go along with your plan."

"Thank you, your Excellency."

Kimpak eyed him speculatively. "This will be your last assignment, I take it."

It wasn't a question but an observation. And a very accurate one.

"Yes. I wish to retire and pursue . . . other interests."

A small smile lifted the corners of Kimpak's mouth. "You've been a good investigator. One of my best. You will be missed."

Jerrod inclined his head, relief that Kimpak hadn't fought him over the issue swimming through him. "Thank you, Regent Kimpak."

Boredom weighed heavily on Kira as she paced Mirage's bedroom. She'd been here for almost a week now, waiting for Jerrod to return. Hopefully with the news it was all over, that they could finally go on with their lives. Together.

With a sigh, she rolled her shoulder. It was still sore and the wound would leave a nasty scar, but that was no worse than the ones on her back. A forever reminder of just how nasty people could be. She loosened the sling and let her arm hang straight, stretching it out. Jaimee had told her it might be a while before she could lift it over her head.

"Kira," Mirage admonished as she came into the room carrying a tray laden with food. "You're supposed to be resting."

Kira scowled. "I've rested enough. If I don't get out of this room, I'm going to go stark raving mad."

Mirage laughed. "All right, I'll tell you what. Eat your lunch and I'll let you go downstairs and help me get ready for tonight."

Kira smirk at her motherly attitude. "What am I, eight?"

Mirage smiled. "Maybe ten."

"Very funny."

Kira sat on the bed and picked at the food. If she continued to eat everything Mirage brought her she'd gain fifty pounds within a month.

"I just want to make sure you're well before you overdo it just like you always do. You would do the same to me if the situation were reversed."

Kira grinned. "True."

Kira picked up her fork and studied the piece of meat dangling from the end. She just wasn't hungry. She dropped it back to her plate with a sigh.

"Lord, girl," Mirage admonished. "If all you're going to do is push the food around your plate, let's go ahead and go downstairs."

Kira jumped up and headed toward the door, ignoring Mirage's laugh.

"You're not in a hurry, are you?"

"Yes," Kira sighed, making her laugh even harder.

"Come on, mother hen," Kira shouted over her shoulder and practically skipped down the hidden back staircase that would take her to the main bar. Once through the door, she glanced around the nearly empty room. Just the bartenders and a few waitresses were around. The normally dim lighting was now bright, casting light into dark corners. The smell of vanilla and spice clung in the air. A man sitting at the end of the bar caught her eye and she sucked in a breath, her heart pounding in her chest.

"It's about time you came downstairs."

She smiled, letting her gaze travel down his dark blue shirt and slacks. The color deepened the sapphire of his eyes, making them sparkle.

"Jerrod," she yelled then slung herself into his open arms.

Jerrod laughed, holding her tighter. "Careful, Gorgeous. Don't hurt yourself."

"I don't care. I'm just glad you're back." She pulled away and stared at him, biting her lip in anxiety. She was dying to know what happened, but her heart raced with the fear it might be bad news. "How did it go?"

"Everything is fine. No one but us knows who the woman in the video was. It's over, sweetheart."

Relief gripped her, making her giddy. With a squeal, she hugged his neck. "I love you, Jerrod."

She froze. She hadn't meant to say that. What would he do? Would he ignore it? Or play it off as nothing?

"I love you too, Kira," he whispered and her heart soared. He smiled and cupped her face between his hands, his eyes shining with all the love he felt. "Let's go start that resort."

She wiped at the tears falling down her cheeks. "Yeah."

One year later

Jerrod stood beside Kira, his arm along her shoulder as they surveyed the new Fantasy Resort. Everything had gone as planned and they were now ready to open the doors. They'd been booked solid for almost two months now. As soon as word had spread of the new resort, people began to call. The opening party they had planned would be a huge success.

Kira smiled and snuggled closer to Jerrod. It had been a wonderful year. Days full of work designing costumes, decorating rooms and working out class schedules. The nights were full of snuggles, long talks and passionate lovemaking that never failed to leave her breathless. But nothing compared to the night before—when Jerrod had placed a diamond ring on her finger.

"Now that everything is in place, it's time we took care of this. Marry me, Kira."

She'd accepted, gladly and without reservation. He was and always would be the man of her dreams.

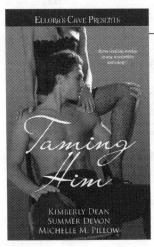
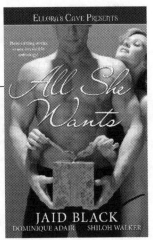

Printed in the United States
By Bookmasters